S0-FFX-305

THE WOMAN ON PRITCHARD STREET

Journal #7 – *Grace*

The Vasile Chronicles

by
jd young

First in a trilogy of Urban Fantasy Thrillers

All rights reserved. No part of this book shall be reproduced or transmitted in any form or by any means, electronic, mechanical, magnetic, photographic including photocopying, recording or by any information storage and retrieval system, without prior written permission of the publisher. No patent liability is assumed with respect to the use of the information contained herein. Although every precaution has been taken in the preparation of this book, the publisher and author assume no responsibility for errors or omissions. Nor is any liability assumed for damages resulting from the use of the information contained herein.

This is a work of fiction. Names, characters, places and incidents are either the product of the author's imagination or are used fictitiously. Any resemblance to actual events or locales or persons, living or dead, is entirely coincidental.

Copyright 2011

Published by: Young Lions At The Gate

Original cover art: Miki Leathers

Editing: Mary Ellen Gavin

For Jerry

G

Acknowledgements

My gifted Muse Mary Ellen Gavin
Without your support, encouragement and editing
the first of this trilogy would still reside on my desk.
We are truly old souls.

My first fan Don Anderson
You strengthen my resolve and encourage me to laugh.

THE WOMAN ON PRITCHARD STREET

Sometimes things just fall into your lap. Some make you smile and enjoy the ride. Others make you grab your balls and pray for redemption. When this job fell my way, the easy money clouded my senses. Though my balls ached, I ignored my gut. I figured, why not?

Another city, another job, another haphazard collection of notes to take up space in my luggage. I don't know why I keep all these journals.

Perhaps one day these chaotic impressions will come in handy.

…Simon Nicolae Gautreaux

Journal #7 - Grace
Entries 1-5

1 – The City

I had just found my oasis on the streets of Washington, DC. Top floor condo with balcony, lots of windows plus Becketts was minutes away and a great place to relax. I enjoyed going there to be alone, regardless of the masses, the busy bar and filled outside tables. Mel, the bartender, always made sure his regulars were taken care of in the best of ways.

DC was certainly a different lifestyle. I had tried New York. It was exhilarating and sexy, but I wanted something less intense on a daily basis. In New York I could depend upon muggings, cops and lots of street attitude, but it wore me out quickly.

My travels toward Newport News caused an overnight stop in the Capitol. The city proved inviting, but was not "in your face" like New York. I would not have the newspaper contacts that NYC afforded, but I figured I could make it work. Muggings, rapes, and politics--they all used the same verbiage.

About a month after arriving and with no really interesting news presenting itself, I rethought my decision to stay. Almost on queue I was presented with an offbeat news article.

2 – Zoe

A young reporter named Zoe Weston, one of those genius minds that gets into college at fifteen and is working by seventeen, wrote for an underground paper in DC. They had published her small article describing feral dogs wandering in the DC area. It stated that several homeless people had been savagely attacked and no headway was being made in solving their deaths.

Zoe blamed the police for ignoring the plight of the homeless. I had to call her for lunch.

When we met she was out-of-control excited to speak with me as I was a senior, more experienced paper pusher. During lunch she could barely sit still.

"Simon, the witnesses I've interviewed told me they saw a group of teenagers hanging around the areas where the people were attacked and killed. In fact, several of the teenagers turned into eye witnesses."

At first, I thought the concept of feral dogs loose in a metropolitan area was unlikely, but the bodies of these victims were torn to shreds with a vengeance. They were ripped open with a violence that I would only associate with dog packs living in mountainous areas."

I sat and listened while this kid exploded with thoughts and theories on the attacks.

"The scary thing is that it's not just homeless people. In total five victims have been found. Three were regular nine-to-five working stiffs. Probably a poor choice of words. But, they were government workers, returning home after their eight hours of toiling in the system. This all started a few months ago and no one is paying attention."

"Zoe, kid, take a breath. You've just shared a lot of information that seems unlikely to me. It could be that these dogs were trained for fighting in some guy's basement and they got loose."

"Simon, no, no, I'm sure it's more. When did you last hear of feral dogs roaming city blocks? Really, one person attacked, maybe even two, but not five. And not all homeless. This pattern is something that has to be investigated."

We finished lunch and I promised I would call her soon.

3 – The Incident

Meeting with Zoe proved to me how crazies reside in every city on the planet. I went to Becketts for a relaxing hour of people watching before going back to the condo. After several glasses of amber happiness, I began my walk home remembering my earlier conversation with Zoe. My thoughts were interrupted when I heard screaming. I wasn't sure if the screams were coming off New Hampshire or Massachusetts Avenues, but they were loud and the fight was fierce.

The hairs on my neck stood at attention as I rounded the corner in front of my building and heard screaming. I ran blindly toward the fight. I saw, or thought I saw, several large dogs gorging on a carcass, dripping with blood, and fighting each other for position. A briefcase appeared thrown to the side and spilled bloodied paperwork across the sidewalk. These animals kept ripping at their victim until suddenly one jolted from the pack.

Now, I was face to face with an unknown entity. It scared me out of my skin. Standing as tall as me, coarse red hair grew out its head. The animal like face contorted and stretched in a most grotesque manner. My body stood frozen and I could not remember how to breathe.

As the sound of approaching footsteps became louder, somehow this entity changed into an average looking person. The other crouching figures simply stood up and took on the appearance of bystanders.

I stood in stunned silence as a crowd gathered. I only remember people touching me and asking, "What happened? Are you okay? What did you see?"

Sick to my stomach, I slipped away from the melee and walked back to my condo. I quickly poured a drink and tried to understand what I had just seen. Did I imagine that slaughter? Were the attackers people or animals? Why wasn't I attacked?

Something Zoe had said must have sat in my psyche and took advantage of my imbibing several glasses of single malt. I could not justify what had happened; what I thought I had seen. It must have been the scotch.

It was a fitful night's sleep – I could not explain what I had seen. It had to have been a dog of some sort. Perhaps an exotic animal some crazy had smuggled into the city. It just had to be. In my head I hoped it was a bad dream or too many scotches. But in the back of my mind, I somehow remembered being a witness to something similar at my father's camp in Georgia. It was likely only the nightmare of a young, impressionable child and the screams this evening must have brought that dream to the surface.

The next morning Zoe called and insisted we see each other. I really didn't want any part of this mess, but told her I'd meet her at her apartment in two hours. When I arrived she was as edgy as a caged cat. It took me thirty minutes to calm her down. She had gotten lunch and we sat in her kitchen drinking microbrew and eating pizza.

"Zoe, I read your article and it's fine, very informative and edgy. I'm not sure your editor will print all the names of the congressmen you believe are involved in some of those shady deals you wrote about."

"Simon, all this crazy stuff is happening and it gets worse every day. I can't get anyone, including my editor, to pay attention. This attack you witnessed last night. Will anyone believe you? You were there and know what happened, but have the police called you? Or a newspaper? Has anyone called?"

"Zoe, I don't know what I saw last night. I had a lot to drink and it was late and I just can't say. Don't read anything into it. I have to go right now, but will call you again soon."

I left her place and walked the streets. Just a little downtime was what I needed to forget the horror I thought I had witnessed.

4 – Becketts

At noon, I made my way to Becketts. It was satisfying sitting among strangers. No demands, no questions. Just my own nightmare to sit on my shoulders.

Becketts was the last bookstore in DC where you could relax. I was free to read a novel, write notes or simply mingle. Able to order a glass of single malt and still enjoy a cigarette were an absolute luxury. The east side of this sanctuary opened onto 19th street and was dotted with small café tables. The outside tables allowed an unhindered view of both 19th and Q streets — likely the reason you could still smoke.

Vacationers' money was neither needed nor encouraged. Grubby children fresh from the National Zoo, parents bitching and tired from schlepping through three of the Smithsonian buildings were not a welcome addition. Rarely did they stay for more than fifteen minutes since the price of their drinks was double what regulars paid. Mel watched out for the regulars.

No pressure, no mumbling high school girls, no cocktail/mom waitresses trying to make the rent. Just a glass of single malt and relaxation. Being a researcher for 2nd rung newspapers did not ingratiate me to the brass-and-glass bunch sucking down white wine and grabbing at any bottom that approached their hand. All were there to have a good time. Selfish bastards, but it worked for me.

5 – The Gig

Beckett's regulars crowded the tables and yet no one bothered me. Except for Leslie. He was pushy and kind of weird in a lot of ways. Always admiring his long, slim fingers – what a nut job. I didn't like him much, but he grew on me in that odd sort of I-should-get-to-know-this-freak kind of way.

I was enjoying my drink, ignoring the masses, when Leslie sauntered over with, "Hey handsome, how are you tonight?" Ignoring my physical revulsion, he continued on and on about so many things about which I did not care. Trying to feign politeness and participate in this inane conversation, I mentioned my Georgia background. Leslie immediately knew someone that needed a bit of work down there. His contact was willing to pay big money, but required a quick turnaround.

My magic button...money...and lots of it.

Leslie went on that there was a house and a girl in Georgia somewhere and well, this guy with a lot of friends on Capitol Hill wanted some photos of anyone that called on her. Some woman on Pritchard Street. No big thing – he wanted someone that could handle any unlikely interactions with the locals. With my Georgia roots and assumed inbred connections I would be perfect. And his guy was willing to pay a lot of cash – no questions asked. I wanted out of town after last night's excitement so I quickly closed the deal. I would get hold of Zoe when I returned.

I rented a car and started the trek south. My cameras, a bumping Nikon D50IR with infrared and a Sony digital with unbelievable low light capabilities were at my side. I did not like to spend money on equipment like this, but cameras had become invaluable tools. My slow digression into the baser, yet more profitable side of investigative reporting paid the bills so I justified the expense. I was not a National Geographic kind of guy and clients did not pay this kind of money for a few pictures of a goat on some hillside. Ya gotta go for the money.

G G G

Journal #7 - Grace
Entries 6-9

6 – Purgatory

Fourteen hours later I pulled into the only motel in town. I remembered it vividly. It was the only place where used car dealers and stay-at-home moms could meet. It had not changed in twenty years as I am sure neither had the bed sheets.

When checking in, old Roy commented how I looked familiar. I feigned ignorance and asked for a room on the end of a hallway. No one stopped here unless they were lost. Then they were lucky to get out. Grabbing the key, I drove to the last room on the flat, ugly span of building. The ice machine was working overtime, yet no ice was in the bin. The soda machine sat idle and the smell of wet mold saturated the carpet-tiled hallway.

I tossed my bag on the worn comforter and returned to my car, cameras in tow. I found the house on Pritchard Street Leslie had proffered. It was vaguely familiar, but it had been eleven years since I traveled this town.

After five minutes of maneuvering to the perfect viewing spot, I parked. Nothing was stirring – not air, not people – not life. Overwhelming quiet, overwhelming sadness, overwhelming neglect.

I was again validated in my decision to leave this place of agony.

As I sat in my car the stifling heat reminded me of my advancing age and narrowing tolerance for anything uncomfortable. Being here was unpleasant for so very many reasons. The longer I sat and sweat, the more the payoff was becoming less enticing and not worth the torment – even though it was temporary.

From my dark, muggy spot under the hundred-year-old magnolia there was barely a breeze to be had and the damn cricket screams were never ending.

I stared at the clapboard house. The corner open window was dressed with an old aluminum screen riddled with rust and dotted with gaping age holes.

My eyes focused on a worn cotton dress clinging to a very sweaty body. She sat looking through the dirty screen as if a lost love would emerge.

An old fan declared noisy, irregular beats in the background and lucid tones of "he done me wrong" songs played on the only radio station available in this patch of hot, humid real estate. Two moldy chairs on the front porch and numerous chimes interspersed with dead plants wrapped in macramé hangers reaffirmed that nothing survives this heat.

What is it about southerners and their fascination with chimes? They hang these ugly groupings on any protruding material they can find. Shells, glass, iron, tin, beads, bones – trash. A simple breeze happens along and the friggin' town sounds like a Freddie Krueger movie. Just waiting for blood to spill and unearthly screams from someone's backyard to fill a quiet evening.

How the hell long was I gonna have to sit and watch? All she did was stare through that filthy screen. I had thought the cash would be worth my trip back into purgatory, but I was reassessing this choice. My condo in DC with air conditioning, view of DuPont Circle and Connecticut Avenue, concierge to fetch me pizza or moo shu pork at 2:00 a.m. was ever more a reason to pack up and go home.

7 – Reflections

My mind wrestled with old memories. I may have been born into this heat, played with the racist bastards next-door and supported the political scum of southern Georgia, but I had Yankee genes.

I hated the South and all it housed. The wet, moldy bathrooms, sweaty faces and necks on the most beautiful of women, dirt running down the back and ass of every redneck in a grocery store. The north beckoned at an early age. After a tour in NYC, DC was my last stop. Anywhere north of the Mason Dixon would have been fine.

I reminded myself that the cash for this job was too good to ignore. Nothing hard and it was a town I was familiar with and could revisit without raising too many suspicions. I even had a cousin on the three-man police force.

What was his name? Gomer? Bobby Joe? Nah, it was Wesley just as it was "Wesley" for the other 1,003 male residents in this simmering pit of torment. Guess Jackson Creek's baby books discounted the first 22 letters of the alphabet.

Everyone's nickname was Bubba so it didn't really matter what your Christ-given, preacher-confirmed, baptized-in-the-creek name may have been. Bobby Joe, Bobby Bill or Bobby Jim -- Bubba was the name to which you answered. I lucked out since my mother was reading the New Testament when she was pregnant. Thankfully, she went with Simon – cudda been Hezekiah.

Here, you just went along. Didn't raise a lot of political fuss 'cause the guy from your district funneled in enough cash to keep residents placated. The locals didn't want much either. Keep the bar going, the post office in the back of Selena's diner, the John Deere lot.

No road upkeep was needed for the dirt-and-rock pitted trail into town, and a steady flow of cash to the mayor and sheriff ensured a no-problem town.

After the gold mining petered out, the cemetery was the only real moneymaking business around. No one cared who was buried in Aunt Birdie's plot. If Birdie died and her plot was being used, the family got a bit of cash and another place for auntie to spend eternity under a newly planted magnolia.

Been that way since Thunder Road casualties filled most of the Tennessee & Bama graveyards. Just push those bones across the border – Georgia was always open to alternative cash flows.

Hell, Marve would bury anyone or anything, for any reason - for a price. Cash opened doors and pushed sensibilities sideways. Even the new yuppie types invading town were welcome. Baptists turned their heads and accepted the cash-flush newcomers. Their large and frequent contributions to town coffers made some of their odd customs seem not so strange.

I thought back on some of my other gigs. They were at least invigorating: shots fired, women fighting, police lights flashing. This was, well, boring, but like the Baptists, the cash was terrific so why make a fuss. How the hell else was I to pay for my needs that dotted my air-conditioned condo?

Just photograph anyone that knocked on her door. Forward the picture, any details with arrival and departure time. Simple.

I wiped my forehead again and looked toward her window.

She continued to aimlessly stare into the humid night, her wet dress ever more caressing her body. Her right arm gently resting on the windowsill, left hand brushing back the sweat running down her jaw, her eyes still searching.

Something about her was mesmerizing and somewhat familiar. Not a top of the line beauty I had brushed against in NYC or DC, but the need in her face was numbing. Three hours of watching, sweating and crap coffee and I wanted to leave - back to the flea-infested carpet that lined my motel room. Not that price determined my choice – just geography.

There have been a few occasions when I longed for the quiet, uninterrupted peace of this wretched ring of hell – admittedly after several glasses of an expensive single malt. As horrific as it was growing up: pimply-faced Bubbas and Billy Bobs, overflowing hips of farm girls in jean shorts, farm animals breeding everywhere you looked, sales women in faded cotton shifts with over-fried permanents and every male chromosome in town spitting tobacco juice on any clean surface, this place held a minor bit of solace.

When I left it, I never looked back. I wanted so much more. My travels north brought me physical comforts, but once in a great while old emotional ties were overwhelming. I got along okay as a kid much like the rest of the barefoot, smelly urchins that lived here. My old man drank way too much, all the time. I expected my ass to be kicked at least twice a week. My mother wiped her hands on the only piece of clothing she ever wore.

No streetlights to condemn your being late to dinner, no cops screaming about loitering on a street corner, no ticket from some righteous meter maid pasted on your primo Camaro, and no girl that thought she was too good to be seen with you. Yeah, a few things tugged at my heart, but just a very few.

Here I am. Spying on someone I likely knew long ago. I could not place her face and the name Baxter was not familiar. Although with the marriage and divorce rates here who could tell. Though she was familiar, back then a face was not important. Whatever was available below their tan line on jean shorts was what you remembered.

And, I do remember a few. The slimming of the waist and slight blossoming of the hip, the in or out belly button, the top of the panties – some with frayed elastic, likely hand-me-downs from older sisters I had previously known. Others were silky smooth from a recent purchase at WalMart. Regardless of the quality, the beckoning prize bore no nametags.

And I could have cared less. I was always selfish that way.

8 – The Stakeout

Dammit! The stinking bugs were feasting on every uncovered bit of flesh on my body.

Am not sure how I could hate being here more than I do at this moment.

From the corner of my eye I saw a shadow skirting the dim porch light. It captured my full attention. My Nikon was set to respond to any movement, it showed nothing for a heat image.

Gentle knocking on the screen door encouraged her to slowly rise up and head in that direction. I positioned my Sony on the rim of the car window, made sure the auto was on and waited for the shadow to turn around. One picture, just one and I might be able to leave this hell in a day or so.

I could not see her when she pushed open the screen door allowing the shadow to quickly slip inside. The Nikon only showed her form, but I took a dozen or so pictures with the Sony. The door rattled shut and nothing else moved. I didn't know where the figure had come from. I had a pretty unobstructed view of the house and had not noticed anyone walking or cars moving on the street. Heat stroke likely or just daydreaming – I slapped myself into alertness.

I never saw anyone leave – I must have dozed for three seconds when the bastard left. The window was now dark so I had screwed up this evening. That meant more nights sitting in sweat-soaked underwear, friggin' bugs the size of candy bars and listening to more chimes. I swear, if there was no breeze, these people walked onto the porch and pushed the stinking chimes themselves.

Driving into the motel lot I saw another guest had arrived. Fancy car for this dump.

People got lost all the time if they got off the interstate without knowing their location. They usually stuck it out for a couple of hours and then left regardless of how tired they thought they were.

The smell from my room greeted my nose before I even opened the door. The air conditioner was laboring to keep the room at 80 degrees, but it was better than outside in that recurring *rehearsal for hell* weather.

I lay across the bed, hoping the fleas had already enjoyed their daily meal and tried to imagine that the limp air was actually cool. The next thing I knew bright, hot sun was streaming through the dirty window landing directly on my throat.

I jumped up and shot into the bathroom – at least the shower would be cold. As long as you ignored the black mold climbing both the wall and shower curtain it was an almost pleasant experience. I didn't bother to check out the towel shoved on the back of the toilet. The towel bar had been pulled from the wall and plaster dust lay in a pile on the asbestos tiles.

Obviously the continental breakfast was a misprint on the room information sheet. No coffee maker, so against my better judgment I threw on shorts and went to the office hoping they would have something to drink other than warm Dr. Pepper.

As I opened the door Roy pointed toward the dirty coffee pot on the corner card table. Ummmm, beige coffee in a thin plastic cup – not even Styrofoam - and barely lukewarm. My day was off to another unsatisfying dance in this pit of despair. I carried the liquid offering carefully back to my room. I opened my door and reality was hard to ignore. The black of night was definitely an effective tool to rent these squalid rooms.

Aw hell, do what ya gotta do and no more complaining – down to business.

I grabbed my Sony and removed the SIM card – plugged it into my laptop. I was hopeful the slightest outline of a body would show. This camera could pick up anything that had a glint of light in the vicinity. My hopes remained high.

I actually got fourteen pictures off in that couple of seconds when the screen door opened. Her reflection was evident – really quite beautiful in the low light – yet not even a glint of a reflection from the shadow figure entering that clapboard house. I was annoyed, not deterred. I studied all the pictures. I found it amazing that the speed of the camera caught the subtle animation in her face. It was as if you could see her face move. I sat for a very long time trying to imagine what she was like. The dim pictures seemed to show a tinge of fear. I needed more photographs.

First, I had to get some real coffee. My mind was digressing. I needed air, even hot, moldy air.

I also figured it was time to stop by the sheriff's office and let my cousin know I was in town. Hopefully, he might not invite me for dinner – especially if he was still living with my aunt, Drema Sue. Now there was a flaky southern biscuit. She reminded me of the sisters in *Arsenic and Old Lace*. Daffy as a deaf bat and didn't have a mean bone in her aptly endowed body.

Arriving at the sheriff's office, I pushed open the door and there sat Wesley. Still as ugly and likely as stupid as when I left town. Now he was wearing a big gun and I could tell that he liked that. It was evident. The hardware made up for his many shortcomings. Probably how he got his dates.

His tooth-challenged mouth opened with "Cuzin! How'a y'all doin'?" spitting as he got out the words.

He tried to jump up from the old banker's chair and as expected made a lunge forward into the desk. Sad thing was, he didn't even realize how stupid he looked.

I stood for ten minutes while he spit and sprayed me and everything else in the room with questions, comments and "how great I am doing" phrases. The only way to get out was to accept a dinner invitation to join him and Aunt Drema Sue.

I should have known better – I should have known better – I should have... Hell, forget the coffee – I need a drink.

9 – The Reunion

Drema Sue was a looker way back when – not much of an intellectual, but a looker and she could cook. Anything, anytime. I liked being there with my momma cause there was always good food: eggs and sausage gravy, chicken and dumplings, bacon soppins' and scratch biscuits with every meal. Ummmmm. I guessed I could put up with her chaotic mind-set for one of her dinners.

I walked onto the porch and could smell her food: country ham, cornbread, slow simmered green beans and those creamy mashed potatoes she always made. My mouth was watering and I could not wait to get inside.

Wesley opened the door and my appetite seemed to leave immediately. I could take Drema Sue sitting across from me, but Wesley with food projecting out his mouth each time he spoke was becoming my line in the sand. Maybe if I talked all night – he would be still. Right, hope sprang eternal.

Drema Sue grabbed me in a bear hug and her wet apron clung to my shirt. Her Midnight in Paris perfume hadn't changed in thirty years and her fleshy arms pinned mine to my side. Her hair held a dusting of flour from her biscuit making.

I wasn't sure what the blotch of green on her arm was, but decided against asking. Her hug was like a straitjacket and I knew better than to try and squirm away. I stood, listened and agreed with her every other comment.

She blurted, "Sweetie you never called, you never wrote. Lord, you have sprouted so tall, you look just like your momma. Bless her little heart that the Lord took her too early in her life and thankfully you have no apparent defects from your father, that drunken bum that drained the life force from your momma and caused her early-calling to the Lord's house."

Yup. Nothing had changed.

Wesley tramped through the house dragging his ungainly form while knocking into anything in his way – even if it was the wall. Drema Sue had the table set, her best aqua blue melamine dishes, paper napkins and flatware from when she was married to Yancy, that great man of God that the Lord took goin' on two years ago now. Bless his sweet Lord-lovin' heart, she loved Yancy so hard and so did his followers. He was the pastor at the Church of Christ and him being that she didn't have to put up with any of those Baptists that threw their noses in the air when she saw them in Butts Family Foods outside Atlanta.

We sat at the table, Drema Sue prayed for six minutes and then started her two-hour "catch up" on life in Jackson Creek. "Now Simon, you would be amazed at how things have changed here."

She continued, "Child, have some of that fresh ham and I made the red-eye gravy you always liked. We got fresh peach pie for dessert. Woulda had ice cream, but Wesley forgot to get it. Him and his busy schedule.

Baby, you're too skinny. You aren't eatin' enough child. You need good home cookin' and a wife. You seeing anyone?

"There are still some nice girls here. Remember Grace, that pretty thing? You dated her sister Maggie as I recall. That Maggie left town about a year after you and she never did look back.

She left Grace to take care of their dying momma and care for that old house on Pritchard Street.

"It's a shame that Grace isn't married. Good Christian girl too. Comes to church every Sunday and sometimes on Wednesday nights. Well, not lately – figured she must be feeling a bit ill. I must remember to go over and check on her.

"Anyway, I can't believe no one has grabbed her yet. You might just want to visit…"

Wesley interrupted his momma with "Hey Simon, getting' anything good up where you are? What's it like dating Yankee girls? Are they as good as…" Drema Sue slapped his arm. "Wesley, shut your demon mouth. You will be respectful at my dinner table. Save your dirty talk for your new friends."

Dinner proceeded with Drema Sue relating each and every marriage, divorce, death, unwed birth, Baptist women seen smoking in the parking lot, back-door romances on each and every street in town and the blasted newcomers that acted like they owned everything.

I listened and ate heartily while trying to ignore the words assaulting my senses. Wesley stayed quiet. He knew where his cornbread was buttered – along with the squash, pinto beans and fried potatoes.

Before I could leave, Drema Sue insisted that I stay with her till my business was completed. She said she would not have kin staying in that filthy motel that was a pocket of Satan's hell while her clean, Christian home was available. Her food would nourish my skinny frame and her house in praise of the Lord would nourish my soul.

Wesley smiled and I knew my choices were gone. I gave away my privacy and freedom of movement – all for a good meal. Rethinking her cooking skills – it was worth it.

I left the house intending to pack my room and relocate to Drema Sue's clean sheets and good food. Instead my mind turned to my job – my job on Pritchard Street. The job offering big bucks. The reason why I was treading heat and filth in this mistake of geography.

GGG

Journal #7 - Grace
Entries 10-14

10 – Grace

I never connected Grace and Pritchard Street. Too many years, too many hard times, too much drinking and too many nights of passing out trying to forget – forget so many things. Times I wanted to leave behind and had apparently done a great job of it.

The moment Drema Sue spoke her name my mind filled with angst and lust. Yes, I remembered Grace. She was an occasional focus of my thoughts, dreams and hormones during senior year. Though I dated her sister Maggie, Grace was still a beauty. Still, at fifteen girls that young are dangerous. Taking one of them behind the barn bought you an ass full of buckshot from a variety of relatives. But, I couldn't pass her up.

Grace never had it easy growing up. A stream of *uncles* visited her house and each had a hard time keeping his hands off her. Her mother was sickly, likely the bourbon she kept close at hand, and didn't care much for either of her girls.

Grace was sweet and physically mature, but an innocent soul in so many ways. She believed the best about everyone and trusted without question.

I loved Grace, but dated Maggie. I thought I loved Maggie too, but at seventeen love is just sex. Hormones, physical satisfaction, lust and time spent waiting for your next easy mark – yeah, they were all love. Your body shaking with tremors on the belly of an untouched farm girl. Her wicked smooth breasts touching your throat, arms and chest. Those tight thighs wrapped around wherever you wanted them. These girls didn't expect anything. Her unknowing hips followed your lead – whatever made you happy 'cause if you were happy you'd ask her out again. Because to her it just might be love.

Even *used* farm girls held a measure of satisfaction. You promised that warm, accepting body the world – you were gonna be there forever, she was the one you wanted and the moment you released the hormones that coursed through your body – you knew better. She was dirt and you would likely never see her again, and you did not care.

Love was not in your vocabulary. Physical release, hormones emptying into an accepting vessel, an uninitiated yet comely body sighing with need because she thought it was what you wanted to hear and hoped to turn you on. Yet, you thought of your next conquest. That is what matters to your ugly soul when you're young and haven't yet grown a heart.

You wanted a future that did not include dirt roads, gravel pits or often used farm girls. The bodies were dispensable, they were adequate for the time you needed – the roads got you where you needed to be – neither had any part in my future.

I maneuvered back to the wretched 10x10 motel room and sat on the bed. All I could do was stare at the water-stained walls. My suitcase on the vile comforter and – I remembered how I had begged Grace to leave – to come with me in search of Nirvana. She could not leave this place and I could not stay. There was something better out there and I needed to find it.

Staring at her beauty that night so long ago pulled at my heart. Still, I stood up, zipped my jeans, looked at her on the sofa and bid her goodbye. Grabbing my backpack, I left and didn't look back.

I did everything in my power not to remember and I had done a pretty good job. Had I not met Leslie at Becketts my life would still be simple - boozy, arrogant and unfulfilling, but simple. I would not have to face my past. I would not be back here in this hole – in this pit. I would not have to remember.

Money was not worth this revisit to hell. Money was no longer motivating. Money became an anchor pulling on my life and soul. Money was killing me.

11 – The Realization

I grabbed my two clean shirts, bathroom items and left the room. When checking out, Roy asked if I had enjoyed my stay. I mumbled he should shove it up his ass, but he paid no attention – he was too involved trying to redo the charge slip for the third time.

Depositing my clothes and few bathroom necessities in Drema Sue's spare bedroom was almost magical. A clean room, fresh bed sheets, sparkling albeit simple bathroom. Inviting, with only the necessities. I was happy. I grabbed my cameras and could not wait to maneuver to the magnolia on Pritchard Street.

Now that I knew Grace was the face staring through the window screen I was needful to see her again. I parked under the tree and waited for her to appear at the window. It was not long before the light in the window cast shadows on her cheekbones. She sat, looking through the screen, exactly as she had the night before. Who was she waiting for? Somewhere in my mind I thought it might be me – yet I knew better.

My cameras at the ready, I waited. Questions shot through my head. Why was she the focus of this job? Had she met someone up north that was checking on her? Had she entertained some errant husband and his suspicious wife wanted photos? Grace was a nothing in the scheme of life – well, almost a nothing.

When the chimes started to move and made a weird tinkling – nothing showed on my Nikon, but now the window was empty as the screen door opened. I sat in the heat, bugs feasting on my flesh, wiping sweat from every corner of my body. I saw her – I think it was her – I saw bodies.

She stood quite still – her wet dress holding to each and every curve of her body. A hand touched her waist, her bottom, and her throat.

A dark figure positioned his head on Grace's shoulder. She seemed to collapse – yet not so. I saw a rivulet coursing down her neck. It was dark – it could not be blood. I sat riveted to the seat and took pictures, and stared. What the hell was this? What was happening?

I bolted from my seat and fell when I pushed open the car door. I had to help her. As I ran to the house, I could see through the window that her head turned and she looked out at me running toward the porch. Her eyes closed and she fell limp.

The moment I got to the porch, I pulled back the screen door – screaming "Grace, Grace – answer me!"

The front door opened. There she stood – a faint smile on her face, asking, "What's going on? What's the problem? Who are you and what are you doing here?"

My body could not move. I froze, focused on her face. Beautiful yet worn. I stood fixated as memories flooded over me. Memories flooded. Who was this woman with blood trickling down her neck?

I pushed passed her, heading for the bedroom looking for the other figure. The bedroom was empty; the house was empty. There was no one else there. I went back to the front room and grabbed Grace. She looked so frail and leaned into my body to steady herself. I got her to the couch and sat with her until she appeared ready to speak. I tried to wipe her neck, but she pushed my hand away each time I attempted to do so.

"Grace, what just happened? I saw someone attack you. Who was it? Tell me and I'll kill him. Let me take you to the hospital."

Grace gently turned toward me and spoke quietly "Simon? Why are you here? Were you watching me?

What are you doing in the house? I don't need to go anywhere, I just need you to be with me for a little." All she would let me do was sit and hold her close and make sure no one else bothered her. It would be a long night.

I cat napped all night. Grace leaned peacefully on my chest, her only movement was her shallow breathing that I checked several times – just to make sure. Her body next to mine felt so good. For the first time since arriving in town, I did not notice the heat, lack of air-conditioning or the chimes on the porch.

When sunrise arrived Grace stirred slightly; enough to make me sit at attention. She woke slowly and was not at all interested in answering questions. She spent time in the bathroom cleaning her self up and when she emerged I had coffee made and a couple of pieces of toast ready.

Grace looked tired, but she was still beautiful. The memories of times past flooded my head and my loins. I filled her coffee cup a second time and finally she spoke. I was definitely not prepared for what she had to say.

"Do you know anything about the undead?" When my mouth dropped she added, "The dead who awake to drink the blood of the living. Do you know anything about them?" She turned the left side of her neck toward me. At first I could not believe my ears, but when my eyes saw severe lacerations and significant bruising around her throat I could only give her the benefit of the doubt.

She slowly began to recount the terror of the years after I left. "I know this will be hard to believe. I struggled with it for the past couple of years, then I got tired of fighting and became part of the insanity. I believed none of this undead stuff before I met Melosh. He arrived here with a group of businessmen that were buying up the old Kruger mining property outside of Ackerman. Melosh was a little weird and not great looking, but he was such a gentleman.

Made me feel like a million bucks. Feeling that way in this town meant a lot.

"They were here for a week and ate most of their meals at the diner. One thing led to another and he asked me out. Took me all the way to Atlanta to a real fancy place. He even bought me a dress and a gold bracelet to wear. After a couple of dates he grabbed me in the back of his limo and bit my neck so hard I passed out. The pain was excruciating. The next thing I knew, I was in his hotel room for three days. He stayed at my neck constantly until I had no will left at all.

"It's hard to explain, but I could not leave. At times he was physically abusive, yet he also treated me well, and with no other way out of this place, I accepted things the way they were. After a while, I actually looked forward to his visits.

I don't know if I really liked it, was addicted or just scared enough to convince myself. Then things changed a couple of months ago. He wanted me to be accessible to one of his friends. Several have showed up saying Melosh told them to stop by and that I would make myself available for them.

"The last time I spoke to Melosh, he swore no one was told to come by. He was very angry and he has a horrendous temper. He wanted their names, but I was afraid to tell him. These *friends* have been coming by and I am afraid of them. They scare me and if Melosh doesn't kill me – one of them will. I'm doomed."

I sat in stunned silence, trying to get my mind around the insanity. I was unsure if I should take her to a hospital, back to DC with me or load my gun and look for her abusers. I told her we had to go and speak to the sheriff. She grabbed my arm. I could feel her fear and see it in her eyes.

"The sheriff is one of them and Wesley is his gofer."

Wesley was stupid, and I wondered why they would want him, but he could serve a useful purpose running their filthy errands.

Grace slumped in her chair exhausted from recounting her horror. I lifted her gently and placed her on the bed terrified to leave her alone, but I wanted my own kind of blood. I wanted dead bodies, I wanted a slaughter, I wanted vengeance and I was not willing to accept anything less.

Sitting at her side I watched her breathe for almost two hours. It was hard to understand, let alone accept, what she had told me. I felt like a caged animal. My mind was racing to try to make sense of the previous night. My first priority was to protect Grace. No matter what it took.

I decided to take her to Drema Sue's. She would stay with me until I could get some answers or kill every last bastard that I thought may have hurt her. Either way, she would be safe. Wesley would never make a move with both Drema Sue and me in the house. I would make sure of that.

12 – The Getaway

I packed some of her things, threw her toiletries into a plastic grocery bag and woke her gently. I insisted she come with me and she did not refuse. She looked relieved. "Drema Sue would love to fuss over you and there was no way any demon of hell would get through her army of angels."

Grace attempted a smile indicating she knew exactly what I meant.

Settling Grace into my room, I insisted she not call anyone. Absolutely no one. I took her cell with me and would handle any calls or texts that might get through. Drema Sue walked into the hallway, saw Grace on the bed and knew something had happened.

She motioned for me to meet her in the kitchen. I let Grace rest and then tried with all my might to explain to this holy woman what had transpired.

It did not take much explaining. Drema Sue had accepted that Satan took many forms and there was enough evil in town that nothing surprised her. She promised no one would harm Grace because they would have to get through her.

Her back straightened and she vowed, "Ain't no demon of hell, force of Satan or vile guardian of the dark side was gonna get past me. I've got my prayer chain started, Preacher Bobby will come over to read scripture and we will not step one foot out of this God-fearin' Christian home that loves the Lord.

And if my angels need any help, I still have Emmett's double barrel in the closet. He always told me to keep it loaded 'cause you never knew when something bad might be comin' through the door."

Drema Sue was even more upset when I told her Wesley was hanging around with this group.

"Well, I knew that boy was into somethin' ugly. He was never rite-brite and always followed the bad kids. If there was money or beer he just went on like he knew what he was doin'. I blame his daddy for letting him jump in that shallow pond off Treaton Road too many times and…"

I interrupted her knowing she was not one to keep her stories short. Now, I would have to deal with Wesley so he did not return to the house and I had to come up with something quick.

Perhaps I would just kill him, but would rethink that choice before pulling the trigger. Maybe I could use him to find the rest of the group. I would kill each and every one of them. Very slowly while inflicting tremendous pain.

Drema Sue told me the new people in town started their own place of worship. It didn't look like a church, no one other than the newcomers went to it and there wasn't a cross anywhere to be seen. They built it up on the Kruger property.

"I don't know where they all live 'cause none of them bought or rented anything in town. Right weird they are, they spend a lot of money so nobody much bothers them.

Still, I always knew there was something unchristian about…"

Quickly interrupting her speech again, I told Drema Sue that Grace hadn't eaten well in weeks and maybe she could make her something. "Lord, yes. Let me work on makin' this child of the Lord well. I didn't see her real close from the hallway, but she looks a might thinner than I remember. Maybe if I made…" her voice trailed off as she headed for the kitchen.

I didn't have much time to plan my next move: keep Wesley at bay until I could put a bullet in his head. Simple actions made me happy.

13 – The Kill

I needed to get up to the old Kruger place. Why were they there? What was it about that property that attracted them here? And then it hit me - the old gold mining tunnels. That's what they wanted.

Georgia was the site of the first gold rush and there were miles of deep, dark, tunnels and caverns. Secluded entrances far enough back from the road that anyone approaching could be seen and stopped. I had to get up there and find out what they were hiding.

Yeah, Wesley was my way in – maybe I wouldn't kill him right away. He might serve a purpose. If he didn't, his time was shortened by a whole lot.

I left Drema Sue to fuss over Grace figuring I could get to Wesley before he left work. I pushed open the office door and was not surprised to see him dozing while leaning his head against the water cooler. I had a perfect shot to his head, but decided he was currently useful. My time would come.

I didn't know exactly how I was going to deal with any of these filthy shits, but I knew bullets weren't going to help. Believe I read that wooden stakes in the chest were what was required, or ripping off their heads and burying them. Hell, where was an instruction manual when you needed it?

Ummmm, Wesley had a lot of hunting gear – gotta be something here I can use.

I kicked his leg and his fleshy, unkempt frame toppled forward. "Cuz, cuz, what ya doin'? I was just takin' a quick nap. Why ya here? What's happenin'?" Wesley had not accumulated any IQ points since fourth grade. He was huge, ugly and stupid. His brawn, slimy character and ability to fart on demand were what got him free beer and cheers from his local scum friends.

"Wesley, hey, Drema Sue said you got some new friends livin' up at Krugers old place. I need some fun. How 'bout you introduce me. Maybe we can party? They got any lookers up there that might be achin' for a good time?"

"Cuz, they got all kinds of good times up there. I can't believe you want some of my funnin'. Why'd you think of askin' me? You ain't never been interested in my parties."

"Wesley, I figure I've never given you a fair chance and, well, maybe it's time I try to make amends. Do ya think we could party today?"

"Sure, Cuz, they raise a lot of hell at night – daytime they don't do much – kinda sleep late and take care of their businesses – when the sun goes down they party big time. Kinda nice you want to hang with me. C'mon, we can take my Humvee."

"Hey Wesley, maybe we could also hunt just a little while we're there. I remember old man Kruger had lots of critters on that property. It's not like we have to eat them – let's just kill'em for fun. Remember how you used to do that when we were kids?"

His eyes lit up with excitement. Killing just for fun. He liked that – real well. He pushed open the back room of the office where Sheriff Buck and the other deputy kept "their stuff" including all their hunting gear. There stood a myriad of violent items: an Arrow Precision Impala compound bow, pump action shotgun, fishing poles, nets, a 30.06 with scope and a cross-bow. A large collection of knives to gut anything on the planet and ugly bait hooks for 300lb pike.

I suggested the compound bow, crossbow and collection of knives – this way we would not be noisy. He hesitated a bit saying the crossbow belonged to the sheriff and we had to be careful. Sheriff Buck had some arrows that were titanium, but he really liked his custom wood arrows from the Cajun Wood Archery place down near Macon. He only used them for serious hunting.

I figured my hunting was serious and wood was wood – stake or arrow – just different shape. "We should take them all." He was afraid 'cause Sheriff Buck might get angry, but I told him, "I'll replace each and every one we use. Won't it be great to just kill things at Krugers?"

He smiled that disgusting semi-toothless grin he did so well and we threw all the equipment into his Humvee and left for Krugers. I asked where he got the money for his new Humvee. He said he did some odd jobs for the newcomers, introducing them to the locals in town. Just little things like that.

When his end came it would be nice to know I rid the world of this insufferable imbecile. Leaving at two Wesley drove hard and fast and never shut his stupid mouth.

He droned on about the girls he dated. Well, not actually dated, just those he got drunk enough to let him crawl over their bodies. He didn't shut up till we hit Kruger's.

Arriving at the property there was nothing moving – not a bird, deer, rabbit – not even a breeze. I read somewhere that animals are afraid of the undead creatures of the night.

Perhaps that was the reason for the lack of any breathing species. I knew there was little time left, maybe three hours before sunset, then darkness would be a problem.

Wesley looked around and was furious there was nothing to kill. He had his heart set on gutting something ever since I mentioned it. I suggested we knock on the door of the house and ask permission to hunt in the woods. He didn't want to do that 'cause sometimes these people got upset if you just showed up. I convinced him we would just knock and ask permission.

He finally followed me to the front door. The heat outside was kissing 102°, but the outside of the house felt cold and odd. There was no answer when I knocked. Wesley stood with that ugly grin saying "We gotta leave, ain't no one home, we better go."

I convinced him that I would just check the door and make sure nothing was wrong. There were a lot of cars in the back yard and someone should really answer. Maybe something had happened. The imbecile agreed with me. As I pushed open the door the smell of decay was sickening. There were few pieces of furniture and dark drapes covered the windows. There was no artificial light and the stench was overwhelming.

We walked into what appeared to be a living room with several chairs and a sofa – a center table piled with burnt candles and other trash. Wesley got real shaky.

"We gotta go, we gotta go, they gonna make trouble for me, we gotta go. I always do what they say and don't make no trouble. They gonna' get mad. I gotta get outta here."

"Wesley, I was wondering, did you ever bring anyone else up here? Did you ever bring Grace to visit?"

Wesley sucked in his breath and stammered "No, no, I ain't never brought her here. I tried to get her to meet some of the guys, but she didn't want no part of meetin' strangers.

The only thing I did was tell some of them guys about her and a few other girls just in case they wanted to invite them to their parties. I told them Grace worked at the diner and a couple of other girls at the WalMart. I think I might have said where Grace lived. I don't remember 'cause I think I was drinkin'. That's all I did, really."

I stood directly in front of him, raised my gun, pointed it at his head and simply pulled the trigger. His look of surprise was pretty satisfying. Those 1.5 seconds of fear, a question in his eyes and then the gory aftermath. Blood dripped from the hole in his forehead while the entire back of his head was plastered against the wall.

It was certainly a scene Wesley would have appreciated especially if he had done it. I thought about gutting him, just as he would have done, but didn't want to take the time.

I don't know how his corpse continued to stay on its feet, but when I pushed my fingers into his chest he delicately sat down on the filthy couch. Just in case there was any life left in his degenerate body, I took hold of the crossbow. Holding it against his chest, I let one of the sheriff's expensive, handmade wooden arrows find its way into his heart.

The force of the crossbow caused the arrow to go straight through his body and through the back of the couch.

I grabbed it from the floor and pushed it back into his chest along with the blood soaked matting from the sofa and dust from the floor. I wanted to ensure the arrow did not move again.

Okay then, Wesley was no longer an issue. I hadn't felt this good since I last enjoyed air conditioning. Now, I was pumped up and had other work to do.

I went from room to room, ripping down drapes and opening windows as I scoured the house. Nothing, no one. No sign of life. This wasn't Krugers old house – it was a new addition of sorts, but it was a dump.

I started down the basement steps and held my breath. The floor was covered with bones. A graveyard of some sort, but none of the bones were recognizable. I could not tell if they were animals or people. When I looked up my mouth dropped open. Cut into the cinderblock wall was an opening. As I walked closer, my feet were pushing bones out of the way. The opening was an entrance to the mine tunnels. Now that was a great hiding place.

Black as night, dank and filled with depraved fiends of hell. This was going to take some planning, but I had little time. How many were there? Where were they? There were hundreds of tunnels in this mountain. I checked my watch. It was 4:15 p.m. I had forty-five minutes at the outside, maybe an hour. This could not wait till morning. I had to take action now.

Going back to the Humvee, I grabbed every arrow I could manage, carried them back to the house and loaded the crossbow. I would kill those bastards one at a time until the arrows were gone. There was no other choice.

It took ten minutes walking the tunnel before I noticed the first coffin. It looked like a cheap wooden box. Sweat was pouring off me. Fear has a way of making your body do strange things. I had no experience fighting the princes of darkness – I could hardly believe what I was doing myself.

When I popped off the lid from the first coffin, a body appeared to be sleeping quite naturally. I quickly took the crossbow and shot it in the heart, but was unprepared for how terrified I felt. This demon's eyes and mouth shot open. Dark black eyes with almost an iridescent greenish glaze and from its mouth came a horrific low guttural moan. One arm tried to reach up to grab me. I pissed myself.

Okay, this was the first one, the hardest. Get your ass in gear and take care of business. I walked up and down the shafts.

At first shooting each and every body I could find – then realized I was running out of arrows. I decided to break those expensive shafts of wood in half and make as many of these undead – dead. I broke my last four arrows in half. The crossbow was no longer any help.

As I lifted each lid I had to stab the broken arrow through their chest. It was not easy and it was not pleasant. I took the half arrow with both hands, kneeled above the coffin and plunged the wood as hard as I could and used the crossbow to pound it further into the chest. Though they all drank blood, none came from their bodies. Only the most foul of odors, and unrelenting, bloodcurdling moans. The look of their eyes would never leave my mind.

The shapes of their mouths were twisted and horrific, coal black and filled with some awful goo. A glass of single malt was not gonna chase these nightmares away.

Figuring I had gotten sixteen of the bastards, I turned into the next tunnel. It held more coffins. This was not good since I had nothing left to fight them. I started running back toward the entrance and immediately knew I'd better start praying.

The tunnel filled with the noise of other lids popping opening, fierce banging and a fair amount of wailing. I glanced at my watch – it was 5:20 p. m. Time was against me.

I couldn't look back and just kept running. Sounds of screeching hurt my ears. Noises I have never before heard echoed through the tunnels. Something flew past me as I ran. When finally I got through the cinderblock opening and up the stairs I was face-to-face with two dark figures. I couldn't make out their faces, but they were big. Very big.

I stood absolutely still, unable to move any part of my being. I didn't know if I was going to be beat to death, ripped apart or just have my throat cut and laid out as dinner.

Though I could see their lips moving, I heard nothing. They pulled my arms and dragged me out of the house, set me on the porch and finally spoke, asking me if I was okay?

My mind was unsure what was happening. Was I dreaming? I needed time to regain my senses. After several minutes I raised my head from my hands, tried to clear my eyes and looked around.

There sat Sheriff Buck and his deputy, Trevor. They explained how they just happened by and saw Wesley's Humvee and came looking for him.

Sheriff Buck said, "Wesley was prone to drinking a bit and then roaming around the old, deserted house and tunnels looking for any bit of gold that might be hiding in the dirt." As I watched Buck's mouth move his face muscles seemed to move in an awkward way. As if they were realigning somehow. I have to get out of here. I'm losing my mind.

"I warned him a right bunch of times about him gettin' his self lost in them mineshafts. Wesley was a bit hardheaded."

They had been in the house and could not have missed Wesley's body on the couch. When I asked where Wesley was, Sheriff Buck said he was taking care of business in the backyard and that his deputy, Trevor, would take me home. Seems some junkyard must have parked a bunch of cars without getting permission.

"Ya'll don't worry, we'll take care of our own little problems here. By the way, what scared you so bad?" I told him that I tripped on the cellar stairs and there were no lights.

"Yup, happens when you go to places you ought not be. Good thing nothing more serious happened boy. You ought get home and see what Drema Sue is fixin' you for dinner. I heard tell you got Grace with you – is that true?"

"For a while. She wasn't feeling well and Drema Sue wanted to help her out."

"Yup, sounds just like your Drema Sue. Got a heart of gold and never makes any trouble for anyone. You need to watch over Grace and make sure she stays safe. Know what I mean?"

"Sheriff Buck, Wesley said there were a lot of newcomers in town?"

Buck came back "Now ya know your cousin ain't the brightest bulb in the box. He does what he's told, but not much of anything important stays in his head. We just had a revival in town and also a bus tour of Yankees thinking they could find gold in those old tunnels. Yeah, they were newcomers, but most have left. Just a nothing piece of information. Ya know how Wesley gets things mixed up in his head.

"Not ya worry now boy. Trevor will take you to Drema Sue's. You get yourself a hot shower and some of her good fixins'. Tell her Wesley likely won't be home right away. Got a lot of work to do trying to sort out this car parking thing and ya know how slow Wesley can be. I'll stop by tomorrow and check on you and Grace. Just make sure all is well. Maybe Drema Sue will have some of her famous lemonade when I come callin'." He smiled and gave Trevor the eye to get me out of there.

Trevor made inane conversation on the way back to the house and I had no idea who to trust. The heat was now the least of my worries.

14 – The Cleanup

Trevor pulled up at the house and asked me to give his regards to Drema Sue and Grace. He thought Grace was a real special kinda person and hoped she was gonna be just fine. He knew Drema Sue's cookin' would make anyone fine. I got out of the car thinking Trevor and Sheriff Buck seemed more than interested in Grace's well being.

I stepped gingerly onto Drema Sue's porch. How would I tell her about Wesley? What could I tell her about Wesley? Slowly approaching the screen door, I was reminded of just how much I missed the comforting sound of the old wooden door against the doorframe.

I also vividly remembered it when I lived here with my momma. Especially when my daddy came home drunk, screeched into Drema Sue's yard screaming for his family and once tried to rip the door from its hinges.

I had to get Grace out of here; make sure Drema Sue was safe, destroy the rest of the coffins and their inhabitants, maybe even kill Sheriff Buck. My God, how was I to do this? Where would I start? Why was killing everything in sight becoming so easy?

My heart was still pounding when I touched the door handle. Drema Sue appeared in front of me and my thoughts immediately turned to what was for dinner. What a wretched soul I had become.

Drema Sue said, "You'd better clean up before you put your dirty butt on my new chair covers." No one came to her dinner table lookin' like I did. I beat feet into the bathroom and I was a sorry sight. Did the best I could and actually said a prayer. What was becoming of me?

I walked into the parlor and there sat Grace. Drema Sue had gotten some food into her wasted frame and she actually looked freshened and pretty damn good.

Drema Sue moaned, "This child has been ignored for too long – not a bit of flesh on her bones and bless her heart, not near enough takin' care of. She needs a spat more food and a whole lot more attention. Now, Simon, your momma is lookin' down on you now makin' sure you do the right thing. This is no way for a child of the Lord to live. Simon, I am expectin' you to do your best."

As if I had any say – I knew what was happening. Drema Sue had thrown down the gauntlet – it was not a choice for me to pick up - it just mattered how long it took for me to do so. And I did it quickly.

The smell from the kitchen was inviting. Pork roast, red cabbage, greens, parsley potatoes, fresh applesauce, gravy and those biscuits. My mouth watered and I felt guilty. Guess I'd have to take care of Wesley's portion.

We started into the kitchen and Drema Sue wondered why Wesley wasn't yet home, but then he'd started doin' that anymore without even callin' to tell her so she could keep dinner covered and warm.

Well, she wasn't going to hold her food till he dragged his butt home so we three sat at the table. Drema Sue prayed for only four minutes this evening. Don't know why she cut it short, but I was thankful. I was hungry.

Grace picked at her food and Drema Sue insisted that she have some biscuits. "Nothing else made you feel better like biscuits, fresh butter and her pork gravy." I did not disagree.

Dinner did not hold much conversation. Grace was hesitant to broach any subject other than how sorry she was about missing church lately.

Drema Sue went on about how Wesley had changed and she always had high hopes for him, but he was the 'big disappointment' in her life. She figured the Lord had given him to her as a trial. She only prayed for his redemption. Still she wasn't sure that was gonna' happen before she personally went to be with the Lord.

We helped Drema Sue clean the kitchen. When she then went to the parlor for nightly prayer, Grace and I went to the back porch. At least the ceiling fan out there promised air movement – not cool, but moving. We settled into the glider and did not speak for several minutes.

Grace took my hand so lightly as not to feel real. She leaned her head against my shoulder and started to cry. She tried to speak saying she felt empty inside and there was simply no reason left to live. She lifted her head, "Simon, why didn't you make me go with you? Why did you leave me here? I have regretted every day since you left - each and every day."

All I could do was sit and hold her. I knew she did not want to talk or hear old excuses. She needed acceptance, solace, someone to hold her. Someone who wanted nothing, but her skin touching welcoming arms. When I put my arm around her shoulder, she melted into me and I knew this was how it would have to be at least for a time.

We sat in the glider for hours and as I listened to her soft, rhythmic breathing I tried to determine my next move. I was unsure what my first step would be, but I knew there would be violence involved. Yeah, and there would be blood. Had to be some of these demons that would run red – and I'd find them.

After carrying Grace to her room I fell into my bed. My mind was a blur. I remembered my daddy talking many years back how the undead roamed the back roads at night, but momma said it was only the liquor talking.

She went on to explain that it was crazy talk handed down from his weird mother, Anastas.

I wondered if momma was looking down from heaven, shaking her head as she watched this carnage. I also wondered where my daddy might be at this moment. Somehow I knew he was not near momma.

I fought sleep for most of the evening. It was a little after 8:00 a.m. when I heard knocking at the screen door. I sprang up ready for battle. Before I could yell out a warning, Drema Sue, already dressed with breakfast on the table, was answering the door.

I peeked down the hallway and saw Sheriff Buck standing like a concrete wall blocking most of the light that should have been streaming into the front room. Drema Sue insisted he come in and have some fresh lemonade and biscuits.

By the time I got clothes on, Sheriff Buck and Drema Sue were already in the kitchen and she was pouring him a tall glass of lemonade. I gingerly sat down, poured some coffee and piled bacon and biscuits on my plate.

Sheriff Buck cleared his throat, took a long drink of lemonade then looked like he was ready to break the bad news.

"Drema Sue, best to say it right out, your Wesley ain't comin' home no more. It's a real tragedy. He was trying to apprehend some violent car thieves. They gunned him down. He was a good deputy and I know he made his momma proud."

Drema Sue was visibly shaken. And as any southerner will attest, she would hold her grieving and crying for her time with the congregation and Pastor Bobby. She would hold herself together for now.

Sheriff Buck took another drink of lemonade and said "I truly would love to share breakfast with you and yours on this sad morning, that is if you would care to have me Drema Sue?"

She immediately rose and got him a place setting of her aqua melamine. "Of course you are welcome to share our bounty, Sheriff Buck. Wesley so loved his job and looked to you as a father figure since Yancy left to be with the Lord. I'm just going to freshen myself up a bit. You boys talk your men stuff. I'll be back in a little."

Sheriff Buck filled his plate and poured himself coffee. He looked my way, "Well, boy, you planning a long stay here with your aunt?"

I stared at him, "Really haven't made my final plans Sheriff. Is there a problem with me staying?"

Buck put another forkful of biscuit and bacon gravy into his mouth and shook his head. "Course not, you stay as long as you like. Jus' wonderin' what kind of business you in that brought you to our parts again? Been a long time since you left. Was right after your momma died if I recollect right?"

My gut pinched because this conversation could only end badly – for me – and Grace.

"I was doing some background investigative work, but that's done now. I might stay for a short visit with Drema Sue and Grace." Pushing the biscuit around my gravy – I wasn't really scared, but I also did not want any confrontation with Sheriff Buck. He could and would make life very difficult for anyone that crossed him. Even if he only thought they crossed him.

Buck continued, "Real hard thing for Drema Sue now that Wesley is gone. I figure I can make sure Trevor comes over here often enough to take care of any fixin' on the house she might need. Her being such a good Christian woman and helping out those less fortunate, I'd make sure she was never in any danger from those panhandlers that come round from over by the train tracks.

Yes, she is a good woman. You are a lucky boy she was here for you and your momma when your daddy got himself killed up in the mine. Yes, you just lucky, son."

I understood exactly what he was saying. He would tolerate me for a short period and he would ensure Drema Sue's safety when I left. There was no "future" for me here. He meant business and I knew it.

Grace came into the kitchen rubbing her eyes and asking if there was any breakfast. When she saw Sheriff Buck she froze. I started to pour her coffee when Buck stood up to leave.

He drawled, "I don't wanna take up any more of Drema Sue's time. She needs her rest and time to grieve for her boy." He would see her over at the church later today. Of course, he personally would take care of the arrangements.

Buck continued to let comforting words slip from his lying lips. "It's right unfair we can't have a viewing due to the tragic and heroic way Wesley died, but the town is gonna take care of all of Wesley's funeral expenses and there was an insurance policy so Drema Sue will be just fine."

We could depend on Sheriff Buck, just like we always could. He was there anytime we needed -- for anything we needed. All he wanted was our friendship and trust.

As he walked out the door, he turned his head. "Boy, next time you plan on comin' for a visit ya might want to let me know. Just so I know when to expect strangers in town."

"Strangers?"

"You know what I mean."

He walked out, tipping his hat to Grace and bidding me a speedy and safe trip home. I started breathing normally when he cleared the driveway. It was odd how he brought up my daddy getting killed at the mine. I wondered if that was a case file from his office I ought to investigate.

Grace sat in silence and a look of true relief covered her body after Buck left. I touched her hand and told her she was coming with me, back to DC. No way I was leaving her in this purgatory. There was no discussion – she would be safe with me. She let her hand relax on the table and a gentle smile covered her lips. She was still so beautiful.

I had thought I would have to make a difficult decision. Stay here and somehow fight these hordes of hell, or leave and find safety for Drema Sue and Grace. It had become abundantly clear there was only one choice.

Drema Sue would be fine as long as I kept my distance. Sheriff Buck wanted me gone more than he cared about Drema Sue or Pastor Bobby, and Buck would continue to take care of his town. Without help from anyone.

What I cared about was Grace, getting her healthy and far away from this pit. I wanted the bastard that did this to her.

I was anxious to get on the road. The moment I got Grace settled in my condo, I looked forward to a nice single malt at Becketts and a long conversation with Leslie.

GGG

Journal #7 - Grace
Entries 15-18

<u>15 – The Ride Home</u>
Grace and I left Jackson Creek. Drema Sue understood I had to leave and she agreed Grace needed more attention than she might be able to give right now. She made up her mind to try and help the young ones at church so they did not travel the same road as her Wesley, her baby, her cross to bear.

Drema Sue packed a basket of food for the trip north. I was gonna miss her fixins' and her gravy and biscuits. It was a fourteen-hour drive north. I gassed up at the Quick Stop and we left town, never looking back in the rearview.

Grace was quiet. She frequently touched her bruised neck, lightly, but with attention. She did not speak of the previous horrors of her life, but only stared ahead and appeared so docile that I felt I was kidnapping her.

Sitting quietly she occasionally looked over at me. "Simon, I so missed you. My mother's illness made me stay in that pit. I had no choice. Then, when you left, my soul was vacant. I thought of you each and every day. And when momma died I had no way to find you. I prayed you would look for me, but then just gave up. My heart broke. My heart gave up. My heart stopped."

Pulling off the highway I parked on the side road. I could only stare at her. "It was not that I wanted to leave you – I needed to leave Jackson Creek. My mother had died and I had to find my way. Something, someplace other than Jackson Creek. And I thought I had."

I could not explain the depth of my emotion right then. My soul was exposed and I was not accustomed to this.

Her eyes smiled at me, "Simon, I have loved you from the moment you touched my hand, the moment you kissed my shoulder, the moment you held me close, the moment our skin touched. Simon, I have never forgotten what we shared. Though you may only remember it as sex. I remember only softness, emotion and love, even if it was one-sided. I wanted to find that again and I have looked in so many places."

I could not speak. I knew what she meant. From the moment we touched that long time ago, we were destined – I left town like the ass I had become, but I remembered the love I once knew. The old love that now was consuming my soul, my heart, my being. I would make amends and I would garner retribution.

I touched her arm, tried to bring her close, but she sat stiff and silent. It was not the time for me to force any emotion. It was a time I should sit and listen. A time to give her the space she needed. My time to reveal my feelings would come. My time to make this up to her. My time to set all the records straight.

It was a long drive and worth every moment as we distanced ourselves from the raging heat and village of the undead. I tried to make sense of the past five days, but there was no way to justify anything that had happened. As long as I could keep Grace with me, I figured I could hold things together. Thankfully, she slept for most of the trip and was not talkative when she awoke. Her recovery was the most important thing in my world.

The minute I got off Rt. 95 and crossed Memorial Bridge, I felt a calm settle over my body. It was Sunday and traffic was almost reasonable. A right turn onto 23rd street eventually brought us to the circle and into Dupont where I was glad to see the parking garage.

Grace followed me to the elevators and hugged my arm as we rode to the top floor. She was still a small town girl and these surroundings were intimidating. She stared at the elevator's mahogany walls and polished brass rails.

The thick-carpeted hallways kept the place silent as a tomb – an unfortunate thought. She said she felt as though she were interrupting someone.

When we got into my condo, she seemed quite impressed. Most times that would boost my man hormones when a woman was impressed with my "things." Now, I was actually pleased that Grace liked it. Hormones aside – she seemed relaxed and happy.

I put her few things in the second bedroom and let her alone to rest for as long as she needed. "Grace, do me one favor – do not leave here for any reason. I have an errand to run, but I'll be close by. You have my cell number and if you want anything: food, magazines or whatever. Dial 633 for the concierge. He'll get what you need. Stay inside. I'll be back soon."

She nodded, showing she understood and lay across the bed. She was asleep before I left the room. I felt the need for a drink and Becketts was just down the street.

16 – The Gauntlet

For a Sunday evening Becketts was crowded. I took a table on the street, pushed my chair against the back wall and waited. Mel caught my eye and he knew what I wanted – a waiter quickly brought my drink.

I sat for forty-five minutes before Leslie appeared.

The little freak sauntered over to my table. "Well, handsome, how did the job go? Did you get pictures? I have the $10k cash when you hand them over." I simply smiled and asked him to sit down. I leaned in and when he bent closer my hands could not wait to grab his collar and twist it - hard. He turned bright red and gagged, his limp wrists and long fingers flailing about.

Out of the corner of my eye I spotted Mel holding up his hand up to a waiter that was headed my way. The waiter stopped. Leslie continued with deeper shades of red covering his face and throat. I loosened my grip ever so slightly so he could speak. "Ugh, uh, what are you doing? What's wrong? Have you lost your mind?"

I suggested that if I were to let go of his neck he should sit quietly at the table and listen to what I said and to make every effort to answer all my questions. He eked out, "Okay, okay – whatever you say."

I let go and he fell back into the chair, grabbing his throat, wiping his eyes and grabbing his legs. "Are you crazy? Why did you attack me? I was happy to see…"

I slapped my hand on the table and he shut up. I told him if he spoke before I asked a question, I would put a bullet between his legs. That way he could slowly suffer instead of die. He sat at attention and didn't move a muscle.

"Leslie, exactly who wanted those pictures of the woman on Pritchard Street? Who paid me to find out who might be going to her house? I want answers now, Leslie – don't think about it – tell me the truth."

He looked terrified. That was gratifying. He stammered back, "I, I, um, just this guy I know, nobody special. I think he knows a guy that met the girl once and just wanted to keep tabs on her. That's all. Why? What happened?"

"Leslie, any reason you did not mention the undead things living in the mining tunnels? You about got me killed and I want to know why. I want this guy's name."

Leslie cried that he didn't know what I was talking about, what undead things, what tunnels? He cried like a baby, but would not give up a name. He asked if I would meet him tomorrow and he would bring me the cash and the guy who hired him.

Motioning to Mel for another drink, I needed a moment to consider Leslie's offer.

I decided to let the slime ball bring me his moneyman tonight – not tomorrow. He would be allowed to live another three hours, but he had better show up with the guy and my money. "If you show up a minute late, you will not have to wonder about anyone noticing your long, lovely fingers. I'll cut them off, one by one, and shove them down your throat."

Watching the time, I stayed at the street side table. I could see Leslie was again approaching and he had someone with him. Excellent, he had only taken two and a half hours. I could taste revenge before they even sat down.

Leslie and his friend thoughtfully took their seats and placed a small leather satchel on the table. Leslie introduced me to his business friend, Mr. Leland. I could only stare at this guy who was a mousey bit of a man, slight of build, bad skin, and quite repulsive. Before I could ask a question, Mr. Leland offered, "I am only a solicitor for your employer.

Mr. Melosk wanted to ensure the well being of that woman on Pritchard Street. He asked me to find a reliable investigator to simply take pictures and gather any other pertinent information. Leslie suggested you, Simon. There was no ill intent and no harm was meant to occur."

"First of all you stupid, little bastard, I didn't say you could use my first name. Second, who the hell is Melosk – where is he? I want to meet him."

Leland continued, "I have never personally met my employer. Our business is conducted via phone and e-mails; funds are transferred when assignments are complete. He is a quite reasonable sort. However, I do believe he is politically connected and has some very influential friends, but I cannot guarantee that information.

"Leslie tells me you spoke of the undead. My personal thoughts aside, I cannot imagine why you would bring such accusations. As for now, my assignment is complete. You have your money – I would like the photos and any other information you acquired."

"Well little man, here's what I got – nothing but bad dreams and a lot of death and destruction added to my resume. I'd include blood except the damn things only oozed goo. No pictures of anyone other than the Pritchard Street woman because none of their undead forms showed up on infrared. Low light shadows and that's it. Even if I did get pictures, after what I've been through, there is no way in hell I'd give it to an ugly shit like you. If Melosk wants anything – tell him to contact me, personally.

"Oh, and thank him for the cash!"

I left Leslie quivering at the table tightly gripping his beloved fingers. Mr. Leland had a look of surprise. I headed for my condo and turned a couple of times to ensure I was alone. Sometimes I got a feeling I'd seen a shadow. I brushed that off and quickly entered my lobby anxious to see Grace and hoping she had rested.

17 – The Makeup

Grace was still asleep when I got into the apartment. I stood for many minutes watching her breathe. She looked peaceful and I only hoped I could keep her that way. I grabbed a cold beer and watched TV in the bedroom, hoping morning would be uneventful.

I was up by 6:00 a.m., made coffee and stood on my balcony, appreciating the fact I did not have to participate in the traffic of government nine-to-fivers in DC. On the other hand, they didn't have to kill the undead. I guessed they got the better end of the deal.

Grace was up by seven and joined me on the balcony. Her throat was still badly bruised, but there was color coming back to her face. She smiled and hugged my arm. I was really enjoying her touch. I liked it and wanted more. We sat for an hour surveying the traffic and drinking my favorite dark roast as she tried to relate all that had happened to her. Little by little it was getting easier for her to speak and I was determined not to push.

I thought about Leslie's satchel of money and decided on a good use for the ten grand. Figured Grace needed some pampering, clothes, whatever she wanted. I wanted to spoil her. She got dressed and we headed for the mall at Tysons. She was hesitant to let me buy her anything, but it got easier the more shops I showed to her. Her smile came easier and she began to enjoy herself. I was eating up every minute.

She said she really liked the feel of silk against her skin. La Perla lingerie was significantly nicer than the sale items at WalMart. She picked several long scarves to hide her marred neck and seemed to develop an affinity for long silk tee shirts. After loading the car, I noticed the Tiffany store at the corner. I wanted to take her there, but she refused. Another time, perhaps.

We stopped for a steak at Morton's, enjoyed a bottle of wine and even split a decadent dessert. We quietly searched each other's faces trying to sort out a host of emotions. She was beginning to trust me and almost enjoy herself. I was more than willing to be patient. When she was ready to be closer, she would let me know. Of that, I was absolutely sure.

When we got back to the condo and were relaxing on the sofa. I handed her a small suede cloth. Something belonging to my mother was hidden in the soft folds. It was a simple gold cross on a chain that I had given it to my mother a year before she died. Used every penny of the first paycheck I got from Westside Hardware.

My mother put it on and never took it off. I took it from her neck before the casket was closed. Leonie Gautreaux would be happy that Grace would now be in possession of her cross.

Grace carefully opened the small piece of suede. She gently lifted the cross and looked at me as her eyes filled with tears.

She knew exactly what it was. As I fastened it, I realized it was the first time Grace had let me touch her neck.

18 - Redemption

Two more days of sleeping late, pampering, listening, probing and Grace began to come back. She laughed readily, ate constantly and watched television curled up on the sofa with a mug of tea clutched to her chest while playing with the cross around her neck.

We enjoyed a salad while sitting on the balcony watching a wonderful sunset. The lights of DC set against the red sunset made the city look surreal. Putting her glass of wine on the table, Grace took my arm. She held me tightly and lifted her head. Her lips found mine and it felt like senior year all over again.

Without thinking, I grabbed her hard. She pulled back almost in terror and I knew what I had done. I smiled gently and coaxed her to come close to me again and held the small of her back. Ensuring there was not an inch of space between our hips, she responded with a small moan and relaxed in my arms. I guided us into my bedroom and we lay on the cool sheets. We hugged, kissed and started to explore each other; something we neither knew about nor understood those many years ago. The years had taught me well while Grace remained a lost soul.

She had learned to be submissive, but I was determined to free her of that binding. I let my hand slowly inch down her leg lightly toying with the silk panties she had become so fond of wearing. She responded with small noises and her body was becoming noticeably warmer. Gently traveling upward, I undid her bra. I had forgotten how amply endowed she was and just how beautiful she felt. I took her hand and placed it between my legs. She unzipped my pants and moved her hand slowly and deliberately.

I pushed her hand harder into my groin, pulled down my boxers and started to massage her inner thigh. Higher and higher until I could feel her moisture slowly slipping down her thigh. She started moving into my hand and I withheld just enough to make her want more. And she did. She pushed me away and quickly moved her head lower. I was losing control.

Gently pulling her up and holding her wrists, I inched her panties down with my mouth. I laid my head on her flat belly and let my tongue slide in and around her belly button. As I let go of her wrists she grabbed my head and pushed it down further. Her hands pulled at the bed sheets and her hips moved faster. I let my tongue explore her gently and lightly. She moaned…a deep, pleasing moan. I took her hips and held her tight.

The longer I stayed, letting my tongue massage her over and over, the more she sighed contentedly, over and over. She grabbed for my head to pull me back up, but I would not move. I wanted to finish this journey. She lay back and gave in to me. I inched back up and again took my time. I wanted her to remember this. I was making up for lost time and I wanted it to be perfect for her.

When she was ready we were in exact sync. We held each other closely and peacefully drifted off to sleep. I remember only the morning sun flooding the room and the smell of a dark roast brewing.

GGG

Journal #7 - Grace
Entries 19-23

19 – The Dance

I was happy, really happy. I did not want it to end, but there was unfinished business that was waiting. Zoe had again left me a voicemail, but I was not yet ready to deal with "feral" dogs. I made a mental note to call her back and put off another meeting till some of my own issues were close to being solved.

I left Grace with a new pile of DVDs and walked to Becketts. Mel nodded hello and I secured my favorite table on the street. I was happy Becketts had put in overhead fans to keep the air movement pleasant. I remembered, painfully, what I'd just been through and counted DC weather as a blessing. A waiter placed my drink on the table. It was nice to have someone know your taste and have it delivered upon your arrival.

As I waited for Leslie, that little rodent, I wondered if he was one of the undead I had just battled. Christ, ya take a job that's supposed to be quick and easy, take a few pictures, that's it. Then you find your fighting the demons of hell. I still could not believe what had happened. It was like a grade B movie and not even worth a rerun. If I had rented it, I would be asking for my money back. I sipped my drink and stared down the street, waiting.

An hour and a half later, starting on my third glass, I heard that bitchy, high-pitched voice at the bar. "Oh, come on. My fingers aren't that special. Well, do you really think so?" I turned my head, pushed the chair out a bit from the table and caught his eye. He turned paler than usual when I beckoned him over. Like an errant cocker spaniel, he came closer at the pace of a snail.

Leslie opened with "Well, hi stranger. How are…"

I yelled, "Sit down you little shit. I'm not in the mood for chitchat. What have you found out? Does your mystery man want his pictures? Is he willing to meet? When can you arrange it?"

He stuttered and started shaking. "Well I spoke to him and he isn't willing to meet with you. He said you should just keep the cash for any trouble you encountered. He's not angry or anything. I think it sounds okay to me."

"Oh no you don't – that is not even close to being okay. This guy hurt my Grace and I want blood – well, that is if he bleeds. I want his name, where he lives, I want everything. And you are gonna get it for me. Do you understand? DO YOU?"

Leslie seemed to have pissed himself. He sat back in the chair, rubbed his crotch with his napkin and looked visibly frightened. He kept looking around, behind him, at the bar, on the street.

"You just don't understand. He's not the kind of guy you can just summon at will. He needs a reason and he has to be the one that makes contact. He won't listen to me. He won't care if you…"

"Listen, you prissy bastard, I will strip the flesh from your bones. I will slowly mash your balls, cut them off and feed them to the rats on the street. I will crush your fingers so they fly like a flag when I plant your arm in the ground. And you will be awake when I do it.

You will slowly bleed to death unable to scream because your throat will be crushed. You will get me a meeting and you will do it soon. Do you understand me? Have you heard everything I've said?"

Leslie fixated on his wine glass, unable to respond. I slammed my hand on the tabletop and he shot up out of the chair. He started running and kept saying, "Okay, okay, okay…"

Figuring I'd hear from him soon, I finished my drink and slowly walked to the condo. As I approached, I looked up and could see a long scarf flowing over a balcony rail. I hoped Grace was in one of her silk tee shirts.

This was the first time I felt good about going home in, well, forever.

20 – The Invitation

Four days later, Leslie crept into Becketts and stood at the table next to mine. I told him to sit, but he hesitated. He looked frightened. I quietly shared if he didn't sit down I would start peeling the nails from his pinky fingers. He immediately sat in the chair across from me.

"Simon, I really don't want to upset you and I think you're gonna be happy with what I have to say, but I'm so afraid of you now. I was just trying to help…" I told him to cut the crap, stop whining and tell me exactly what he had. "Well, okay, just take it easy. I have an invitation for you to meet your employer. There is a private party here at Becketts on Sunday night and I got you an invitation. It's black tie. He will be here and meet with you. Just like you wanted. No strings. Does that make you happy?"

"Leslie, you finally did something right. What's his name? What does he look like?"

Leslie stammered, "Well, that's the only thing. He said he will introduce himself to you at the party."

I went to slap the table and Leslie froze in his seat. I smirked a bit and asked if he ever got the piss stain out of his pants the other evening." Leslie whined for a few moments then asked if he could leave. He hoped we could still do business and this momentary lapse in our relationship was not fatal. He quickly took off and I left.

This was now a promising option. I'd finally meet this bastard and I could kill him. First, I would hurt him, just like he hurt Grace. Whatever it took – he was gonna die.

I spent the balance of the week taking Grace to museums, the Smithsonian, the Vietnam Memorial. She was childlike in her awe of the city and all that it offered. She loved walking hand-in-hand on the mall along the reflecting pool and the National Gallery was her favorite. The September weather was lovely and the slightest hint of leaves turning made the days magnificent. I did not ever remember being this happy. This just could not end.

Grace and I spent sunsets together on the balcony, sipping wine and feasting on the city lights. We spent the nights together, clutching each other, making love, sleeping, making love again and awaking in each other's arms. Sitting across the breakfast table, holding my coffee cup I looked at her. "Grace Jenat Benoit, I love you."

She tilted her head so her eyes looked up at me and softly replied, "I know that now Simon. I love you too and always have."

21 – The Gathering

Sunday arrived quickly. I made Grace promise not to leave the condo - under any circumstances. I put on my tux, and ensured my .32 was loaded and fit nicely in my cummerbund. Nice thing about a Walther PPK – big enough to make a point, small enough to hide. I kissed Grace and embraced her for a long time. She asked me to please come home safe. She would wait on the balcony.

I left, hoping I would survive the evening. In the least, I wouldn't be the only body taken away in a cheap black plastic bag. I entered Becketts about 8:00 p.m. It was crowded and noisy for a Sunday. I looked around for a party, but it was not apparent.

Then I noticed Mel at the bar. He was in a tux! He motioned for me to come over. As I approached, he opened a door on the side wall of the bar. Funny, I had never before noticed a door there. But then, I always took a table – never did like a barstool.

When I stepped inside and looked around, I was stunned. The room was magnificent. It was decorated with hand-carved mahogany, expensive art, bronzes, and silk brocade furniture. I stood staring around with my mouth hanging open.

The male guests were all dressed in black tie, the women beautifully attired in long gowns and serious jewelry. Waiters passed seamlessly through the crowd with glasses of champagne and crackers with the crushed liver of some unsuspecting bird. I'm sure there was a chamber ensemble playing, but I could not see past the guests to the end of the room. I wondered if my .32 would be a welcomed addition to the festivities.

The waiter asked if I would like a scotch, which he already had on the tray. I took the glass and drank it down in one swallow. He went for my refill. I stood and surveyed the group. There were at least two congressmen and one senator, several police captains and I swear I saw two cabinet members laughing and hanging on the arms of some skinny, young models.

As I made my way around the room, I also saw the Washington Bureau Chief of an extremely powerful newspaper. I could see why Leslie's friend wanted to meet here. Not like I could cause a huge problem. He was probably one of them.

This party included an elite group of Washington insiders. Being here put the guest on entirely different level than the peons outside the door sucking down beer and nuts. I was going to have to play this carefully. I had to have my head around everything going on here before I made any move. Each time I looked around another face I had seen in the Washington Post emerged: laughing, back slapping and having an exceptionally good time.

After several more scotches, I was making small talk with a partner of a top law firm. His latest picture in the Washington Times could not have been pleasant for him or his family. I felt a tap on my shoulder and as I turned Leslie was there smiling with his pinched face. He said my meeting was about to start and if I would follow him he'd take me to the room. I excused myself from the group and turned to follow him.

I was feeling quite relaxed. Almost too relaxed. The hair on my neck started to bristle and my gut told me the single malt had not been the only ingredient in my glass. Leslie guided me toward the back of the room. Beautiful people, laughing, drinking and paying not the first bit of attention to me. I wondered if anyone would find my body.

A door opened and I was ushered in and shown to an overstuffed red leather chair. I settled into it thinking this was like the chairs in an expensive men's club. Leslie left the room and when I looked up, Mel was seated across from me. A bottle of my favorite scotch and two glasses were on the table between our chairs.

I stared at Mel and asked why he was there. "Simon, you asked me here. It was you that wanted this meeting." I sat for a moment and tried to get my head around the moment. Meeting? What meeting did I ask for with Mel? What was he talking about? And then it hit me. Mel! Mel the bartender was Melosk. He was the son-of-a-bitch that hurt Grace. It was him I had to kill. I grabbed for my gun, but could not move my hand. I could barely move my arms. Mel quietly sat and smiled, enjoying each moment of my frustration and pain.

He poured himself two fingers. He pushed back into his chair and crossed his legs. After enjoying a long swallow of that amber liquid he looked at me, "Simon, take your time right now. Calm down. I'm not planning to kill you this evening.

When you get your senses and your anger under control we can talk. Until then I'll just sit here and enjoy your company."

"Why the hell are you a bartender? What exactly…"

"Simon, appearing as a bartender allows me unhindered entry into many conversations. People ignore the bartender. He is a non-person. It is truly hiding in plain sight. Don't you agree?"

22 - The Revelation

I sat, paralyzed watching this darker persona of Mel as he sipped his drink and smiled. I could feel movement coming into my hand and arms. I thought I'd be able to grab my gun and maybe make a break. Too late, Mel had read my mind.

"Simon, your gun is of no use. You will only make this an ugly evening. With my guests outside it would be quite easy to kill you, attest that you attacked me while under the influence of drugs, which they will find in your pocket. After a few moments of remorse, I would simply apologize for the rudeness of this guest and bid my friends goodbye. That is, after they removed your body in a cheap plastic bag. I cannot imagine that is how you want Grace to remember you."

I felt like he hit me in the head with a hammer. He knew Grace was here. He knew why I was here. What the hell! I figured it was worth going along with him if only to ensure Grace's safety. Fine, I'd play nice – this time.

Mel's new personae, not as a bartender, reminded me of Pacino when he finally became the *Godfather*. Sitting in a chair, exuding total control, perfectly dressed, a drink by his side and then he lit a cigarette - unfiltered. Mel stared ahead with his coal black eyes and calmly continued his chant.

"Look Simon, did you think it was unexpected providence that Leslie offered this job to you? I knew exactly whom I wanted to go to Jackson Creek. It was not simply a random opportunity. I handpicked you. I knew what I was doing then, just as I do now. It is unfortunate you inherited your temper and impulsive approach to life from your father. Did you ever know your grandfather? And, you received so little from your mother's side of the family. It would have served you much better."

"How the hell do you know my father? My mother? Who are you? How dare…"

"Simon, we shall not successfully finish this conversation if you continue you're useless whining. I know everything about you. So many more things than you will ever know. Though the past has its own merits for our purposes this evening, it is the future, well yours and Grace's future, that we shall concentrate on. Does that sound good to you?"

Movement was now possible in my arms, but I only grabbed for the scotch. I knew all else was useless. I threw back the scotch in my glass giving Mel a questioning look. He offered, "That drink was fine – no pharmaceuticals mingled with the liquid. However, should I…"

"No Mel, I'm fine. I won't make any aggressive moves, but I want a bottle of single malt on the table not house scotch.

"Certainly Simon." Mel smiled and tapped on the arm of his chair. Immediately Leslie entered the room with a bottle of Glenfiddich, smiling as he backed out of our sight. I hated that piece of scum. Really hated him.

Mel continued saying that Drema Sue was fine and would continue in good health as long as I was able to contain my violent nature. Sheriff Buck had taken care of all the immediate issues that had surfaced. Buck was a quite competent associate and would keep everything in order.

He had already resolved the involvement of the tunnel inhabitants. There would be no further problems in Jackson Creek. At least not for the time being.

Mel told me he had met Grace while he was buying the Krueger property. They frequented the diner where she worked and he was taken with her. "A naive girl, quiet, sweet and not at all worldly." She was trusting to her own detriment and she fit ever so nicely into his plans. He wanted her as his host body in Jackson Creek. She was lovely, innocent and gratifying.

"I had been preoccupied with other matters and neglected Grace. All would have remained calm had not some underlings taken advantage of the dear girl without my express permission." Mel's eyes widened with intensity, and became quite intimidating. "I wanted proof of their transgressions and optioned your services."

Mel admitted there had been some unexpected stresses with newcomers joining his fold. He was willing to listen to their minor issues, but his word was final. There would be no argument. He was in charge and that would not change. He had proclaimed Grace as off limits. This breach to his authority was dealt with harshly.

He took a long swallow of Glenfiddich and slowly raised his eyes toward me. He said, "I could kill you at any time and reclaim Grace, but I'm not now inclined to do so." He thought my background, bloodline and new appreciation of his *kind* would be valuable to him - in a way no other investigator had been previously.

"Of course, there will be rewards. Frequent rewards for any help you might give." First and foremost he would declare Grace off limits to anyone other than me. There was no doubt his followers would now listen. Mel owned my building so my condo was now paid in full. Anything required to complete an assignment would be supplied, without question.

If I required entrance to the hallways of government, an open door to the FBI, CIA, NSA or local police departments, he was happy to oblige. He had many friends in those agencies, all would be more than happy to grant a request from him.

Mel smiled, recounting the many favors he had granted for these people and how they valued his friendship. I never doubted they would accommodate his requests.

I sat silent, unsure if it was the scotch or the unexpected pleasurable drugs lacing my drink or my own mind. I seemed to have no problem with Mel's offer of a partnership, though I was unsure how to proceed. Should I grab my glass and lift it to our partnership? Should I throw it in his face and damn him to hell? Should I ask for time to think about his offer? Should I ask for more money?

How would I explain this to Grace? More importantly, how would I keep this from her?

I had no idea how long I had sat in the red leather chair. When I became totally aware of my surroundings, I was alone. No noise, no music, no anything. Just the Glenfiddich on the table and my hand grasping a crystal glass. I slowly stood up, steadied myself and headed for the door.

When I pushed it open, it hit the wall with a loud crack. Guests at the party turned, looked at me with annoyance, and went back to their drinks and chatter. I stood as a fool, alone and without any arm to hold to take me home.

I exited the back room and stood at the bar for a few moments to compose myself. Mel was nowhere to be found. That slime Leslie was also gone. I tried to remember if I agreed to anything Mel had offered. My thoughts would not separate from each other. My mind was blank. I had to get my shit together.

I prayed it was a dream. A blackout of sorts, perhaps from the drugs. Anything other than what I perceived had just happened.

I made my way home hip-hitting every concrete planter strategically positioned by the District to thwart any terror threat. Yeah, my ass was a threat. Actually, the way I felt – I was a threat. I got to the condo, slipped inside and stood silently – my back pressing against the mahogany door and my eyes staring out the balcony windows. How could such a beautiful view exist alongside the depravity of this city?

There was no choice but to accept Mel's request. I figured the best course of action was to keep my mouth shut and accept his protection until I could figure out how to send his demonic ass back to hell.

Thankfully, Grace was asleep. I needed time to clear my head before trying to explain what had happened or if I should even try to explain. Keeping her worry free and out of Mel's reach was most important. I made my decision; I'd go this alone, for now.

Dropping my tux and gun on the floor, I snuggled in beside her. Her soft, even breathing made me feel safe. She smelled so good and her body generated peace.

Strange how we had traded places on the planet.

23 – *The Request*

It didn't take long for Mel to request the use of my talents. A week or so after our "discussion," I was summoned to Becketts by that ferret Leslie standing at my front desk. My balls had felt this ache before and today was the first of many curtain calls.

Arriving at Becketts, I walked in and took a table. I spotted Mel at the bar, motioning for me to join him. Like a trained beagle I did just that. We walked into his side room and sat down. A bottle of Glenfiddich was already on the table flanked by two crystal glasses.

"Simon, I assume we now have an understanding of what our partnership requires and a viable working relationship?" I simply nodded in agreement and grabbed for a glass. "I've never been one to criticize another's vice, but you drink too much. Did you want something to eat?"

"Look, this is not a social call. What do you want?"

"All right, Simon, no small talk - all business. I like that. I have a need for some information that has been, shall we say, a bit difficult to obtain. I feel quite certain it will be an interesting first assignment."

"I'm all ears. Get to the point." I found myself wanting another drink. This was not a good sign cause it was only lunchtime.

"There is currently a list of possible candidates for the newly created czar position to the president. I need…"

"Whoa, wait a minute cowboy. Are you crazy? Are you kidding? How do you remotely think I can…"

"Simon, you jump too hot too quickly. I do hope this is not the way you regularly run your investigations. I don't want to be forced to rethink our arrangement. Now, as I was saying, this is a simple list of potential individuals vying for the czar position. The president makes the appointment, but the czar selects committee members. I require the names of all current recommendations."

I could feel a migraine tapping at the back of my skull. "Look, you said you had all kinds of friends in government and all kinds of high places. Why do you need me to…"

"Since this is our first attempt at an assignment let me be precise because I will not repeat myself. I call you, we meet, I give you an assignment, the tools you may need to complete it and unlimited funds for its completion. You do not ask me why or why not, how come, do I have to? The only exception for potential questions would be for perhaps a phone number, or contact that you don't have available. My reasons are none of your business. You will complete it, to my satisfaction, or you will have failed, at which point our original contract is null and void. Now, are we clear?"

"Yeah, I understand, I understand."

"Here are several names and phone numbers which may be assets in your search and an invitation to an event at the Kennedy Center this weekend. This is a private affair and invitations are a hotly sought commodity. Use your time there wisely. Now, do you have any questions?"

I sat and stared at the cruel look he now wore on his face. Questions, I thought? Yes, I had questions. How the hell was I supposed to accomplish this feat? I had no contacts inside DC politics. How would I insert myself into this society? I looked at Mel and replied "No, no questions right now."

"Good then. Never approach me during work hours unless you want a drink. If you must speak with me, tell Leslie and I will arrange a meeting time. I expect to hear from you soon. Oh, give Grace my regards." He disappeared through the doorway and I sat wondering what had just happened.

Give her his regards? Yeah, right! Like that would happen. I opened the envelope and looked over the five names. Good Lord, I recognized two who were frequently in the news. Was Mel one of their friends? The invitation was for this weekend, black tie and a guest. And cash. Lots of cash. Looked like $50K to me. This guy didn't fly cheap.

Now, what was I gonna do to keep Grace outta his sight while I rummaged around the bowels of DC's high society? I stopped for lattes and returned to the condo. Grace looked better each and every day. She loved lattes and always put extra cinnamon on the foam.

We enjoyed a late lunch and I mentioned I had a new gig. She accepted that I was going to be busy, saying it was really okay because she had been offered a position, but was unsure how I would react.

I was surprised when she told me it was to be a volunteer position with the National Gallery. Grace had gone there frequently and loved all the paintings, but in particular, she admired the centuries old European sculptures. She had never realized they existed. This was not something she thought about in Jackson Creek. She had struck up a friendship with one of the curators, named Lilly. "Lilly told me that it would give me access to the entire museum and I could review new acquisitions prior to the general public."

It was the first time I had seen Grace excited since we left Georgia. She was broadening her horizons in a major way and I was proud of her. I told her we didn't need the money and if she wanted this, I was in total support. My only caveat was that she use a car service to and from work. I wanted to know that she would not be stuck on a Metro platform or city bus during the evening rush.

She agreed and I think she may have squealed when she ran into my arms and hugged me hard. She did not let go till we finished a wonderful afternoon of making passionate love. I was becoming quite fond of her reaction when she was happy about something. Quite fond.

This museum position for her was fortuitous. It would give her something to take her mind off my absence. She called Lilly and started work the next morning. I arranged for a car service to be at her disposal at any time, day or night. I now had to concentrate on my job.

GGG

Journal #7 - Grace
Entries 24-30

24 – The Event

The week flew by. Grace was in and out of the condo – and smiling all the time. I was doing research on everything. I had to create my cover and know what I was talking about if questioned at the Kennedy Center event. The gala was for big money supporters of the administration and many of them were newspaper hierarchy.

Saturday arrived with a dreary, rainy sky and traffic stopped as far as I could see. Grace was going to the Gallery for an evening soirée with clients. I wasn't sure I liked that she appeared happy and comfortable with this new road in her life.

I put on my tux, but could not take my .32. They would have metal detectors and all I needed was ten Homeland Security guys on my tail. There were limos, blocking limos, when my cab arrived. Jumping out, I walked to the entrance line. I was warily eyed by several very large and ominous looking men. There must have been a height and weight requirement to work at this event. After reviewing my invitation and me several times I was allowed through.

I made an entrance as if I owned the place – just like every other penguin there. I still had no idea what I was going to do, but I guessed a drink would help clear my mind. The bar was crowded, but manageable. No matter, a couple of hours of free booze might loosen lips.

I presented myself as a freelance investigative reporter, indicating that I did a lot of work for New York and California papers. I made charming chit chat and listened – listened to every word I could possibly take in, with, or without the speakers' permission.

One of the magic names on Mel's list was Jerome Tremont. Well-known, very politically connected and owner and Editor-in-chief of NewsWorldPapers – a mega conglomerate of print, TV and radio news outlets. I looked up his resume, photo and any other bits of info I could find. His private life was apparently the lust of all the tabloids. His penchant for female and male partners had become legendary in DC circles.

I made my way toward the elevators and saw Tremont. He was holding court with several underlings. I joined the crowd and waited for an opportune moment to mention that Mel sent his regards.

Tremont stopped and looked at me closely, not with fear, but a measure of apprehension. He asked if there were anything in particular Mel needed. I said Mel would appreciate Tremont giving me a few moments of his time. He immediately turned from his fans, touched my elbow and ushered me to the side of the hall. Boy, this was prime access I could come to really enjoy.

Tremont asked a few mundane questions then "Well, Mr.?"

"Please, just call me Simon."

"Well Simon, how may I assist you this evening?"

"Sir, I'm doing an article on presidential appointments and was wondering if you could help me complete my list of the proposed candidates for the new Czar?"

Tremont looked like I had slammed his fingers in a car door. His eyes popped and he stammered ever so slightly. "Well, not at this point. What other names do you have? Did Mel give you any? Does he know..."

"Mr. Tremont, Mel only asked that I give you his regards. He has no concerns about the appointment. I'm looking for information. Is there anyone you can identify as a candidate?"

"I've heard speculation, only speculation. The name Thomas Rushton was privately mentioned to me, but I beg you not to make that public. At least not with my name attached. I really do have to go back to the party Simon, best of luck with your assignment."

My curiosity piqued. How did he know it was an assignment? I had mentioned only an article. Okay, at least I had one name. This gig might not be as hard as I thought. Mention Mel's name and they grab their balls, just like I do.

I moved around the crowd and met some really valuable contacts. The kind that might be helpful when I got my real life back - when Mel was out of it completely. I looked forward to that day.

Feeling satisfied with the evening I excused myself, grabbed a cab and headed for home. I replayed the evening in my head and could not believe how easily I traded quips with the power players in DC. The head of Home Land Security was quite nice and seemed more knowledgeable than his usual portrayal in front of CNN cameras. He actually did know the difference between Shia and Sunni Islam. Public speaking classes would definitely help him out.

The Secretary of State was quite personable, although her knowledge base appeared taken directly from Wiki pages. One surprise was Supreme Court Justice Bertram. He was not at all what I expected. I had been led to believe he was a middle of the road justice yet this evening his comments were decidedly liberal, in fact, ultra liberal. Considering the next bill before the court was immigration I made a mental note to watch closely the summary arguments on this bill.

Connecticut Avenue was at a standstill so I jumped out at 18th Street and figured I'd walk through Dupont Circle. The rain had stopped. I crossed the street and entered the Circle.

No one roamed Dupont Circle this time of night. The regulars had usually vacated earlier in the evening.

Out of the corner of my eye I saw a shadow coming up my left side. The form slowed slightly allowing me to take the lead. Dammit, where was my .32 now! I started to quicken my pace when I felt a hand on my shoulder and something pushing into my back.

"Hey there fancyman, you all dressed up and makin' us not-so-rich folks feel bad? It ain't nice to parade through here looking like you own the place."

I immediately offered my money clip bulging with bills, telling him I'd be happy to drop it on the ground and continue walking straight ahead. He said that was just fine, but he still felt the need to slam the back of my head with his crappy gun. Damn, he hit me hard and it hurt. I went straight down.

As I lay on the ground I saw him bend to grab the clip of bills. Then, I heard growling. Angry, loud growling and the sound of nails scratching along the pavement. It was terrifying.

I tried to raise my head, but decided to lie still, all the while trying to cover my head and listening as these animals ripped apart the guy trying to defend himself. There must have been three or four of them grabbing the flesh away from his chest and throat, shredding his face and chewing off his ears. He was flailing on the sidewalk when they disemboweled him. I was petrified I would be next.

They disappeared as fast as they showed up. I heard voices in the background screaming. I tried to get up. My hands were in a puddle of blood and I wasn't sure if it was mine. The man who had just bullied me with his gun now lay next to me in an unrecognizable pile of flesh, blood and entrails. My clip of bills was clutched in what appeared to be a partial hand with only a few fingers remaining.

I felt someone grabbing me from the back to help me stand. Some guy behind me tried to help support my weight and then started to vomit. A woman was screaming so loudly my ears hurt. I saw police cars flooding the area. The lights and sirens were overwhelming.

An officer came to me and asked if I saw anything. Did I know what happened? Did I hear anything strange? He insisted I go to George Washington Hospital. I refused. He stared at me so oddly and I then realized I was covered in blood. My head, face and arms were dripping red. There were pieces of human flesh hanging on the sleeves of my tux and pants.

The medics insisted I remain with them until the investigative team came by and examined my clothing and me. I tried to argue, but there was no way they were letting me go. Sitting in the ambulance, getting examined, stripping off my clothing, being asked the same questions over and over - I could not wait to get out of there.

The cops were talking outside the ambulance when I overheard one of them say it was the fifth time some pack of dogs ripped the hell outta someone. One witness up on New York Avenue swore they saw wolves. Hell, unless some fruity pebble was breeding wolves in a basement and using them for dogfights, there was no way they were wolves. For my money, they had to be pit bulls or crazed shepherds.

My heart continued to race. That incident by my building did not involve feral dogs. I'm still not sure what I saw that night, but the fierce growls were the same. The fear was the same and at each incident I was spared. Zoe was on to something and I needed to call her.

With this latest killing it was a sure thing that the mayor would be on the early morning news telling the citizens that everything was under control. It also went without saying the papers were going to trash the force again.

The cops said the mayor was consulting with some government types to determine if these attacks were some sort of threat. If anything sounded stupid. That would be it. On the other hand, it was Washington DC. Here they practice stupid.

The paramedics finally released me as long as I'd sign paperwork that I refused going to the hospital and that I would be available for any further questions from detectives. I signed, told them I'd be available and they gave me my money and a pair of scrubs to wear back to the house. My set of clothes was now evidence. Hell, I needed a new tux anyway.

Thankfully, Grace had not been with me. The thought of her seeing that carnage was sickening. When I arrived, the condo was quiet. Grace had already drifted off to sleep. I got a hot shower, a drink, and gently wrapped myself around Grace. Thankfully, sleep arrived quickly.

25 – The Stink

Grace had the coffee brewing and there were fresh bagels on the table. Seeing me walk in, she shrieked. "What happened to you last night? Your face is rubbed raw." When she came to hug me she put her hands round the back of my head then pushed away. "Simon, you have a huge knot on your head. Tell me what happened."

I sat at the table, grabbed the coffee cup and gently explained I had been mugged, but luckily the police were quick to arrive. My face was fine. It happened when I lay on the concrete and my tux had been torn. Everything was fine. A bump was all there was to it.

She pampered me the rest of the morning since she was going to the Gallery at noon, but would spend the balance of her time taking care of me. I told her the mugging happened by the Kennedy Center. She did not need to know I was involved in the Dupont Circle attack.

That would be difficult to explain and I doubted she was up to that kind of information.

She turned on the TV and, as expected, there was the mayor and city council members decrying the attack in Dupont Circle. They were confident these dogs would be caught soon and taken to the Humane Shelter. Of course, they could not say they'd put a bullet in each animal's head because PETA would go insane. I guessed the cops should go out with Kibbles and Milkbones to catch these misunderstood fur balls.

Anxiously, I waited for Grace to go to work. I needed a bit of downtime and a plan with which to approach some of the other names Mel had given me - four more people to coerce into spilling confidential material with someone like me.

When Grace finally left, I poured a drink. Maybe this was becoming a problem for me. Well, I'd think about it after this job was over, not now, definitely not now.

I called Zoe and got her voicemail. Even her voice message was peppy and upbeat. Hubris is wasted on the young.

After all the schmoozing I had one name – not bad for a night's work. Since meeting Tremont I figured I could drop his name without too much issue. After the attack last night and police activity, I figured Bill Rousch was the ideal contact for today, what with the ravaging packs of poodles roaming the city. I could not imagine what he could offer, but I was quickly learning not to second-guess Mel. In the least, Rousch might shed some light on these wild animal attacks.

Checking his credentials on the Internet, I found out he had been in his position for two years: Chief, Special Assignments Task Force. The post had been created to track atypical serial murders in DC, Virginia and Maryland areas.

The post also would be the primary investigative unit for some of the more bizarre crimes that dotted East Coast cities and possibly might have some connection. He was not the typical rising star that populates the ranks of DC's law enforcement. The media described him as a no-nonsense kind of cop that needed to polish his play-nice-with-others skills for TV cameras and the press.

I called his office and mentioned I was the victim in last night's murder in Dupont Circle. His assistant said he could give me fifteen minutes mid-afternoon. Dressing quickly, I arrived at his office on K Street. It was jammed with reporters, each asking the same question, "What was going on with these dog packs roaming the city? What was the plan? How safe were residents?"

Rousch's assistant ushered me into his office amid the stares of media that had been there prior to my arrival. Rousch grabbed my hand, welcomed me and hoped I was okay after the attack. His detectives were going to contact me for an update, but if I didn't mind, he had a few questions.

The moment I sat down, I was the one answering questions. This guy was good. He reminded me more of Columbo than the slick detectives on *Miami Vice*, but he knew his stuff. He asked for a quick rundown of what happened, then as expected, wanted to concentrate on the animals. Did I see them? What exactly did they look like? Had there been any warning?

Bill stared at me. I sensed I was going to like this guy. He was blue collar, in-your-face sort of people. He knew his new job put him in a game with heavy hitters. He wasn't impressed with them. Still, he was clearly aware of how the power structure worked in this capitol city. He had been given a long leash, but was not allowed to pull on it too often or too hard.

I recounted my steps and then tried to describe the animals.

"They were large and very broad. They had ears more like a husky, but it was their eyes that had gotten to me. They appeared reddish gold – weird I know, but I was trying to keep my head down and face covered. The deep, guttural sounds they made scared the hell out of me."

Bill was thankful for my description. He did say there had been several attacks like this, but the department was not having any success in tracking down the animals. Several unsolved deaths had also been attributed to a single animal attack.

Adding to my comments, I admitted I had seen something before, but was hesitant to broach the subject at the time. "I saw the attack, rather the aftermath of an attack, on New Hampshire Avenue some weeks ago.

Bill sat at attention and wanted more information. Had I reported it? How many dogs? What did they do when they saw me?"

I had not wanted to get involved in this unbelievable situation, but was compelled to answer him. I told him, "These were not regular dogs. What had stood in front of me was unearthly. Though it was hairy, big and could be a dog – it was like no dog I had ever before seen on this planet. I was frightened and wanted to forget it happened." Now it seemed I would be involved regardless of what I wanted.

Bill wanted more conversation about these demons of hell, but I was very reluctant. I promised him another meeting because anything I might add would not be the answer he was looking for.

I then mentioned I was doing a piece on the new Presidential Czar appointment and wondered if there was anything he might be able to share – of course, it would be on an absolutely confidential basis. He hesitated at the question. I explained I knew Mel and he had off handedly mentioned Bill's name as a friendly voice.

Bill sat up a bit straighter and asked that I please give Mel his best wishes. He seemed surprised that I was there as a victim and also as an investigator. He shared he had met Mel through his teenaged sons. They were sixteen and seventeen and were introduced to Mel at some sort of ball game.

One thing led to another and Mel befriended him in his bid for this job. Mel seemed a good man that wanted to immerse himself in the community and ensure the safety of the residents. He particularly supported all the schools and the programs that were woefully underfunded. He had a beautiful camp in the mountains of West Virginia and often allowed the older teenagers to spend weekends there. Of course, they were always supervised.

Okay, I started to wonder if I knew the same Mel that Bill was talking about. I politely agreed then vaguely intimated I knew the possible candidates and said I had been chatting with Jerome Tremont about the possible names being bandied about.

Bill said his only connection to the current frenzy about the czar appointee was his department was tasked with lending support to the Secret Service. More like backup to the convoys transporting proposed Czar appointees on the city streets to and from the White House for the interview process. He did not know the candidates names.

He admitted this was something never before done with the Secret Service – getting assistance from local law enforcement. Someone was pulling rank. He personally thought he was there to take the blame should anything happen.

He did say he had heard some Secret Service types had shuttled a couple of candidates from the corner of 34th & Massachusetts Avenue NW – right near the Embassy of Vatican City.

He thought I might want to check around that area. Other than that, he was a 120% committed to solving this latest animal attack. He had to put all his energies into the scorching headlines.

I thanked him for his time and left. Curious, I went for a name and I'll be damned I got a whole lot of information that would be helpful somewhere down the road.

It was noon since my last drink so I figured I deserved at least that. I made my way back home and passed through Dupont Circle. There were remnants of blood still dotting the concrete path. Guess the fire department missed some spots. Thankfully it wasn't mine. On second thought I wondered why the pack had left me alone. Still, I was happy walking over the pavement instead of being part of it.

It would be an hour before Grace got home so I stopped at Becketts. I really didn't want to see Mel, just wanted my quiet table and a drink. A little time to sit and not listen or look for anything – or anybody. I sat at the outside table and skulked into the corner. Hopefully, the only person to see me would be the waiter. Grabbing the paper, I realized I hadn't read the news in a week.

I was deep into the Lifestyle Section when my drink arrived. A familiar name popped out at me, Daphne Cosic Delaine. She was the inimitable hostess in DC. She knew everyone, everything and the glitterati fell at her feet. An invitation to one of her soirees was worth big bucks.

I had done a small job for her a while back. A discreet photomontage that she put to good use. She was recently divorced and suspected that her new girlfriend had other interests than her company. Daphne always hedged her bets.

I planned to give her a call and wangle an invitation to her next gathering. If anyone had the info I needed, it would be Daphne or one of her close friends.

After a second drink, I was feeling pretty satisfied with myself. Life seemed to be coming together. I let out a long breath and ordered a third drink. I felt good.

26 – The Invitation

Grace and I were becoming more comfortable with each other. She was thrilled with her new found freedom, her job and living with me. We got along and that was a gift.

Though we sometimes only passed each other in the condo, we always spent the night together in bed. It was our time and we enjoyed every moment. The late night love, early sunrise coffee and those wonderful extended mornings just lying close, our bodies wrapped around each other. Life seemed to finally be going well for both of us.

Grace left and I relaxed on the balcony while I called Daphne. She cooed over the phone she was sooooo happy to speak with me. She had actually been thinking about me for a small, intimate job, but had just been lazy about picking up the phone.

I said I had read about her latest party and asked if I might join the group. "Of course darling. I would love to see you. If you want to bring someone feel free. I'll put your name on the list immediately. Oh, you do remember where I live?"

With tongue in cheek I offered, "Daphne, do you still live in that tiny 5,000 square-foot condo in Georgetown?"

She laughed softly. "Well, yes I do, but I'm having this at my Watergate apartment. You do know where that is?"

"Of course Daphne, I don't know how I had forgotten your *intimate* parties were held there. See you on Saturday." The lives of the idle rich! Although if I continued doing these odd jobs for Mel I might also get a Watergate address.

The week went well enough. I spent a lot of time researching on the Internet. Government agencies, ambassadors, high profile investigations, there was more than I could absorb in a lifetime. I did find several articles on those dog attacks. There had been more than what Bill Rousch shared with me.

The single attacks were on people in the area. One in Georgetown, one on New York Avenue and the other by the Naval Observatory. They appeared to be the work of a single animal. All had their throats ripped out. This was not looming as a pleasant investigation. The other attack had been on a group of campers in West Virginia. Seemed they were backpacking and stumbled into a lair of sorts.

Originally authorities reported them as bear attacks, but several follow-up stories indicated that bears were not involved. Wolves were being cited as the attackers.

I found an article from 2003 indicating several counties in the Allegheny Mountains of Virginia and West Virginia were "ideal habitat, some of the best wolf territory in the southeast", officials from the U. S. Fish and Wildlife Service and the U. S. Forest Service announced the planned initial release of six gray wolf breeding pairs in the Monongahela and George Washington National Forests during January, 2003.

Additional breeding pairs are scheduled to be released during 2003 and 2004. The wolves were raised at the USFWS breeding station in Maine and transported to an undisclosed holding area in Virginia. Due to security concerns, exact dates and locations of the releases will not be made public."

Okay, looked to me like wolves were likely in this area. Maybe not in Manassas, but certainly in the area.

Another of the articles was in the UnderSide Press bylined by Zoe Weston, my innocent reporter in waiting – waiting for that big story that would make her reputation.

She was definitely scrappy and didn't mind rummaging through the dumpsters on U Street to get her story. It reminded me that she had not yet returned my phone call.

Grace came home early. She spoke nonstop about several new acquisitions at the Gallery and how she was among the first to view them. She was having the time of her life and I was so happy to be a part of it. I grabbed her around the waist and she melted into my arms. It was a feeling and a place I had never thought I would experience. I couldn't imagine a better spot on earth than here with her in my arms.

27 – Daphne's Domain

Luckily there had been plenty of time to get a new tux. With my newfound financial freedom, I decided to splurge on a primo Hugo Boss affair. This was living. Walk in, try it on, and have it delivered.

I picked up a couple of pair of Cole Hahn shoes at the yuppie paradise at Tysons Corner and a nice Pineider wallet. Perhaps I needed a card case? Yes, of course I did. It had to match the wallet.

Next stop Tiffany's. I needed cufflinks and maybe a small trinket for Grace. I was beginning to see how Grace felt the day she went shopping. It was great, like a kid in a toy store and no one to tell you no.

Saturday morning the tux, shirt and shoes arrived by messenger. I had a cummerbund made to my specs. It contained a small, inside pocket. Just enough to keep my .32 from falling out unexpectedly. Grace was on her way in as I was readying to leave. She whistled at me and said I looked really good. Ummmmm, I had to admit to the mirror that I was feeling hot and looking smart. I grabbed a cab and headed for the Watergate.

Nothing but the best for Daphne. Top floor, waterfront - all windows facing the river.

Furnishings hand culled from the best shops in Europe. Art covered the walls – no haphazard splashes of green and purple paint moved around the canvas by some chicken on steroids.

No, these were mostly watercolors, predominately English painters, and my particular favorites. The bar was set up on the front glass wall giving instant access to the huge balcony.

Daphne had seemed like an okay broad. Always served top shelf liquor and besides the silly little hors d'oeuvres passed around for her guests she also ensured that there was real food available. Jumbo shrimp, sliced filet on crusty breads, baked Virginia ham on southern scratch biscuits. Almost as good as Drema Sue's. Almost!

Daphne had gotten her social status by strategically planning her marriages and divorces. She was smart, statuesque, and a redheaded beauty that was quite adept at using her charms. She had been on the arms of a former vice president, a media mogul from LA, an Italian businessman with suspect interests in Las Vegas and a hedge fund superstar who practiced dubious ethics.

Her divorce from Cal Hastings, the media wizard in LA, reportedly increased her already substantial net worth by over 125 million. All of her settlements contained gag clauses so no one actually knew what she was worth. More importantly the contacts she had made from those marriages were priceless.

Daphne caught my eye and I made my way over to her. She looked stunning for her age. I guessed she was early fifties, but looked fifteen years younger because she had kept her figure trim and taut. There was a long list of hopeful suitors, but she chose to stay unencumbered until it suited her specific need.

She gracefully put her cheek to mine. "Simon, I didn't realize how much I missed seeing you. Please tell me you will join me for a private dinner one evening. You always made me laugh."

"Daphne, you are absolutely stunning. I expected nothing less. I would love to have dinner with you. You tell me the time, the date and I'll be there."

"I will have my secretary, Sofia, call you in the morning. Now, have a good time. If you need something you don't see you just give me a nudge and I'll make sure you get it."

This was a promising start to the evening and I would definitely do dinner with Daphne. I walked around the room looking over the attendees and checking out all the nooks and crannies in Daphne's place. I passed a beautiful room I assumed was a den and poked in my head. Her secretary, Sofia, was at a desk going over some materials.

When I cleared my throat, she jumped. I apologized and introduced myself. Sofia said she indeed remembered me. Daphne had been very pleased with my work.

I told Sofia how Daphne wanted a dinner with me and whenever Daphne was free I would be available.

Sophia smiled and looked over her schedule. She would not be available for a couple of weeks, but she had a just had a cancellation for a brunch - tomorrow. Would that suit me?

I jumped at the chance. "Sure, I'm free as well. Shall I meet her here?" Sophia said Daphne was fond of a restaurant in Georgetown and she would make the reservation and give me a call in the morning. This was providence -- Divine Providence.

As long as things were progressing nicely I asked if I might look over tonight's guest list and see if anyone I knew was coming. She hesitated, but relented. "Sure Simon. Why not?" My stars were all aligned this evening. I picked up the list and ran through the names. A veritable *Who's Who* of power brokers, moneymen and heads of state.

One name caught my eye: Boyd Wesley Braxton, 5th term Congressman from Georgia's 15th district. I thanked Sophia again and headed for another drink. Knowing that Braxton was an avid cigar smoker, I knew exactly where he would be settled.

28 – The Disclosure

Boyd Wesley Braxton was your textbook southern political leader. He was conservative, or liberal depending upon what county or district he happened to be speaking in during his campaign. He liked expensive bourbon, cheap woman, rare steaks, off-color jokes and power.

After insisting on Bible Breakfasts, he could turn around and hire two hookers for his Sunday afternoon of fun. His wife, Flora Jean, kept the family on track, the kids out of trouble and his affairs quiet and out of the headlines. She was a perfect southern wife.

I got my drink and an extra bourbon on the rocks just in case. Boyd was fond of good bourbon. I made my way to the balcony. I could smell the cigar and hear his famous drawl.

I followed my nose directly to Boyd's corner. He was lifting his drink to someone's toast and emptied his glass. I offered him the one I was holding. He smiled at me with "Son, you are a savior. I was gonna have to make my way back for a bit more bourbon and these people would miss my jokes. I think they need to give you a round of applause son."

Hard laughs and clapping ensued. Hands were put forth to shake and I did so willingly. I mentioned to Boyd that I was one of his constituents from Jackson Creek and he lit up. "Do you know Sheriff Buck down that way? He's a good man to know."

This was going to be a fruitful evening.

We stood on the balcony for an hour before the group thinned down to just the two of us and I felt comfortable enough to pose some questions to Braxton. "Congressman, you said you knew Sheriff Buck. Do you know his deputy Wesley?"

I sure do, well, haven't seen him in a few years, but I do believe I'd recognize him. Why?"

"He's my cousin and he was just killed by some car thieves down that way – up around the Krueger mining property."

"Son, I am so very sorry for the terrible loss you are sufferin'. Is there anything I can do? Send flowers or a note to his momma?"

"Congressman that would be terrific. My aunt Drema Sue would feel honored to receive a card from your office. I'll leave her address with your secretary on Monday. Is that okay?"

"That's fine. I'll make sure it goes out. If possible, I'll see if my wife Flora Jean could stop by and say some prayers with her. I'll tend to it straight away on Monday.

"Ya know, I helped broker that land deal down in Jackson Creek. Krueger had that property up for sale for years and never wanted to accept any offers. Finally got him to talk to a business group that one of my valued contributor's had put together. Yes, that was a good deal for all involved."

"Yes, I believe Mel headed up that buyout. In fact, he asked me to give you his regards."

For a brief moment ole' Boyd lost his concentration, but picked it right up again.

"Well, tell Mel thanks and my return regards to him. Are you and he close?" He asked a bit too eagerly.

"We have common interests. In fact, I'm doing an article on this new Czar appointment at the White House and Mel has offered any resources I need. Is it possible you might also be able to offer some assistance? Are you familiar with any of the candidates?"

His face lost its smile for a microsecond as he looked around to see if anyone was paying particular attention to our conversation.

"I hear little bits and pieces, nothing definite mind you. Don't know why it has been so hush-hush. The President seems to have come up with this new Czar position outta nowhere. Like he got up one morning and it had come to him in a dream.

I don't agree with him on much and this is another item, but who's gonna argue with the man? Seems like some "no names" are being considered along with a couple of heavy hitters – not politically connected. I think the President really ought to look for a good southern boy to help him out."

"Congressman, any name in particular that might slip off your tongue? I would consider it a personal favor and if ever I might be able to help you in any way, us being almost related and all, I'd be happy to oblige."

"Whew. Son, that is a big request. However, let me have another bourbon while I consider this." I offered to go grab his drink and refill my own still hoping our mutual background and friends would be enough to loosen his tongue. Just in case, I slipped the bartender a fin and got three fingers of bourbon – no ice this time.

By the time I returned, Braxton had busied himself with a comely redhead. I pushed in and asked if we could finish the conversation before I left. He looked as if he was relieved to hear my plan to leave. He also seemed quite fond of massaging the thigh of the redhead pushing against him. He told her to go powder something and he'd be with her right away. Grabbing the bourbon, he threw half of it down before addressing the subject.

"Now, you do understand you never heard this from me and I can never confirm and will only deny that these words ever left my lips, but the one name I hear is Phil Zarega. You can look anywhere and find out about him. A quick note of advice, you do know you are asking big league questions. Son, you best be suited up to play in a big league game.

"Now, excuse me. There is a lovely constituent waiting to discuss my voting record on something. Have a good night. Am sure our paths will cross again."

The night was not only charming, but also it proved to be a valuable source of information. I must remember to bring Daphne flowers tomorrow. I wanted to remain on her "good" list of friends.

It was time for me to make my exit. I found Daphne, hugged her and whispered in her ear that we'd meet for brunch. Turning to maneuver through the crowd, I spotted one of those "black suit" types Bill Rousch had discussed with me. Figured there had to be someone at the party who required their presence. Although I really wanted to know more, I was sure Daphne would chat with me tomorrow.

I was not in the mood for a walk in the Circle this evening. The doorman got me a town car and I headed back to the condo.

When the condo door shut behind me, I found the place silent. Grace had fallen asleep on the sofa watching *Casablanca*. I knew there was something more about her I loved.

29 – The Brunch

It was a beautiful Sunday morning. Grace and I took our spots on the balcony while enjoying our coffee and fruit. It was becoming more like autumn each day. Some mornings were pretty brisk. We read the paper and Grace chatted about her job at the Gallery.

She was enjoying this new life. Learning about things she did not know existed was intoxicating for her. She could not get enough and was beginning to leave her old life behind. She still wore her scarves, but her hand touched her neck less and less each day.

Grace had decided to go out and sightsee while I went for brunch with Daphne. We agreed to touch base around three and decide on a place for dinner. Within thirty minutes, Sofia called to confirm the brunch at 11:30 a.m. at DelaGards on 30th & M Streets in Georgetown.

I dressed, bid Grace goodbye and grabbed a cab. Sundays in Georgetown could be dicey with traffic. I was pleased when the ride went smoothly. Daphne loved peony and white rose bouquets. The driver stopped at Whole Foods and I secured seventy dollars worth of admiration for her. I got there about 11:15 a.m. and Daphne arrived at 11:30 a.m. on the nose. She was a classy broad.

Daphne swooned when I put the flowers on the table. Remembering this small item garnered me big points. The brunch was starting off well.

She ordered a Mimosa, while I stuck with coffee, a plate of assorted fresh fruits, yogurt and whole-wheat toast. Maybe a Bloody Mary would not be too far off. Daphne looked stunning yet again and commanded the center of attention regardless of where she might be. She had presence and confidence and had learned to use it with expertise.

"Simon, did you have a good time last night? Did you get to meet the people you were interested in seeing?"

"Daphne, it was lovely. You certainly know how to entertain and you're acquainted with absolutely everyone. You always amaze me with your talents."

"Simon, if I could still blush I would. Listen sweetie, I had wanted to call you about a small bit of work I need done. Photos, of course, also a little more information than last time. Nothing too strenuous and as usual, cost is not an issue.

A new suitor actually that I'd like to ensure is telling me the truth. You know how I am."

"Daphne, no problem. Give me the details and I will get it done and, yes, I did meet a lot of people last night. I had a pretty good conversation with Boyd Braxton. He was surprised that I was actually a constituent. He is a ummmm…"

"Simon, Boyd Braxton is a lying sack of badly cooked grits. He tells you only enough truth to keep you on his list of contributors. Be careful of Boyd, he is out for himself and whatever little shaky puddin' he has on the side. Flora Jean, his wife, knows where the bodies are buried and one day that is going to serve her well. I know from experience."

She moved closer and smiled coyly. "Speaking of dead bodies, how is Mel doing these days? He, my dear boy, is a master of misdirection and manipulation. I stand in awe of his abilities. How long have you been involved with him?"

"Just over a month or so. He hired me for a quick job and it's turned into a bit more. I find that…"

"Let me interrupt you, sweetie. You need to know a couple of things about the way things happen here in DC. You must be aligned with the correct power base, but not so close that when something hits the wall you get smeared in the fallout.

There is a safe, respectable distance you must keep regardless of the war raging around you. It's very hard, believe me. For instance, Mel is in a horrid battle for control of his little empire. Bet you didn't know that?"

"Battle? Actually I didn't. Can you tell me more? What should I know?"

"First, I need another Mimosa. Would you get one for me sweetie, while I go powder my nose?"

30 – The Lowdown

Daphne sat back in the barrel-shaped cloth chair. She was settling in for a long chat. I slipped a fifty to the waiter to ensure Daphne would not have to wait for another refill.

"Daphne, tell me what's going on."

"Simon dear, I just need you to be informed so you don't get yourself killed. After all, I don't want to lose the best investigator I ever hired. I can't tell you everything, but you are a bright boy, I have no doubt you will fill in the gaps."

I sat quietly trying to control my anticipation. It was hard.

"Simon, I don't know how long you've known Mel or exactly what your transactions have been with him and I really don't need the details.

I've known Mel for quite a long time. It was my second husband, Anthony, my Italian stallion that first introduced us. Mel thought I was just another pretty face, but as you know Simon, Daphne Cosic Delaine is nobody's dupe.

"As I was saying, I first met Mel in Italy. Anthony had some business dealings with the Vatican and he and Mel met at one of the many social gatherings in Rome. They seemed to hit it off and Anthony had further business dealings with him – mostly overseas contracts.

"After several social functions, Mel felt comfortable with me. Dare I say he was looking for something more. However, I am not a dessert to be picked up by a random appetite. Mel quickly understood, but he started using me as a confidant of sorts.

"I think it was more that I was a convenient way to spread info he wanted put out on the streets.

"Simon, Mel is an extremely powerful man. His connections reach into the governments of several countries and even our White House. What is happening is there is a bid for Mel's power position in this area. Men like him are not elected, they take those positions with force, connections and fear. There is now someone that is attempting to overthrow Mel. He is rich, connected and has a significant power base of his own."

Daphne's cell phone vibrated. She looked at the caller ID and said she needed to take the call and would I order some fresh strawberries and ensure her waiter had the Mimosas close at hand.

As she walked away, my mind was trying to sort out what had just happened. I could not believe she was sharing this info as easily as giving me a new recipe. The lines of power were becoming difficult to follow. Daphne would not talk about Mel this way if she were remotely afraid of him or felt she was in any danger.

Who was her protector or what undead souls might be in her closet? I was sure I would find out. I also ensured there was tape left on my recorder.

Daphne returned and began picking strawberries off the plate and sipping her Mimosa. I decided I would not push her and let her take the lead.

Finally, she was ready to continue her conversation. "The new anxious heir to the throne is Philip Zarega. He is the editor-in-chief of Zarega-Pierce News Consortium. Perhaps you've heard of him? I would venture to say he is on equal footing with Mel in terms of power base and connections. Might even have a slight edge.

"I've been around these types long enough to always play my cards close to the vest. Phil also lived in Europe for a while. I believe it was Rome or Venice perhaps. We did not meet until I arrived in DC with my Anthony.

"Admittedly, this my-gun-is-bigger-than-yours episode is going to get ugly. I'm not making light of the situation because it will be quite unpleasant. I am already tiring of the battles." She took a long sip of her drink.

"Daphne, I'm having a hard time wrapping my head around this. What is this escalating intensity about the new Presidential Czar?"

"Simon darling, Zarega is the short list. He will have the President's ear, and as such, he will have tremendous power. Just imagine if Mel were in that position. I do understand there are several on the list including the son of our ambassador to Vatican City, well, actually it is called the Holy See. However, I am unsure he has enough political backing or experience to successfully traverse Washington politics.

One interesting point I hear, but cannot confirm, is that Zarega has one of the other candidates under his thumb. That gives him a two out of five shot at controlling the appointment. Not bad. And no, sweetie, I don't know Zarega's pawn. I would love to know myself."

"Daphne, you are, I don't know, magical, I guess. You have it all going for you. Would you mind a personal question?"

"Of course not, sweetie. I'd love to know what you would find fascinating about me."

"Everything about you is fascinating. I have never equated the words mundane or ordinary with you. My question though, have you ever married for love?"

"Interesting question, Simon. Is it so obvious that my marriages have been for power and money?"

"No, it's just that with a woman like you if you were truly in love you would move heaven and earth to keep your lover at your side. Well, at least I would think so."

"Very perceptive Simon, you're good-looking and observant. My only true love had neither money nor power, and though I so loved him, I knew our lives would be ordinary. Perhaps that is selfish of me, but I took the other road.

I think of him often. He is living in the States and has not married. Sometimes I think of contacting him, but I know better. Life would not be the same.

"Now then, I need to get back. I have another affair to host this evening. A fund-raiser for Thomas Rushton. He is one of the other candidates on the short list. Aren't politics interesting? Look, I do love you darling, but I need to go. Have the waiter get my town car, would you? And, I've been told that your friend, Grace is a lovely child. Please bring her by for a visit. I'd love to meet her."

Daphne picked up her flowers, kissed my check and went to meet her town car. I sat silently finishing my drink. Daphne was amazing. She gave me fifty hours of investigative footwork in an hour meeting.

I did not tell Daphne that I had been taping all of our conversations. Certainly not to use for blackmail. Simply a venue that when combining notes I had an accurate account of any meeting.

Occurs to me I never mentioned it to Mel either. Smiling, I wondered if it would ever come up?

G G G

Journal #7 - Grace
Entries 31-37

31 – The Evening

Returning to the condo I was tired and yet energized. Wanting to put down the information I had gathered in the past few days, I pulled out my Mac and started transcribing my tapes. The sound of a key jiggling in the door immediately turned my attention from work to Grace. I shut down my computer.

It was enjoyable when Grace came home. She was exuberant; an innocent filled with hope, excitement and the promise of things to come. Somehow she had deleted the horror of her past, or in the least, hidden it in a dark corner of her soul. She embraced life and so loved living every minute that was now granted. Nothing seemed to darken her outlook and I was determined to protect that small sphere of peace she now enjoyed.

She threw her purse on the sofa and sat lightly on my lap. Hugging me tightly, kissing my face and quickly telling me all that had filled her day. She had learned so much and wanted to learn everything she could about the nation's capitol. She only hoped her mind would accept all the history and events that had built this city.

We sat and held each other for a brief moment until Grace got up to open a bottle of wine and we relocated to the balcony. It had become our favorite resting place. Sunsets and each other...perfect, as it had never been before.

Grace spoke about Lilly, her new boss. She liked her well enough; yet sometimes felt that Lilly kept a close eye on her. Grace assumed it was because she was new to the art world, but occasionally the scrutiny made her feel uneasy.

In particular, Grace thought it odd that Lilly also wore scarves around her neck. Each day they traded information about stores that had the best selection. Grace suggested we invite Lilly and a friend for dinner. Seemed reasonable since Grace needed friends and perhaps Lilly was the perfect candidate.

Grace was tired and went to shower. I rebooted my Mac. I had to get my tapes onto the hard drive.

32 – The Briefing

Grace and I always had coffee together in the morning. It was the best possible way to start the day. When she left I got my notes together in anticipation of meeting with Mel. We had not met in a few days and I knew he was expecting an update. It would be best for me to make the first overture.

Waiting until noon, I left for Becketts and was happy to get my regular table. Leslie was already annoying the outdoor guests with his prissy commentary. I wondered why Mel allowed this useless piece of humanity to exist, but figured it was best I kept silent. Mel had his reasons, none of which remotely made sense to me and should I question Mel it would likely result in my demise.

As I was sipping my single malt I saw Mel beckon from the bar. Okay Simon, it's show time. Moving to the bar, I thought about running away screaming that I had been attacked. Could that be enough to throw me into a cushy asylum? I kept walking because I knew that would not be the case.

As I approached the bar, Mel waved me to the back room, always clever not to speak within earshot of his customers.

"So, Simon, how are you progressing with your task?"

Thankfully, I had carried my scotch with me and was able to sip steadily till I had to answer. Mel's eyes were starting to turn that intense coal black.

"Not too bad, Mel. I actually have a couple of names for you."

"Just a couple?" Mel sneered.

"I'm working on the balance. Thought these two might be helpful. The first is Thomas Rushton, CEO RedSand Cyber Security. Your contact Jerome Tremont shared that bit of info. The second is Philip Zarega, editor-in-chief Zarega-Pierce News Alliance."

Hearing that name, Mel sat up and I could see he took notice. "Philip is a candidate for the position?"

"According to the information I've received, he is. Zarega also appears to have a close ally on the short list as well, but I have not yet obtained the name nor have I confirmed. He may somehow be related to our ambassador to the Vatican, but I will need more time to verify."

"Exactly why am I giving you protection when you fail me? Do you think your escape the other evening in Dupont Circle was providence? Do you believe I have nothing better to do than handle you? I expect results and not when you think you have time. I want those names – NOW!"

Instinctively, I knew our meeting was over. Mel stood up, brushed his pant legs and left the room. I guessed the information was not what he wanted to hear. I also wondered what he meant about my being protected in Dupont Circle. What the hell would happen if he decided not to protect me?

As I was walking out, Leslie touched my arm. "Simon, Simon do you have a minute? I just want to chat for a quick second. I won't be long. Promise, handsome."

"If you call me handsome one more time, I will break every bone in your slimy body."

"Sorry, I won't do that again. Just give me a couple of minutes, please?"

Another scotch seemed critical and well deserved, so I figured what the hell. This mistake of humanity might have something relevant to say.

"Simon, I just wanted to ask if all is okay with Mel? We've been friends, well not friends, rather associates for a long time and he doesn't seem himself lately. Is there anything I can do?"

"Yeah, Leslie, die on the floor now and rid the planet of your annoying presence." I put down my empty glass and left. I had no intention of discussing anything about Mel with Leslie.

33 – The Twist

I woke with Grace cuddled next to me. Edging out of bed, I tried not to disturb her when I headed for the kitchen. Dark roast was what I wanted – forget the shower.

When she finally arose, she joined me on the balcony. It was comforting to have her beside me: the silk teddy, the tousled hair, the night's sleep still fading from her body. She had a mug of coffee and settled in her seat. Satisfaction covered my soul. So many years, so many mistakes and finally happiness.

Grace wanted to arrange the dinner with Lilly. "Anytime, any day is fine with me," I said. She would set it up and let me know. Hopefully, my work would not interfere with plans. Kissing her gently, I assured her that I would make it happen. I would not let her down.

It was imperative that I resolve the issues with Mel and Zarega. Yet, I had no idea how to make it work. I thought about calling Daphne, but hesitated. She had shared more than I thought she would. It was likely that I had gotten all I could with the peony and white roses.

Perhaps Bill Rousch would be a further resource. I called him and he was able to meet at 11:00 a.m.

As happened at our last face-to-face, his office was filled with newspaper and radio types asking all manner and sort of questions. I could not make out all the screaming queries and was relieved when Bill's assistant ushered me into his office. My face was now an irritant to the media and I was sure my getting in ahead of others would not be a plus.

Bill seemed out of sorts. As I entered his office he started into an interrogation "Simon, I'm going over the details of your attack and have a few questions. Exactly how many dogs did you see and did they attempt to attack you during or after they disemboweled the mugger?"

I could only tell him that I felt blessed the animals stayed away from me. It was as if the mugger was the object of their assault. They did not move away from his body and seemed to totally ignore me.

Bill looked visibly upset. He said another attack had just occurred at the Watergate. An attendee at a posh fund-raiser had been viscously attacked and it was touch and go if he would survive.

I watched beads of sweat form on Bill's brow when he told me that it was Boyd Wesley Braxton, the Georgia congressman who was fighting for his life.

He apparently was summoning his car and driver when a pack of dogs attacked him. The doorman and bodyguards tried to fight off the animals, but to no avail. Several were bitten badly, two were hospitalized and the Congressman was not expected to live.

Rousch admitted that he was now in the middle of a media war as well as unimaginable pressure from his superiors. Anything more I might possibly share about my attack would help him immensely. And he would be very grateful.

"Bill, I spoke with Boyd at Daphne's soiree. I have no idea what might have occurred."

I could not imagine what Boyd may have said that would result in his carnage. Regardless, Boyd had crossed a line, or crossed someone. Rousch was interested that I had attended the party and asked about other attendees, what happened there, did I see anything suspicious?

My ass was on the line. I asked for this meeting and now I was blindsided with nothing prepared.

34 – The Fabrication

I looked at Bill with resolute eyes and compassion on my face, only sharing that Boyd and I had chatted over a couple of bourbons. My last sight of Boyd was with a comely redhead who had gained the interest of the Congressman. I had no idea what, if anything, had transpired after our conversation since I left shortly afterward.

Bill shook his head. "I was hoping you could give me something that I could use. This wild pack is becoming chaotic. My job and credibility depend upon me solving this case.

He shared with me how he had gotten weird calls from gypsies and psychics that these free roaming packs were not dogs, but werewolves. We both shook our heads. Bill figured it was the full moon bringing out all the crazies.

"My sons have even talked about roaming wolf packs, but I attribute this fantasy tale to their Xbox. Hell, these kids play so many attack games they sometimes get lost from the real world."

I wished I could agree. My mind raced at his comments. Mel had a place in West Virginia that catered to teenagers. What if Mel had a hand in these attacks? Perhaps he had somehow turned these kids into werewolves? Maybe he was using them as bodyguards or his own personal hit squad? My mind was starting to go outta control.

Bill and I sat for another twenty minutes, shaking our heads and barely speaking. I had to get out of there. Though I wanted to help the guy, there was a lot more going on than I could share – or resolve. My first priority was to keep my ass, and Grace, safe. I could not take on other liabilities.

I promised Bill I would share any additional information I found on the attacks. He seemed reluctant to accept my promise and I did not blame him.

I definitely needed a drink. Maybe a bottle. After Jackson Creek I was open to most anything, but this was getting too weird. We were talking vampires in Congress, the White House, the Watergate, in my local Waffle House. I needed to find a bar. This was more than I could absorb.

Though unsure of my next steps, I knew it included single malt.

35 – The Regret

Never before had I wanted Grace next to me as I did that night. Her warmth, acceptance and love would soothe my soul. Closeness, skin on skin, affirmation and redemption. I had no idea what was happening in my life. I wanted simple approval.

How had all this started? A simple gig to take pictures of some woman on Pritchard Street. How stupid could I have been? How did I allow this to take over my life? Now, I was battling vampires, the undead, werewolves and some reprobate destined to become the right hand of the President.

Sure, I had money – lots of money and access to the hierarchy of the Washington elite, but my soul was being assigned to the devil – bit by bit.

If not for Grace, I would have rolled over and feigned death. I loved her so many years ago, but did not understand the passion that took over my body. The warm feeling in the pit of my stomach was not sex. It was love. I knew at that moment that we were meant to be together. I made a promise to never let her go, nor allow anything to cause her harm.

Scary how we promise ourselves, and those we love, protection and redemption when we are in the presence of evil and extinction.

When I got home, I finished off my scotch and fell into bed. Grace returned home and quietly slid in next to me. No questions if I had been drinking or where had I been. Just her skin on mine. Soft, comforting, and calming. I had done nothing to deserve these pleasures.

Though Grace was warmly cuddled beside me, I awoke with a headache. I was unsure if it was the scotch or the issues of the previous day.

Where was I to start? The papers screamed about Braxton's attack. The city was crazed with the possibility of rabid dogs roaming the streets. Mel was incensed, Daphne was unavailable for calls, and Bill Rousch was being crucified. It would be a hard day ahead and I had no idea where to start.

Hell, a cup of dark roast was a beginning.

36 – The Acceptance

It was a great relief that Grace had the volunteer position at the Gallery and she was happy. I had no idea what I could have accomplished if she had to stay in the condo alone all day. This comfort was a gift I could not have imagined back in Jackson Creek. That seemed so long ago.

Answers were nowhere to be found. I called Daphne again and got Sophia. Daphne was resting and I would be put on her return call list. I called George Washington

Hospital to check on Boyd. He was in critical, but stable condition. No visitors were allowed.

How would Mel react if I contacted Zarega now that Zarega was on the short list? I had to decide what, if any benefit, putting my ass on the line might produce. I found Zarega's number and placed the call. What could I lose?

Zarega was unavailable, but I was told he would return my call. Daphne had not yet called and Boyd Braxton was fighting for his life. Computer digging was the only viable option to get information this morning.

There was no shortage of data about vampires, werewolves and a myriad of other entities that were all unpleasant, physically nauseating and the cause of nightmares.

Websites offered membership to all demons of the night or their fans or any demented mind that relished the gory details and life habits of the undead. Handbooks were cheaply available on dress, makeup, blood supply depots and web stores containing every wacko herb. The odd combinations of eye of newt, ground snake tails, oils made from the crushed skin of poisonous frogs, pulverized bones from most anything that had previously lived on the planet was available for purchase. Liquid potions, with undisclosed ingredients, were critical items used to either render someone "undead" or return them from their undead state.

This might be handy for a demon Christmas list. Perhaps they sold sunscreen in the convenient bucket size. Bet Mel would like that.

It was 9:30 a.m. and after much investigation I wondered where I might find verbena or a dark amethyst stone set in silver to wear against my skin. I damn well deserved a drink.

I found out that the undead had a long history of animosity with werewolves and it was reciprocal. They were both neck biters.

The two groups had been enemies from the beginning of time. Crap, I had a long-standing feud with Wesley and never ordered frog oil to make him sick. Since I was a novice at this, I was feeling quite overwhelmed.

Either I had to accept the premise that both of these creatures not only existed and were residents of Washington, DC or everything I had seen was caused by a psychotic break and required an immediate psychological evaluation in a secure mental facility. Either way, I had to take a stand. If I weren't crazy, I shortly would cross the line to insanity. I decided to simply go with it.

It was stated on several websites that there was precedence for a trust of sorts. The two could work together as long as both could benefit. Still, truces were tentative at best and alliances were not always successful in the long-term.

As I continued my search, a couple of things started to almost make sense. Bill Rousch said his teenaged sons spent time at Mel's West Virginia cabin. Bill also mentioned that Mel was deeply involved in the local schools and sports teams.

What if? What if Mel were using these kids for some sick purpose. What if Mel had entered into a truce with a local group of werewolves? Maybe he allowed them free reign over his cabin and property in West Virginia. Maybe it was a training camp and Mel would have untold hordes of teenagers to initiate into a pack. Hell, any one of these kids would love to run with wolves. Naked, howling and beating butts – what male teen full of testosterone would turn that down?

A pack of roaming killers could be Mel's security guards; his muscle. That would explain why I was spared at Dupont Circle. What about Braxton? I had been given his name specifically by Mel.

Somehow Braxton must have screwed up, and I was there when he did. And it happened at Daphne's party. I wondered if she was in danger then realized Daphne must have aligned with Zarega. Which would mean she did not fear Mel.

This was gonna get ugly and bloody. More so than I had ever suspected. I tried to plan a way for me and Grace to keep our bowels intact during this power struggle.

37 – The Curve

The phone rang and it was Zarega. I must have stuttered because he said, "Simon, don't worry. Mel won't care if you speak with me." I stumbled about trying to think of a decent question, and finally spit out, "Forgive me for bothering you. I just wanted to ask your opinion on the new Czar appointment."

"Simon, let's cut to the chase. I know you work for Mel. I also know you've been asking questions. Let me put you at ease. First, if Mel has a question for me he knows he can simply pick up the phone and call. He won't. He thought he could get around that by hiring you. Daphne speaks highly of you and tells me you are a very good investigator. However, you do not have my contacts and this is an end game.

"I would loved to have seen Mel's face when you told him I was on the short list. However, just knowing that his ass clenched is enough to keep me happy for a bit. I assume you are looking around for the other names. Well, let me just give them to you.

"You already know Thomas Rushton and me. There are three others. They are Daniel Mark Leighton, Griffin R. Marino and Michael Grady Flynn. There now, you have your list for Mel. Oh, when you speak with him, please give him my regards."

I hung up the phone and stared out the window. My head started to pound and I was unsure of what to do next. This was an unexpected change in the playbook and I was totally unprepared.

The phone interrupted my numbing stream of blank thought. Staring at the call screen, I saw the number was blocked. I could have thrown up. Picking up the phone I was relieved it was Daphne. My bowels started relaxing and the nausea subsided.

In her practiced sweet voice she asked, "You didn't mind that I spoke to Phil about you. You're better served to have him as a friend rather than an enemy."

I mentally agreed knowing Mel would think twice about throwing me to a pack of dogs if Zarega was in my camp.

Daphne wanted me to meet her friend, Quinn Malone. She thought we would be a terrific team if ever I needed a partner and in the least he seemed to be a really nice guy. She would have Sophia arrange a dinner with the three of us this week. She had to cut the call short to go and visit Boyd in the hospital.

"I thought he couldn't have visitors?"

"Oh sweetie, he can't. Talk to you soon."

It was show time. Determining how to break this morning's events to Mel was heavy on my mind. Oddly, Jackson Creek seemed a breeze assignment compared to the upcoming conversation. After showering a second time and changing clothes I left for Becketts. My newly acquired stammering trait that speckled my conversations of late was bothering me.

Closing my condo door, I heard myself say, "Okay Simon, just hold yourself together." Realizing that I was talking to myself, I wondered if this was the beginning of my mental end.

It was mid afternoon. The short walk from my building to Becketts was pleasant. I loved this time of year. Perhaps if I kept walking I could get lost and never have to deal with this madness. Then Grace would be alone to fight off the demons of darkness. Okay, I'd stick it out a few more days.

Grabbing my usual table, I settled in for a drink and some nachos. No better nourishment than salsa, jalapenos and sour cream. The bar was not crowded and the speaker music was at a tolerable level. The television was showing the local newscast. With the last finger full of nachos headed into my mouth, Leslie appeared. I tried to ignore him.

"Simon, Simon, Mel needs to speak to you right away. Really, he wants you in there now."

I threw down my napkin and forcefully pushed back my chair against the wall. Leslie drew back, his eyes wide and his hands holding his throat.

As we proceeded to Mel's office, the volume of the television was suddenly turned up. "Congressman Boyd Wesley Braxton died an hour ago from injuries received in an attack by rabid dogs. He had appeared to be gaining strength early this afternoon, but he succumbed to his injuries. Full details on our late evening newscast." The newscaster changed subjects.

"Also in our early edition tomorrow morning, the President will announce his new Czar. The decision had not been expected until early next week, but the White House has scheduled the announcement in the morning."

This was not good. Daphne had gone to visit Boyd this afternoon. Was there a connection? I hoped not, I really did.

GGG

Journal #7 - Grace
Entries 38-46

38 – The Scrutiny

Mel was sitting in his red leather chair when I entered. There was no bottle of single malt on the table. Not even water. Leslie silently backed out of the room leaving me feeling naked as Mel stared at me.

"Is it okay if I sit down?"

"Of course Simon. Why would you ask?"

"You seem in a mood and I thought you might prefer I stand."

"You are clairvoyant? Another of your many talents, Simon? Perhaps you can tell me why I'm upset."

"Mel, things have not gone quite as you had planned and you..."

"Enough! Sit down now. Simon, I am annoyed. I ask you for a few names, give you contacts, send protection with you and what do I get in return? I get a dead congressman that was very important to me. I get aggravation. I don't get the names I need..."

"Mel, I have them right here. Let me read..."

"Don't interrupt me ever again, Simon. I don't like you that well. Give me the names, now!"

"Okay, there are five: Thomas Rushton, CEO RedSand Cyber Security, Daniel Mark Leighton, Griffin R. Marino, Michael Grady Flynn and, uh, Phil Zarega editor-in-chief of..."

"Philip Zarega? Zarega is on the short list?"

"Yes, and the news just reported a decision has been made and it will be announced on the 8:00 a.m. news in the morning."

I sat absolutely still. My gut was in turmoil. Maybe nachos had not been the best choice for a snack.

Mel sat silent for a long time. If I would have taken a video of Mel when he learned about Zarega I'd be golden forever. A smile almost crossed my lips, but I quickly regained composure. That would have been a fatal mistake.

When Mel finally spoke, he was in complete control and quite calm. I had no idea what he had decided and I hoped it didn't involve me. Mel tapped the arm of his chair and the door opened with Leslie's pinched face peering in. Mel wanted a bottle of scotch and glasses. Leslie was back in three minutes.

"Simon, have a drink and let's discuss the next steps."

Next steps? He was allowing me to live through the evening? This was an unexpected gift and one I would not turn away.

"Simon, you have no concept of how things will change in DC if Zarega is given the position. If he is not chosen and his handpicked minion receives the appointment, there will be movement in the balance of power though not as quickly. My plans going forward will depend upon the President's choice tomorrow morning. And you will find out exactly who Zarega's minion is before it is announced in the morning."

My mouth dropped. "What difference would it make if it took a couple of days? I would find out a day late, but that would not change the announcement."

"I want all the information before the announcement, Simon. Please do not disappoint me, again."

39 – The Screw

Only one name flashed in front of my eyes. Daphne would know for sure. She had to know. Zarega would have known if he were the appointee. He just wanted Mel in a steady boil for as long as he could. I headed for the condo and my computer. There had to be something obvious that would give me an edge.

Daphne was not yet available for a call. I pleaded with Sophia, but she would only say Daphne was resting.

I started pounding the keyboard with all my strength. Perhaps hitting the keys harder would bring quicker results.

In researching the names, several items were becoming apparent. Each new revelation turned up another possibility.

Bill Rousch had mentioned two pickups that the Secret Service had on upper Mass Avenue NW. The Czar had to be in one of them. My bet was on Griffin Marino. Not much was known about him.

Thomas Rushton was CEO of RedSand Cyber Security. He did not seem like the minion type, especially when it came to taking orders from Zarega. Rushton presented himself as a tough, in-your-face opponent and was not prone to backing down. He had the physical attributes and demeanor of a dockworker that successfully passed a Dale Carnegie course. He had a lively discussion on Washington Today arguing security issues on our southern border. The media chose him as the clear winner.

Daniel Mark Leighton was a relative newcomer to the political game. With his yuppie good looks he was a poster child for living in the Hamptons and wearing LL Bean slacks.

Being unmarried and the nephew of an ultra-conservative Republican, his experience was limited, but not without controversy. His opposition to immigration and proponent of strict enforcement for both our northern and southern borders was not popular with the Administration. Leighton was likely the token candidate from the opposition party.

Michael Grady Flynn had an impressive background. In his early fifties, he was the oldest and more experienced of the group. The lines on his face had not yet benefited from botox treatments that seemed to be running wild within the administration.

He worked with the UN in several capacities, was ambassador to Ireland and Germany and had been an undersecretary in the DOD. He had a marriage of fifteen years, but no children.

His attendance at daily Mass was fodder for the papers, since he had a complaint about an altercation with a hooker. Since this administration had received similar complaints about sitting cabinet members, that misstep was not likely to hurt Flynn's chances. Arbitrarily dismissing him would be a mistake.

Griffin R. Marino was senior partner in the Wall Street law firm of Madsen, English and Edwards. He was married to a top rung of the social register with two kids - a son at Stanford Law and a daughter at Smith. Marino was fortyish and portrayed a stable presence.

His dark hair, 6'3" frame and good looks completed the package and definitely helped him when appearing on stage with the other candidates. He owned the geography upon which he stood. His wife's exceptional pedigree and his kids' spotless arrest record all but guaranteed he was the appointee.

The information highway drew me in deeper. Marino had, in his early years, done work with many companies and nonprofits, one of which was the Vatican. Even though he was inexperienced, he offered his expertise at no charge to the Holy See. He was doing work for the Lord.

Daphne had stated that Rome was where she had met Mel. Also, Zarega had lived in Rome, but they hadn't met till her arrival in DC. Zarega's background was becoming more interesting.

I was unsure of how much more of a beating my keyboard could withstand. This list of possible links was mapping out like andromeda. I needed help, but Grace could not get involved. I needed another me.

40 – The Newscast

Grace arrived home and I hugged her for so long she asked if there was something wrong. I simply told her I had missed her and loved it when she walked in through the door. She quieted my soul and made me happy.

Grace smiled and kissed me, then went to make us a snack before fixing dinner. She asked if some veggie nachos were appealing. I insisted nachos required meat and chili sauce – not veggies. She decided on fruit and cheese, and a bottle of wine. We enjoyed our snack and peacefully sat on the balcony for quite a while. Regardless of Mel's time limits, I was determined to enjoy every last minute with Grace. We found that the light tray of fruit and cheese was satiating. When Grace left to lie down and watch some television, I went to the computer.

I was deep into reading "Vampire Relics, Rituals and Responsibilities," when Grace shouted to come and listen to the news. The reporter was on a roll about Boyd Wesley Braxton's death.

"This five term congressman had been unanimously re-elected every time by his constituents in Georgia. He was a beloved figure on the House floor and was known to always have time for a question or a favor regardless of his workload."

Grace asked if I had known him. I simply shared I had met him at a party without going into details. The reporter continued, "Braxton's death is being investigated on the federal level as well as by the DC police. Animal control has been enlisted to search out reports of rabid or feral dogs or any animal that appears violent or is new to an area. Residents are advised to keep their pets confined until the case is solved. Any animal found running the streets will be picked up and detained until the search is over. Any animal that is combative or aggressive in public will be shot immediately."

It was a given that PETA would have something to say in the morning papers!

I left Grace to feel sorry for the furry four-legged animals now under attack and went back to the computer.

Watching the television I realized there was not much of a tribute for Boyd, but I had no doubt that the next week of news feed would reiterate every step and misstep the man had taken in his life. A special election would soon loom in Georgia. I wondered who his replacement might be? With my luck, Sheriff Buck would enter the race.

When Grace had drifted off, I figured it was time to face Mel. Going with my best guess for the info he wanted was all I could do. At 11:00 p.m. Becketts was busy, but not out of control. I walked right to the bar and faced Mel. He turned his eye to the side room, and like a trained seal, I followed his direction. He came in behind me, but there was no sitting in chairs, no drink, just his black eyes staring at me.

"Mel, Griffin Marino is the only candidate that is viable."

"Simon, do you know that for a fact?"

Taking a deep breath, "No, but I have researched the possible candidates and he is the only one that makes sense. Braxton may have been the one person who could have confirmed this, but he's dead.

Here is a complete write-up on each of the candidates. This is my best and all that is possible by tomorrow morning. If the dogs follow me home, I'll know you weren't pleased." Waiting for his response was torture.

"Simon, we shall speak tomorrow."

Mel turned his back and left the room. I wasn't sure of how an aneurysm felt, but at that moment I would have bet that it started with a stabbing pain in the eye and went clear through to your ear.

41 – The Wait

Walking through the door of my lobby, I counted myself as blessed not having lost an appendage to a ravaging horde of wild beasts. My only solace was that I would soon be snuggled next to Grace, at least until the 8:00 a.m. news.

It was a fitful sleep. Rest would not come and by 5:00 a.m. I was finished tossing and decided a dark roast would be the answer. I rummaged around the kitchen looking for some half and half, trying not to wake Grace.

Standing on my balcony, the shadows of first light eerily peeked over building tops. Streetlights began dimming and traffic had not yet become a prelude to the Indy 500. The hot coffee mug felt good in my hand. It was comforting and with my feet propped upon the other chair, it felt like a normal day, for a normal person, with a normal job and normal friends.

Why aren't the simple things in life ever truly appreciated?

Three mugs of dark roast later, I edged inside and turned on the small flat screen in the kitchen. Braxton was still the headliner. Followed by the soon-to-be press conference from the White House. Whatever the announcement, I had done my best – as long as my best kept Grace out of harm's way.

Leaning against the kitchen counter, I stared at the screen somehow hoping a bomb threat would bump the White House announcement. The press secretary appeared at the podium and smiled. "This appointment is so important to the President that he decided he would like to make the announcement personally." After the press corp settled down, the President appeared and took over the microphone.

"I would like to thank all the potential candidates for their time, professionalism and commitment in this important and formidable process. Each of them possesses tremendous talent and would bring a clear and concise perspective to the workings of our government. The final decision has been very exacting, yet there is one person that best completes the needs of this position.

May I present, Mr. Griffin Marino, as our new Czar for Special Committees Public Affairs. Please welcome him."

The Press Corp stood and applauded along with the President, Press Secretary and other cabinet minions now lacing the stage.

Vindication felt intoxicating. Mel would now have to respect my investigative talents. Or, he might just have me torn limb from limb.

The proverbial "shit hitting the fan" was nowhere near descriptive enough for this announcement. Slipping back into bed, I hugged Grace and let our hormones take their pleasurable route. I don't know how I existed before having her in my life.

On the other hand, I had not met vampires, werewolves or the undead in Washington DC. Ummm, I much preferred the warm, soft feel of her body and her leg intertwined with mine.

42 – The Conversation

Grace was so warm and comforting that I hated to leave her side. Yet I knew Mel would be waiting for my visit. I left Grace hugging a pillow and enjoying the last few moments of a particularly satisfying moment.

Slipping into pants and shirt I managed to get myself to Becketts. The breakfast crowd was already thinning out and thankfully Leslie was nowhere to be seen. Mel stood behind the bar pouring Mimosas for patrons as I walked by and entered the side room.

Mel entered behind me, took a seat and stared straight ahead. "Well, Simon. You proved to be on target. Marino will now be the President's Czar and most assuredly his right-hand man. With all the information you provided, he is definitely Zarega's point man. Do you have anything to add?"

I wanted to scream, "What do you want from me now? It's not my battle. Not my cross to bear. What the hell more do you want?" However, I knew this was not the end - of anything. Mel had a minion of his own, me, and it was my job to pay for Grace's freedom for eternity.

Mel's sudden exuberance caught me off guard.

"Simon, Simon. You should learn to control your emotions. A small setback must not shake your entire base. You have a lot to learn my friend."

My friend? My friend! When did this become a friendship? It had originated with strong-arming and terror. How was I now a friend? God help me I was on a ring of hell and knew not how to escape.

Mel continued in his slippery way, saying that though this Czar appointment presented a deviation to his plans our contract had not changed. "I feel secure in our continued working relationship." He made reference to our common goal: the continuation of Grace's good health and happiness on this planet. He ended by informing me there were other "items" with which he would require my help since I was now more in tune with his needs. No one else would do.

43 – The Disclosure

Sick to my stomach, I fled Becketts and made my way home. Utilizing ignorance and stupidity, I had made an everlasting deal with a devil. Now, I was caught in his web. His filthy, nauseating, violent web. Nothing was going to help. Not dark roast, not single malt – nothing. I ran through the front door and for the first time in years I dropped to my knees and prayed.

While deep in childhood prayers, the phone rang. Daphne's sultry voice filled the earpiece, wondering if I might be available for an early dinner with her and a friend, Quinn Malone. "I feel sure you two will hit it off and you certainly have a lot in common."

The rest of her conversation was how upset she was at Boyd's demise. Especially since she had just had him as a guest at her soiree. She had no idea how something could have happened and she was anxious to put it behind her. "I surely do not want my guests to be afraid to accept my party invitations."

Yes, true concern on her part. Let's not forget her guests' comfort level at her parties.

I told her I was fine with a dinner and really didn't want to continue the conversation so I quickly bid her goodbye. As I dropped down the phone, Grace came into the living room. She was filled with a warm, loving spirit. I knew I had to react to her love, but my body arched with anger. I had to keep this from her. She was my soul. Not the target of my anger.

Grace had decided to take a class offered at the Smithsonian and wondered if I minded. "Sweetie, there is nothing that would please me more. Which class are you taking?"

"Simon, it's going to be so interesting. The class is about 18th and 19th century European literature. I'm so excited. This world of art, sculpture and literature overwhelms me. I cannot believe I'm here and am able to see and touch these beautiful items. Simon, you saved me. You love me and you want me happy and I am filled with emotion each time I think about it. I love you Simon. With all my heart."

"Grace, you are my life. I want you to do all the things that make you happy."

We kissed and hugged for a long time. Nothing else in my life mattered except removing the dark cloud that had invaded our piece of the universe.

Grace enjoyed her bagel and coffee and left for the Gallery. A few moments later Sophia called and confirmed dinner reservations with Daphne and Quinn for Wednesday evening.

44 – The Plan

My only chance of surviving this battle was to gird myself with information. Any and all I could find. A new computer would be needed when this was over. I made another pot of dark roast and settled on the balcony. At least this momentary fresh air and sunshine would make this journey into darkness somewhat bearable.

The Internet was nothing short of miraculous. If I had to do this research in a library, I would never find all the information available. Since I am not interested in hunting down written text, it is great to type in VAMPIRE and have eighty-five pages of links pop up. Crap, where did all this data come from? Who the hell is interested in this stuff?

The more I read, the more intimidated I became. Vampire lore stated that they lived at least 800-900 years and it was believed many lived into the thousands. Worse, they could take the form of a bat or a wolf at will.

According to Serbian legend, vampires were the next incarnation of a werewolf. When a hairy wolf died, voila, a vampire popped up. It is written that there is, regardless of the inevitable incarnation, a violent war between the legions of werewolves and vampires. Each vying for ultimate control and incurring many long battles between the two. Reading about the depths of this underworld made me wonder if breakfast could be considered too early for a drink.

Romania seemed to be the origination of many werewolf and vampire myths or case histories, whichever way one might believe. There were many stories throughout history alluding to the power of these undead.

A poem by John Keats, *La Belle Dame Sans Merci*, is thought to identify a female werewolf. A knight-at-arms falls into her trance and is haunted by ghostly echoes of her victims.

Female werewolves? I definitely went for the scotch. This was beginning to feel like an episode of *The Twilight Zone* or *Ray Bradbury Theater*. My mind was not ready to accept all this, not this early – if ever. Werewolves could be recognized by their reddish hair and glowing amber-red eyes. I paused, thinking of all the redheaded femme fatales on the silver screen.

Nah, that could not possibly be true. How would they hide red eyes? Perhaps colored contact lens? They could dye their hair or have electrolysis.

My shaking hand poured a second glass of amber comfort. After three hours of Internet research, I shut down the computer. My mind refused to take in any more information. There was only so much a person could absorb about the dark side, vampires, and undead entities. Now I was sure dark suspicions would flood my mind the next time any redhead crossed my path.

Draining my glass, I went toward the shower and stopped dead in my tracks. Daphne was a redhead.

45 – The Admission

Wednesday arrived with a vengeance. No sleep and too many scotches were likely the reason. By late afternoon, I was dreading the dinner with Daphne and her friend. My mood was lousy at best. The phone rang and Leslie was on the other end. Just what I needed. I growled, "What the hell do you want?"

"Uh, uh, Simon…uh, Mel wants you to come by."

"When?"

"Well, uh, now."

"Fine!" I slammed down the phone then checked it for any broken parts. Just what I needed before seeing

Daphne. I changed clothes and walked the block to Becketts. On queue, Leslie was waiting and ushered me into Mel's little sanctuary. There he sat as always, like a king on a red leather throne with his idiot jester, Leslie, backing out of the room.

"Simon, how have you been?" Knowing he still had the ace in his hand I was accommodating and damn near subservient.

"Fine Mel, just fine."

"And, Grace? I hope she is happy and well in her new surroundings."

"Yes she is quite happy, and getting healthier by the day. I had my doubts when I found her in Jackson Creek. She had been so badly abused that I feared she would die. Apparently decent food and a caring spirit is what she needed. Now, is there something in particular you wanted?"

"Simon, I've been thinking about our partnership going forward."

"Partnership? We have a partnership?"

"Let me rephrase. Our *working relationship* going forward. You are bright, Simon, and nobody's fool. I know you have investigated each and every person and event that has transpired since bringing Grace back to DC. I also know you are aware of the varied backgrounds of many of the players.

"Let me be absolutely clear. I have many interests, in particular, our government. Though I have several influential senators and congressmen that I count as very close friends, the recent czar appointment by the President is somewhat distressing for me. That particular position will have a great deal of input on many decisions, many contracts, many additional appointees and, most importantly, how these decisions, contracts and appointees are presented to the general public."

"Mel, I really don't need all this bloated informa…?"

"Simon, your interruptions are always rude. You will listen to my thoughts and no more comments will be required. You realize that Philip Zarega is an adversary. I don't know if you realize his power and I must assume that Griffin is his pawn. As such, Philip will be aware of private discussions and decisions within the White House and Congress. And that, Simon, is where I expect you to intercede.

"I know Philip has spoken with you and you have a relationship with Daphne. My expectations are quite simple. You are to keep me updated on any discussions you have with either one, particularly as they relate to Congressional issues. Of course, if there is something of equal value going on in foreign relations or the White House that too would be of interest.

At the moment, the upcoming special election in Georgia to replace Congressman Braxton holds my attention. I was not at all pleased with his assassination. Not in the least.

"Going forward, you may not find this job as interesting as your time in Jackson Creek. However, let me make you clearly aware that what you left in Jackson Creek is only a prelude to your future encounters here in Washington.

"For the present, you and Grace will remain under my protection. I will revoke that status only if you force me to do so. Of course, you will be very well compensated. Now, do you have any questions?"

I sat in silence, trying to take in all of Mel's directions. It was painfully apparent I had no real choice. My only problem would be the fragile balancing act between Daphne and Mel. One of them would lose – and when either went down for the count I was pretty sure I'd be under them.

"Mel, right at this moment I have no questions. I'd like to feel if something comes up I could ask at that time."

"Absolutely, Simon. If you need specific information get in touch with me. Would you like a drink?"

"No, not now. I've got a dinner engagement tonight."

"Yes, I know. With Daphne. Do enjoy your evening."

He had to be tapping my phones. Tomorrow I'd start using untraceable cells and discarding them after a couple of uses. Why did he need me if he knew all this information? Well, maybe not all. Not the close-to-the-vest info he desperately wanted. Not the conversations between Phil and Daphne.

And just how the hell was I going to manage that?

46 – The Dinner

I arrived at The Palm on 19th Street at 8:00 p.m. Sophia had picked this restaurant and I often went there. It was a quick three-block walk from my condo and I hoped Sophia had gotten us an end booth. It allowed for more private conversations. Though, I am sure, Daphne would desire front and center stage.

I had no idea who this "friend" was and after my counseling session from Mel, I was hesitant to ask. The maitre'd seated me and within minutes a man was shown to my table. He introduced himself as Quinn Malone and sat down. Thankfully, Sophia had garnered my preferred spot. At least there would be some privacy.

Quinn seemed like a regular guy. He didn't have pointy ears, long fingers, red eyes or excessive hair. I felt relaxed with him when he ordered Jack Daniels neat and joined me, picking an olive from the relish tray.

After we each finished a drink, conversation came much easier. Daphne was late, not one of her signature traits. I wondered what had kept her. Quinn said he was a private investigator specializing in discreet cases.

He worked mostly with Phil Zarega and one job a couple of months ago for Daphne. He was unsure why we were all meeting up, but conceded that dinner with Daphne was never dull.

We were working on our third drink when Daphne arrived. She wore an emerald green dress that accentuated all the right places. Her dark red hair fell loose on her shoulders and she wore a diamond bracelet that would choke a horse. She reminded me of some high-priced call girl seen on a Mike Hammer episode.

She slid into the booth next to Quinn and a martini was immediately placed in front of her. Obviously she was a regular here. The seating arrangement made me feel like I was being interviewed, which was probably the case.

Daphne sipped her drink and silently encouraged us boys to continue our mundane conversation. Daphne could work a room or a table. She was good.

The waiter quickly took our orders. Three steaks, two mediums, one rare, creamed spinach and tomato/onion/bleu cheese side. Of course, another round of drinks. Our waiter thought a bottle of wine would be a great accompaniment and none of us argued.

Daphne started slowly. "Quinn, I know you have had a long relationship with Phil Zarega. He has spoken about your talents on many occasions and in quite positive terms.

"And Simon, though you and Mel have worked together for a short time, Mel seems to feel you offer a fresh perspective. I know I certainly liked our previous working relationship."

Daphne wanted me and Quinn to work together and keep tabs on several people. She felt one person would not be able to successfully do it alone within the time span she anticipated. We were to keep everything we learned between the three of us – only. She would let Zarega know what was essential.

As far as Mel was concerned, she would review any information I felt I had to share with him. This job was for her alone, but she was keenly aware of the close rein Mel had on my time and would allow me certain time lapses in garnering information.

That was it. Simple really. Just basic sleuthing on top of sleuthing. Daphne said, "Philip has already briefed Quinn on the important particulars, but I did want the two of you to meet and start a working relationship of sorts."

As I started to ask questions, the steaks arrived so conversation was somewhat hindered. Daphne certainly did enjoy her steak dripping red. Too much blood for my palate.

As we finished dinner and ordered coffee Quinn announced that he had a meeting with Zarega and would need to leave. He handed his card to me with his private numbers, mentioning we would chat soon. I did not like when men used the word *chat*.

After Quinn left, Daphne looked me in the eyes. They were so blue and her skin so smooth and fair. With that red hair, I would bet there weren't many men that ever told her no.

She said, "I know you feel that I put you in a difficult position. My intent is to actually help you." She explained there was a range war escalating exponentially and some would make it, many others likely not. Mel would be on the losing side and regardless of what he may say, she could arrange to have me and Grace protected. Daphne added that Phil had certainly lived up to his previous promises and there would be no reason to expect anything less now.

Daphne intimated that she was the go-between in this *range war*, but the hairs on the back of my neck weren't as convinced. I'm not sure what or how I felt except I was again in a hell of a position. It would be a balancing act placating each side.

She commented, "The Czar to the President will not need to pass congressional hearings."

When I attempted to ask how, she interrupted. "Simon dear, you are a love, but you need to listen not question.

"The President will also announce the Czar's advisors tasked with researching and approving new contracts for goods, services and miscellaneous items with some of our European neighbors. These are the immediate people you and Quinn will investigate and keep within your sight.

"Of course, there will be other items that pop up. We will address those as they arise. Philip has previously briefed Quinn and I hope you boys can get together in the next day or so. I'll have the list of potential members on Friday."

"Friday? The President hasn't announced this committee yet. How could you have a list?"

"Simon love, Griffin Marino is the President's new advisor and he has also worked with Philip for years. The committee has already been presented to the administration and will be final on Friday."

"Griffin hasn't been in the office more than 48 hours?"

"As I said Simon, the war is escalating. We must be prepared."

Daphne then excused herself and said, "I'll be in touch." She asked me to give Mel her regards. Her driver had opened the door to the restaurant before she even rose to exit.

I sat in silence. They were fighting for control over the White House and one of them was going to win. The rest of us on the planet would lose and I knew my life would not be easy, regardless of the victor.

I guessed dinner was on me this evening. All I wanted to do was get home and forget the past few days. Hell, the past couple of months would be better.

47 – The Letdown

Morning came all too quickly. I decided to stay in bed and feigned exhaustion to Grace. My mind was overwhelmed and I was beginning to doubt everything I did. Grace insisted that I spend the day lounging about at the condo. She ensured that I had coffee, sliced fruit and a bagel before she left for the Gallery.

Information input from any level was not allowed. No computer research, phone calls, newscasts or meetings. I needed a few hours of nothing. Maybe I'd watch a shopping channel as I languished in bed.

It was only Thursday and I was totally beat. Along with being mentally overwhelmed, my body was ambushing me. Too many single malts, too many late nights, not enough time resting and snuggling with Grace.

I drifted on and off till 1:00 p.m., but trying to get out of bed was a chore. I rethought my decision and simply lay back down. Since I had the television remote and cold coffee at my bedside I could not imagine anything else that I needed.

The afternoon news flickered across the screen. Blah, blah then…the President was announcing that his "new czar would review and investigate all negotiations for a myriad of goods and services with our European neighbors, as well as identifying new educational curriculums that would benefit all countries.

"The proposed members would report directly to the czar and would not require the confirmation nor support from congress. The members included academics, businessmen and religious leaders that had succeeded against overwhelming odds in the business, religious and academic world resulting in significant strides within and among their disciplines nationally and internationally."

The President believed this proactive step by the new czar would benefit our country and the world in achieving peace and equality. At this stage of our development we are a global village and must respect, appreciate and cooperate with our global neighbors. The six-member committee would be announced tomorrow evening.

The members were not a surprise yet the mission didn't resonate with Daphne's description. I figured we would be importing plutonium from Russia. This group did not sound like a nuclear alliance.

Members that included religious leaders and did not require confirmation from congress or a nod from the UN? I realized Mel and Zarega had their connections, yet I could not fathom how this was going to work.

After the news I waited for a call from Mel. It would come and I knew it would be soon. There was not a doubt in my mind.

GGG

Journal #7 - Grace
Entries 48-53

48 – The Call

My cell was off and recharging. Unfortunately my home phone was not. Picking up the receiver I heard Leslie's familiar whine that Mel needed me right away.

Lately, walking to Becketts was like heading for a hangman's gallows. Thinking back, I remembered when I enjoyed this walk and looked forward to it. Now it was a chore and most days, dangerous for my health.

Leslie ushered me into Mel's presence.

"Simon, any news you need to share?"

"Mel, you heard about the task force reporting to the Czar. I should have the names this evening or first thing in the morning. I will call you the moment the information is in my hands."

"Simon, please stop by when you receive the names. I dislike using the phone. How was your dinner with Daphne?"

"Just fine Mel. She wants me and another friend of hers to keep tabs on the committee members. Basic shadow work."

"Simon, everything concerning Daphne is a big deal. You will remember to keep me updated on any information you share with her? And, of course, Zarega. Any news from him?"

"No. Not a thing. Haven't spoken with him at all. I will definitely let you know."

"Thank you, Simon. Oh, I wanted to let you know Mr. Jerome 'Jerry' Buck is running in the special election for Boyd's seat. You likely remember him - Sheriff Buck. Enjoy your afternoon."

With that I was dismissed like a child in the principal's office. Just what DC needed, another corrupt politician. Wonder if Sheriff Buck would have closed door sessions for his House members on "How to Identify and Kill Vampires?"

49 – The List

The moment I cleared the door to the condo I saw my message light blinking. I was not surprised to hear the voice of Zoe Weston. She was a really great kid. Well, she was 24, but kid described her to a tee. Full of energy and a huge appetite for news, especially if she was possibly getting a scoop.

Her message sounded semi-urgent. "Simon, have I got news for you. I came across a news article my boss had put to the side and decided I'd check into it. Weird stuff naming the administration and lots of big names in DC. We have got to meet! Call me ASAP."

As I picked up the phone to call her back, another call came through. Daphne's voice purred out of the speakerphone saying that she wanted me to come to her place in Georgetown. She had already dispatched her driver to pick me up. I barely put down the receiver when the desk called to alert me that Daphne's car had arrived.

I decided to let my call back to Zoe wait until I returned. Maybe her news didn't involve vampires or werewolves.

It wasn't a far drive to Daphne's place. When I knocked at the door, I was let in by a uniformed butler and directed to the sunroom.

"Simon luv, how are you? I so enjoyed last evening's dinner. Did you like Quinn?"

"The evening was great, Daphne. Is that why you wanted me here?"

"Sweetie, I have the names for you…"

"Already? You just told me you would have them in the morning."

"I told you things were moving fast. I'm sure you've already discussed our dinner with Mel. That's fine.

However, there will be certain things we shall keep between us. It will be quite clear when we discuss such items.

"The panel of candidates that will report to the new Czar is comprised of six people. They include: a monsignor from New York City, a Nobel Prize recipient from Eastern Europe, the head of a well known law school, a successful Wall Street hedge fund manager, a curator from the Smithsonian and the head of the President's Council on Influencing Human Behavior Studies, Discoveries and Influences.

I have decided you will keep tabs on Monsignor Antonio Darica, recently relocated here from Rome, Elyse Johnson from the President's Council, and Vladimir Dragovic a Nobel Prize winner."

"Why did he win the Nobel?"

"For his work in physiology. I think it was serum therapy and blood disorders specific to isolated European communities. Or something like that. Why do you ask?"

"Just curious. So, what exactly do you want me to do? What does 'keep tabs' on them include?"

"I want to know anyone they meet with, any dinners they attend, any guests that may visit them in their apartments. I have included their addresses and phone numbers."

"And, the others go to Quinn?"

"The others are not your concern. You pay attention to your wards, not his. Are we on the same page luv?"

"Absolutely, Daphne, absolutely."

"Now, they will be announced tomorrow morning. There may be some eyebrows raised in certain areas, but that is a non-issue. This is the way things will be and, in a short time, opposition will simply become nonexistent.

And Simon, please pass any info by me before you give to Mel. Okay luv?" Before I could get a word out, she pulled my arm towards the door. "Well, you best be going. I'm sure you want to start as quickly as possible. I'll have my driver take you..."

"No, Daphne, I want to walk for a bit. I'll grab a cab later."

I walked out the front door and stood for several minutes in front of her house. I did not like the way this was going. Not remotely. I hailed a cab and headed for the closest bar. Blues Alley was an excellent choice.

The scotch was just what I needed. The music around me was soothing. My mind tried to digest Daphne's info. Just what in the hell was a Nobel blood specialist doing on this committee? And a Monsignor? I could not begin to connect the dots in this puzzle.

For two hours I sat, drank and went over each and every detail. As I raised my finger for another drink, my cell rang.

"Simon, this is Bill Rousch. There's been another attack. We found your card in the victim's wallet. Can you come over to my office, right now?"

I threw a fifty on the table, left and hailed a cab. Took me thirty minutes to get to Bill's office and I was afraid of what was waiting for me. Most of his staff had left and I walked directly to his desk. He was ashen-faced and his chin was balanced upon his hands. His head shot up when I entered.

"Bill, who is dead?"

"Simon, it's a reporter named Zoe Weston. She works for..."

"Dammit, I know where she works. She's a friend. What the hell happened? When did it happen?"

"She was found at Columbia Road and Wyoming Avenue, NW right after 5:00 p.m. We found your card in her wallet. She had an envelope of materials marked for you."

"Zoe and I worked a couple of cases together. She was a good reporter. Gutsy broad and true to her story. I cannot believe this has happened. Who would have killed her?"

"Like I said, it was another dog attack. Just as violent as the incident at Dupont Circle. A couple of drivers saw four or five teenagers running down the street. We found them and they were clean. Not a bit of blood on them, nothing. They checked out to be track team members out on a run.

"I have to ask you Simon, do you have any idea, any idea at all what all of these attacks are about? Even the smallest detail might be helpful. I need all the help I can get."

I sat quietly praying the entire day would be blotted from my mind. I wished Grace and I could just leave. Just disappear. Just not be here in DC. Looking back up at Bill I asked, "Can I have the materials Zoe had in her backpack for me?"

"Simon, I must tell you that I had to look over that paperwork in case it would point to her killer. What were you two working on? I read some pretty disturbing things. Things I cannot reconcile. Things about werewolves, secret meetings and a host of other obscure items. Do you have any idea what she was doing?"

"No, not at all." My interest was piqued. I had to have those papers. "Bill, she probably wanted a second eye to read over whatever is in there. Maybe she was working on a novel. Please, may I have the materials?"

"I'll give you a copy since the originals are needed as evidence and I know you will keep it to yourself. But please, if you see anything you think might be remotely helpful, I would appreciate your calling me."

"Absolutely, Bill. Promise I will. And if you find anything more on Zoe's killers I'd appreciate a call."

He gave me a large manila envelope and we shook hands before I left. My body ached from the intensity of the day. I wished I could disappear and just not remember anything of the last three months.

Zoe was a kid and not in a position to hurt anyone. Whatever she had in her backpack I was going to use. I wasn't sure who had ordered this killing: Mel, Zarega or Daphne, but someone was gonna pay and I was going to enjoy every minute.

50 – The Plan

There was no way on the planet that I was going to continue as a pawn. Mel, Zarega and Daphne had crossed a line. I was unsure which one was responsible, but from my perspective, all were guilty. It was my game now. My rules. My plan. My retribution.

I returned home around nine and was tired and cranky. Any more phone calls and I would scream. Grace was home waiting for me with a wonderful dinner of braised chicken and asparagus. I was not remotely hungry, but could not disappoint her.

She was excited about work. Her volunteer position was being considered for additional responsibilities at the Gallery. She was to meet Lilly on Saturday evening for dinner. She hoped I would be able to attend.

I put the paperwork from Zoe on the side table and tried to let Grace think I was enjoying dinner. I barely tasted any of the food and made as much polite conversation as I could. She was bubbling with happiness and anticipation. It fed my soul.

We cleaned the kitchen and sat watching television. When Grace went to bed, I grabbed Zoe's paperwork. I was hesitant to open the package, but knew I had to read her notes.

In several places the copies were stained with blood spatter. I was sickened knowing first hand what a pack of wild animals can do. Pulling out her notes, I started to read.

"Simon. You will not believe what I've been tracking. You're gonna think I've lost my mind, but – really – this is all true. You know me. I don't make up stuff.

"I got a tip from some guy to contact a couple of teenage kids about these dog attacks. Simon, this is incredible. These kids told me the attacks are from werewolves. WEREWOLVES! This is insane. I can't believe I am writing these words.

"I believed these kids when they told me there was some kind of camp in West Virginia filled with kids that were turning into werewolves. Somehow they have the power to turn back and forth at will. I've tried to find out more, but I keep getting doors shut in my face.

"Two days after I used my computer at work it was shut down. The IT guy looked scared when he said it was server problems. I used my home computer for research and then, well, I know this sounds insane, but shadows were following me everywhere I went.

"I told my editor and he dismissed my concerns. That was not like him to ignore me about an article like this. I removed all my stored information from my computer at work and carried the file on my key ring flash drive. My key ring with the flash drive was stolen the next day. I hid another copy on a flash drive at my apartment.

"Simon, I'm scared. I don't know what's going on, but I've got a bad feeling. This guy tipped me about a meeting at the Serbian Embassy. He said if I staked it out and identified participants it would help answer a lot of my questions.

"Simon, he told me about really weird tests being done and if I ... hold a sec someone just knocked at the door. Gotta go, will call you later – we <u>have</u> to talk ...Zoe."

Nothing in her backpack mentioned her source. I had to get into her apartment. Now!

51 – The Search

Grace appeared to be in a deep sleep, so I headed to Zoe's place. As I approached her apartment in Adams Morgan, I saw a single police car leaving. Carrying several trash bags of materials to the squad car, they appeared finished for the night.

As they left my sight, I parked and entered her building. Yellow police tape covered the entrance to her apartment, but it was easily removed after I picked the door lock.

Her place must have been tossed before the police arrived. Not even DC cops would make this mess. Her laptop was nowhere to be found. The police must have confiscated it.

A knock at the door startled me. I slowly opened the door to find Zoe's neighbor staring at me in fear. She said her name was Phoebe and asked if I had a moment to talk.

Phoebe started crying, "What has happened to Zoe? Where is she? She's dead, isn't she? She was so afraid the last few months. I told her to go to the police."

"Phoebe showed me your picture Simon and said you were to be trusted. She thought the world of you. She's dead isn't she? Isn't she?"

"I'm so sorry, Phoebe. She was just killed and I am going to find out just what has happened. I will bring those responsible to justice – my justice."

"Zoe made me promise if anything ever happened to her to make sure I got this to you."

Phoebe handed me Zoe's small laptop computer. "Zoe has this password protected and I can't access anything. Simon, maybe it will help you. You have to find out who killed her. You have to!"

Phoebe finally left the apartment and I tried to absorb our conversation. I walked around Zoe's place trying to fit together the pieces.

Zoe and I had shared pizza and beer here a couple of times when we worked on an article. I knew Zoe well enough to believe she would have a hiding place for information. She said she had hidden a flash drive in the apartment and if she had a second flash drive she may have had three. It had to be in this apartment. She was definitely not the type to rent a safe deposit box.

Her cabinets and tops of the kitchen counters were pretty well tossed and cereal boxes had been emptied on the floor and thrown to the side.

I opened the refrigerator and grabbed a beer. One of those infamous microbrews she loved. As I sat down, I remembered the last time we met and sat at this table. She, with her wide-eyed exuberance and me, with my cynical eye on life. "

I looked around her kitchen hoping something would jump out at me. She had magnets of every sort, shape and color on her refrigerator door. They were her passion and, she loved funky.

The kitchen floor was strewn with cereal, coffee grounds, broken dishes and her eclectic magnet collection. Alongside the baseboard was a funky pair of red plastic lips cocked at an angle. As I reached down and picked it up I felt sticky tape on the back. No magnet, just tape. I pulled at the plastic and it came apart. There was a flash drive. These gimmick things that every company on the planet uses as giveaways. Zoe – you were a smart little broad.

I grabbed her computer, inserted the flash drive and saw it also was password protected. I had to find someone to break the code and tried to decide if it might be Bill Rousch.

Driving home, my mind was overloaded with the horrors of the day. Something bad was going on and I did not know where to turn for help. My gut not only ached, but so did my balls. Finishing this was going to be fast, hard and take no prisoners. At least, that was my hope.

When I climbed into bed, Grace stirred ever so slightly. I moved close and held her. I slept peacefully.

52 – The Rub

Friday morning and I had a hell of a lot to do. I had just stepped out of the shower when Grace came in with my mug of coffee. She sat on the bed, reminding me that Lilly had asked again if I were coming to dinner on Saturday. Grace wanted this dinner and I promised I would be home in time to dress. Cocktails started at eight so I'd be home in plenty of time. She kissed me sweetly then left for the Gallery.

My first stop was Becketts. I wanted answers. I pushed through the door and looked for Mel. He was nowhere around. Leslie was not there either. The hostess said that Mel would be in late. He had some unexpected business.

I sat at a table, ordered a drink and started calling. First was Bill Rousch. He denied having additional information on Zoe's murder except to add that apparently someone had broken into her apartment last night. They could not tell if anything was taken, but they were questioning neighbors to see if anyone might have seen the intruder.

Second was Phil Zarega; he was not available.

The last was Daphne. I figured Sophia would give me the brush off, but Daphne came to the phone. "Daphne, tell me exactly who is responsible for murdering Zoe Weston. I want to know this minute and don't give me any crap."

"Simon, all I can say is that you should speak to Mel. He may be able to shed light on this unfortunate occurrence." Before I could speak, she hung up.

My mind exploded. I was sick and tired of being some line-item pawn. Zoe was dead, Braxton was dead and I lived in fear for Grace's life. I was no longer a journalist or even a private detective. I was a low life gopher, a slimy paparazzi, and a hellish incarnation of Leslie. This stopped now.

I grabbed a cab and headed for Zarega's office. He would see me this morning. I pushed past his assistant and entered Zarega's office when I stopped dead in my tracks. Zarega and Mel were meeting. China coffee cups, little pastries, cloth napkins - just like old friends. They were sitting comfortably in overstuffed chairs in Zarega's office.

This I never expected. They turned, looked at me then nestled back in their respective positions in hell. Zarega was the first to speak. "Simon, I would have returned your call. This interruption is unnecessary. You should have waited, really."

Mel spoke up, "Simon, you have always been headstrong. You can't leave things be, can you?"

"Leave things be? That's why you blackmailed me into working for you? You bastards. You filthy bastards. What are you doing here together? What are you meeting about? You put me in the middle to play off each other looking for weak spots. You - you've joined forces haven't you? You made me run around like some trained dog and now you're gonna partner up. You lousy…"

Zarega and Mel both jumped up and looked at me. Zarega suggested I go home and cool off then, perhaps, we might get together and plan future steps. Mel nodded in agreement and added "Simon, why don't you meet me this evening and have a drink. I'm sure we can reasonably discuss our future."

"There is no future – with either of you. I'll send you both back to hell."

On the way out, I slammed the office door and hit the street. I had no idea what the two of them were planning, but somehow I would lose. That was inevitable.

Getting hold of Grace, Bill Rousch, Quinn Malone, then Daphne was critical. The passwords for the computer and flash drive had to be broken. To calm my nerves, I stopped at Hoban's Irish bar on Connecticut Avenue.

They gave me a back table and the first two drinks went down quickly. My third arrived and I was preparing to call Grace when my cell rang. It was Quinn Malone and he wanted to know if something had happened. Apparently, Zarega had called him and was extremely agitated. He wanted Quinn at his office that evening. I only shared that I had just left Zarega's where he and Mel appeared to be conspiring. Other than that I had no idea.

I was not going to meet Mel tonight or any other night. I decided to go home and meet Grace, sit on the balcony and try to figure out my next moves. Arriving before her, I made a salad, sliced French bread and assorted cheese. I opened a nice bottle of wine and waited. By the time she arrived, I had opened a second bottle.

53 – The Preview

We sat on the balcony late into the night. I loved watching her. She was a gentle spirit and her laughter lightened my heart. She spoke about our dinner on Saturday with Lilly. Her eyes glistened with excitement, as there was a possibility of accompanying Lilly on a trip to Europe to search for lost manuscripts and black market artifacts.

We finally agreed it was time to go bed. As I turned off the light, she put her hand on my shoulder then kissed me long and hard. She said, "I have never been happier. You're stuck with me." It had never been just sex with Grace; it had always been love. Our life together was more meaningful than ever. She was part of my soul and I adored her.

Saturday morning arrived and we shared a light breakfast and dark roast. She was going to run to the Gallery to pick up some things and be back by 1:00 p.m. I was happy because there were a few things I had to address. I turned on the news and sat frozen on the edge of the bed. "Breaking News Flash -- Another attack by dogs has taken the life of a Quinn Malone. Mr. Malone was walking down 23rd street past George Washington University last night when he was attacked. As was the case with the Dupont Circle killing and other reported mutilations, Mr. Malone had been mauled and viciously torn apart."

I started getting sicker by the moment. I cannot believe what is going on. The news continued, "Two witnesses swore they saw three teenagers leaving the scene. There were no descriptions given."

I was numb. What the hell had changed? Why was Quinn killed? The room began to spin and I put my head between my knees. This just wasn't happening. Who did this? Daphne, Mel or Zarega?

I called Daphne and as usual, she was not available.

Mel was my next stop. I went into Becketts and slimy Leslie saw me first. He dashed to the bar and alerted Mel. I walked over and said, "We need to talk, now!" Mel motioned toward his side room. I followed him in and we sat down.

"Simon, what does seem to be your problem?"

"Mel, dammit. Why the hell did you kill Quinn Malone? Why? And Zoe Weston – that was you too wasn't it?"

"Simon, I have no idea what you are talking about. I don't know a Quinn Malone."

"Damn it all, Mel. This has got to stop. Zoe Weston was killed the other night. Did you do that too? Why were you meeting with Zarega? Are you planning on taking over all of DC?"

"Simon, you have no idea what you are doing. At one point I thought I could work with you. I reasoned you had incentive to keep still and follow directions. Yet, you now ignore everything I say. You go shooting off your mouth to complete strangers and now threatening Philip and me? I don't know what your plan is, but I fear our partnership may be coming to an end."

"Fine Mel, just fine. This entire charade has been masterminded by you? Zarega? Why? What is the final goal?"

"Simon, be a good fellow. Go outside, have a drink or two and go home. We shall discuss it at a later time."

"No Mel, the only thing we shall discuss going forward is you dying. We will not see each other again."

I left and the only question on my mind was, "How was I gonna kill this bastard?" That was definite. By the time I got home my blood was boiling. I called Bill Rousch on his cell, but got his voicemail. I left a message that I had the computer from Zoe's apartment – the flash drive would stay with me. If Bill had someone he could trust to break the password, the computer was his. I only wanted in on the ongoing details of his investigation.

Another call to Daphne resulted in Sophia promising she would return my call shortly; Daphne was on her other line. Crap, it was 11:00 a.m. and I was already pouring a scotch. I grabbed my .32 and put it in my pocket. It was definitely time to be proactive. I could not sit still. Up and down. Out on the balcony, then inside. My cell rang.

"Simon luv, what's going on? Philip called and said you seemed upset."

"Daphne, I don't know where you stand in all this, but Mel and Zarega are up to something. They were meeting together. I thought they were enemies? Now I don't know what to think except that I am going to take them down, if it is the last thing I do. I'm taking Grace away. When I return their blood, or whatever the hell it is flowing in their veins, is gonna run."

"Simon, I have no idea what they were doing. And, what flash drive are you speaking about?"

I thought, "Flash drive? I didn't mention anything about a flash drive. How did she know about that? Was she tapping my phone?"

"Forget it Daphne. I've gotta go. I'll speak to you soon."

GGG

Journal #7 - Grace
Entries 54-56

54 – The Calm

Sure, another drink is just what I needed. I poured it heavy. Grace was running late and that bothered me. I heard the door open and Grace breezed in, anxious to start getting ready for dinner. When I said we still had five hours she smiled, "Darling, I have to shower, do my hair, my makeup…"

"I forgot. It takes you longer than me."

"Simon, I think you should start now. Get that sexy tux out and let's just get to it. We can arrive early at the restaurant and have a drink. Just me and you."

Tonight I would carry my .32 in my little custom-made inside pocket. I was not taking any chances. I waited on the balcony while Grace finished dressing. She looked absolutely stunning as she entered the living room. She had chosen a cobalt blue silk dress that hugged her beautifully. Her hair was smooth and flowing. My mother's cross was the only jewelry she wore; she didn't need anything else.

I popped a bottle of champagne and we stood on the balcony toasting the evening. We kissed and walked into the living room to get our coats. The phone rang and the front desk said our car had arrived.

Grace was so excited she fidgeted all the way to Citronelle in Georgetown. The dining room was exquisite and Grace was awe-struck. Her eyes widened and she stood absolutely still. I had to touch her arm to get her attention.

Grace saw Lilly at a table and we were escorted over by the maitre'd. The table was set for six people. Grace introduced us and Lilly said, "I feel quite embarrassed, my date is running a few minutes late and my other guests should be here shortly as well."

Grace assured her it was no trouble. Lilly ordered a bottle of champagne, but I opted for my usual.

We sat and made small talk for a few moments then Lilly raised her hand and motioned to someone behind us. Her date had arrived and I was not prepared when he sat at the table. Grace froze, let out a frightened moan and clutched my hand. Lilly's date was Mel.

"Good evening. Simon, so nice to finally see you and Grace together. And, Grace, how lovely to see you again. You look ravishing. I do hope you enjoy French food. This is one of the best restaurants in town."

Lilly smiled at Mel, touched his arm and gave him a small kiss on his cheek. Grace grabbed at her neck and stared in disbelief.

"Lilly, why would you do this to me? You knew all along about Mel and what he did to me. Why would you help him?"

Lilly smiled, removed the silk scarf from around her throat and put her hand to her neck, "Grace, you and I have so much more in common that you might think." Lilly proudly stroked the bruised area of her neck. Lilly appeared proud of her macabre wound.

"Mel, you sonofabitch. You had Lilly hire Grace, didn't you? You've kept tabs on Grace every minute she's been here. Why have you done this? Why are you hurting her all over again?"

Mel looked at me, "Simon, Grace will always be mine. Always. And, I will do whatever I like regarding Grace, and you. I simply asked Lilly to give her something interesting to do while you ran about the city doing items I needed addressed. Now, why don't both of you relax and we will order dinner. Our other guests will be here in a moment."

I pushed aside the chair and went toward Mel when Grace grasped my arm and begged to leave. I pulled her close and we went for the door. Pushing through the crowd, I saw Daphne entering the restaurant. She quickly stepped aside and let us out.

I hoped she was not the other dinner guest, but I was not waiting to find out. Grace and I were leaving DC tonight. I'd come back and kill Mel at my convenience.

55 – The Storm

Grace was inconsolable on the ride home. "Simon, why didn't you tell me Mel was here in DC? Why did you keep me in the dark? Oh Simon, I just can't deal with him."

"Grace, listen to me. I love you and only wanted to protect you. I swear Mel will never touch you again. I had no idea he would be there tonight nor did I know his relationship with Lilly. I'll keep you safe. We're going away tonight. You won't have to worry about Mel ever again."

We got to the condo and I tried to console her. Holding her close, I let her cry into my shoulder. I could not let her go. I told her when we left DC she would never have to come back. I called the front desk and told them to have my car gassed and ready to leave in thirty minutes.

We finished packing and as we prepared to get the car, a knock at my front door startled me. Opening the door, I saw Daphne and two well-dressed men flanking her sides.

She asked, "May I come in for a moment?"

"Yeah, come in."

All three stood in the living room. Daphne asked me to introduce her to Grace. I did, but Grace hesitated when Daphne put her hand forward to shake hers.

"Okay Daphne, what the hell's going on? Why are you here? Were you the other guest that was late for dinner with Mel and Lilly? Who else should have been there? Zarega?"

"Simon, I'm here to set the record straight. It's time you understood exactly who makes decisions, who asks the questions and ultimately, who is your boss." She excused herself for a moment and put her head down toward her lap indicating her contacts were bothersome. A minute later she raised her head and my heart stopped.

Her eyes glowed red - a fierce, bright red. Grace grabbed at my arm and then inched backward toward the balcony. I stood frozen staring at Daphne's hellish eyes. She was the boss? She was the "big dog" and it was Daphne calling all the shots? Mel and Zarega were her puppets?

"Simon dear, do you now understand? Are you finally clear on the reporting structure? You have been quite a trial, Simon, truly.

I had originally hoped that you being agreeable would last for quite a bit longer than this. You were given Grace as a, well, sort of an incentive to do whatever bidding I had by way of Mel and Philip. And now, you disappoint me so. I really have no option left. There is always punishment. Not so much physically for you, but something you will remember."

She looked to her bodyguards. I tried to run for Grace, but the taller bodyguard tackled me. His strength was more than I could handle. The other went for Grace. She backed up and onto the balcony. Her eyes were filled with fear, searching for me to help. And I was unable to protect her.

This minion of hell simply picked her up and threw her off the balcony. He stood and watched as she fell to the ground. I heard her scream - then nothing. My arms were pinned. Although I kicked and fought, I remained on the floor. All I could do was screech Grace's name, over and over.

"Now Simon, killing you is of no benefit. Of course, you could kill yourself. I would think your anger and taste for revenge would keep you from that nonproductive effort.

"There are many things happening in DC at the moment and you are not remotely capable of changing them. You are only capable of making life more difficult. And I will have none of that.

"Now, I do hope you will take some time and gather yourself together. I need to leave right now. I assume you won't be joining us this evening for after dinner drinks? Do take care, Simon. I have no doubt we will do business again."

The bodyguard left me on the floor and kicked me in the ribs before they all left. I was finally able to get my breath back and go to the balcony. I stared down at the ground and saw Grace's body. It was as if she had lay down on the sidewalk. She was on her back with one arm above her head. Her legs were almost straight and her dress slightly below her knees.

I wanted to jump. I could hear myself screaming. My heart was ripped from my chest. My head was spinning trying to make sense of what happened.

As I stared down, police cars were arriving and a crowd had gathered. All eyes were looking up at me. I was incapable of movement. My hands were glued to the balcony railing and my knees finally gave out.

I was kneeling, looking up at the black night and the beautiful stars. And I was alone.

56 - The Grief

Bill Rousch appeared at my side helping me to stand. The apartment was filled with police and the noise was overwhelming. I stood frozen, unable to communicate for a long time.

Bill got me to the sofa and tried to understand what had happened. "Simon, I know you loved Grace and would not hurt her. Tell me what happened."

I knew I could not tell him about Daphne. Not yet. "Bill, she jumped. I don't know why. I can't understand this myself."

"Simon, I don't believe you. I also don't believe you had anything to do with her death. For the time being, I'll classify this as a suicide. I know there is a lot more that you can tell me, but I won't press you. We will continue this conversation in a couple of weeks."

The police left and I continued sitting on the sofa staring out the balcony windows. The stars were no longer beautiful, the night held nothing but terror and sadness.

I could not breathe. I could not understand what had happened. I moved from the sofa only to open another bottle of scotch.

Everything I had ever dreamed of was granted and too quickly taken away. This is God's fault. Hell, why am I being punished? I'm the one trying to save people. I'm trying to do good. Dammit, why take Grace? Why?

Simon heard his mother's voice telling him how he was a survivor. Deep in his heart, he knew that revenge was the only thing that could satisfy his soul. But now, he had no plan. He had no strength. He was losing his taste for revenge.

After two weeks of no food and a constant flow of scotch, Simon was near death from alcohol consumption. Bill Rousch had left many voicemails and the concierge had left messages about food baskets being delivered to the front desk. Simon ignored everything.

Late one evening there was a knock at his door. Simon ignored it as he had many times before. He then heard a vaguely familiar voice "Simon. It's Maggie. Grace's sister. Would you let me in please?"

Simon thought he was dreaming. Nothing had made sense to him since Grace had died. Thoughts became voices; voices were simply whispers in the wind.

Nothing alive was in his world now. He sat and ignored the knocking. A few minutes later his door lock was clicking and the handle turned. He never stirred.

When the door opened Simon heard a gasp and then "Simon, my God, are you okay? Oh my God!" A voice screamed to call 911. He felt hands grab at his shoulders; knock the drink from his grasp and then everything went black. He was relieved to soak up the black, noiseless place between life and death. It was comforting, quietly satisfying and restful. He didn't feel sadness, pain, love – he felt nothing and that pleased him so.

He didn't dream anymore. He was quiet and still and he longed to stay in that place. This was safe and fulfilling – there was no pain.

GGG

Journal #7 - Grace
Entries 57-58

57 – The Awakening

Simon woke with the sun streaming in through the gated window at George Washington Hospital. He was pissed off. Looking around at the tubes and monitors, he wondered how he could still be alive. His mood was bad and not getting better.

As he moved in the bed, alarms began ringing. Three nurses flew to the sides of his bed.

When one smiled and asked if he was feeling better his response was, "Why the hell don't all of you leave me alone? I don't want to be here – get these damn tubes outta my arm. I'm going home. You can't keep me here."

Two orderlies showed up and tied his wrists to the bed-rails. It was for his protection. They injected his IV with something and his muscles quickly relaxed and he lost his fight to get out of bed.

When he next opened his eyes someone was in the room by his bedside. He turned and tried to focus. She stood up, came to his side and gently touched his neck. Tears streamed down her face and she could not speak.

When he finally emerged from his drug haze Simon spoke, "Maggie? Is that you or am I dreaming?"

"Simon, oh my God, I thought you were going to die. I, I don't know what to say. I am so happy you are okay."

"Maggie, why are you here? I have to get out of this place. Maggie, Grace is dead. They killed her. She's dead and I couldn't stop them. They…"

"Simon, be still for a moment. Let me talk. Please, just be still and listen to me."

Maggie pulled her chair close to the bed. She gently touched Simon's arm and started to speak very softly.

"Simon, I'm not sure where to start so please be patient with me. When I left Jackson Creek, I moved a lot trying to find peace. I bounced around for years and finally settled in DC. I've been here for five years living in Chevy Chase. I work as an escort. It's not the career I had planned, but the hours are good and it more than pays the bills.

"I opened the *Washington Post* two weeks ago and saw Grace's name in the Obituaries. I didn't know what to do. My baby sister was dead. I didn't know if it was really Grace so I tried to call her in Jackson Creek and finally got in touch with Drema Sue. She said Grace had come north with you. You were both here in DC and I didn't know. The police finally confirmed your address as Grace's last known apartment.

"When I tried to get the concierge to open up the apartment he said no one had seen you since Grace jumped from the balcony. My mind was crazed and I didn't know how the pieces fit together.

"When finally the concierge got your door opened, I thought you were dead. And you were right on the verge. You've been here for eight days in and out of a coma-like state. Simon, I am so thankful you are okay. There are so many..."

"Maggie, stop for a second. I can't grasp all of this right now. Grace was killed. They killed her."

"Who killed her, Simon? The police noted it as a suicide. The investigation is closed."

"Maggie, I can't get it all out now. I need you to call a cop I know. His name is Bill Rousch and his office is on K Street in DC. Tell him I need to see him now. Would you do that for me, please?"

Maggie walked out of the room, cell phone in her hand and a determined look on her face. She returned and said, "Bill is happy that you regained consciousness. He'll be here in about an hour."

Looking around the room I saw several baskets of flowers and fruit. I asked Maggie to see who had sent them and she brought the cards over to the bed. One was from "your friends at Becketts," one from the National Gallery signed by Lilly and one simply signed "Daphne."

My blood pressure went off the chart and the monitor's beep became significantly louder. Maggie immediately started to remove every last flower and piece of fruit from the room. I tried to calm myself, but hoped the blood pressure spike would encourage another shot of morphine. This liquid gold was becoming quite nice, almost as good as a single malt.

Maggie sat next to me and the calmness in her voice was quieting for my spirit. I started slowly trying to explain to her what had transpired – in Jackson Creek with Sheriff Buck, and in DC with Mel, Zoe and Daphne. The whole sordid affair. I tried to tread lightly on the weird paranormal things going on, but Maggie stopped me cold.

"Simon, don't hold anything back. I know you think it sounds crazy, but I know these creatures are real. Especially here in DC. I've had the unfortunate experience of being an escort to more than one of these reprobates from hell. Like you, I lived in disbelief for a long time never imagining anyone would take me seriously. I thought I had lost my mind."

"Maggie, are we the last two people on earth to know these things exist here?"

"No Simon, there are far more minions of hell in DC than most other cities. I have been to State dinners at the White House, regal affairs at the Kennedy Center and private parties at the Watergate, that involve not only these demons, but many of our government officials and law enforcement brass.

I have learned to turn a blind eye just to keep from being killed. I don't give anything of myself to these creatures lest it look like I enjoy their company."

Just then Bill Rousch walked into my room. I introduced him to Maggie and she left us alone. Bill looked tired and stressed beyond his limit. He sat at my side and it was minutes before he opened his mouth. "Simon, I am so glad you are okay. I understand it's been touch and go for a few days, but am very happy to see you on the mend."

"Bill, they killed her! One of those bastards picked her up and threw her off the balcony."

"Simon, take it easy. Look, I knew you didn't kill Grace. From the short time we've known each other I knew you loved her. I couldn't start an investigation without putting you in imminent danger. Suicide was the only quick answer. I called you the next day to start working on finding out the truth, but you never answered. I could not leave a detailed voicemail, because in this town, I didn't know who else might be listening. I'm glad that you are okay now."

"Suffice it to say, we both know there are things going on and the people involved are both powerful and dangerous. All I need for you to do is get well. Get strong and keep the facts to yourself. When you get out of here we can meet and determine the best path."

I picked up on Bill rolling his eyes, motioning that the hospital room was not safe from listening devices. He continued with inane conversation until he left.

I needed to get out of the hospital, and fast. I wondered if Maggie would undo my restraints.

When Maggie returned a few minutes later she had specialty cups of coffee sold in the lobby, a welcomed relief from the beige swill served in the hospital cafeteria.

"I have got to get out of here. Just sign me out, will you?"

"Simon, the doctors want another day of you here – just to make sure. Even though you didn't put a gun to your head they think you tried to commit suicide. I know,

I know what you are gonna say. Just listen to me. Please, stay here this evening."

She smiled, "I'll stay in the room with you." Behave tonight and play nice with the nurses and let's try to get out of here tomorrow. Okay?"

She made sense. She was a trusted soul – at least I hoped she was one. I made nice with the nurses, joked with the food server and placated the doctors. My very best behavior – I had to get out.

Just as Maggie had suggested, the entire staff was pleasant and more than accommodating when I wanted to leave the next morning. Maggie had brought a couple of shirts, pants and underwear from my apartment. She threw all of it into a hospital bag and we left.

Thankfully, I had the wheelchair to take me to the curb. I had a hard time walking after two weeks of lying on my ass. Since the morphine had worn off, my taste for single malt was getting stronger by the minute. Maggie was the first to ask "Simon, how about a drink and a bite to eat before I get you home?"

She was an okay broad even though her preference had always been Patron Tequila!

We stopped at the Busboys & Poets restaurant on 14th & U Streets, NW. Noisy, but I welcomed the change. I didn't have to think or make conversation. The drone of the crowd took care of any gaps in conversation.

We ordered drinks and I acquiesced to a bowl of soup. Sitting across from each other was comfortable. Though silent, we didn't worry about the long pauses. We were trying to sort out the past events in our heads.

"Simon, we should probably try and meet tomorrow and talk through some of this stuff. We have to make things right. I need payback for Grace dying. I want those bastards and I want them to suffer."

"Maggie, look. I have some real concerns at the moment for your safety and mine. Just knowing me puts you in danger. I am really concerned for your safety. I don't think you should be working at the escort service. It's too dangerous. I have some money so you don't need to worry about that. I think we should stay close. I have an extra bedroom and a secure building."

"Simon, it didn't help Grace."

I felt her fire her shot from across the table. Still, I knew why she said it. She agreed about joining forces, but not living together. If things did get dicey, we could talk about that later on. She felt safe enough at the moment. If that changed, she would be the first to say so.

We sat, almost silently, for the better part of two hours. We grabbed a cab and I got out first. I slowly walked into the building not looking forward to reentering my apartment. The thought was paralyzing.

As I entered my condo the stench was overwhelming. My two weeks of vomiting, less than adequate flushing of the toilet and massive spilling of scotch had taken its toll. I simply walked into the bedroom, opened the balcony doors and let the air rush in. Graces' smell was still in the bed. I stripped off all the coverings and lay on the naked mattress. I fell asleep hugging Grace's scarves - her smell still permeated the silk.

58 – *The Settlement*

When I finally woke, the sun was shining and the room was cold. Evening temperatures were in the low forties and the open balcony doors allowed for a brisk start to my morning. I went to the kitchen and waded through empty scotch bottles and potato chip bags to make a nice French roast. My first call was to the concierge to ask him to arrange for the building's maid service to do a thorough cleaning of my condo – that afternoon.

I poured my coffee and went to the balcony, but could not look over the edge to the street below. For a long while I thought about going to Becketts and simply destroying Mel. Find a wooden stake, pin him to the wall then take my knife and gut him slowly – ever so slowly. Causing him the same pain I felt from the moment Grace died would be comforting.

I must be feeling better - the thought of revenge was becoming sweeter each time I took in a breath.

GGG

Journal #7 - Grace
Entries 59 – 67

59 – First Breath

Maggie stopped by to check on me. I had to admit it was nice having someone care whether or not I was still breathing. We sat with a fresh cup of coffee and a couple of cheese Danish she had picked up at the bakery. Maggie tried hard to keep our conversations light.

"Simon, I was thinking we might take a trip. How about we visit Drema Sue and see how she is doing?"

"Ummm, go back to Jackson Creek? Well, guess it couldn't be much worse than sitting here and licking my wounds. Sure, why not. I'll pack a few things and we can leave in the morning."

"Simon, I'll call her and let her know we're coming and see if we can stay for a while."

Next morning Maggie arrived early with coffee, juice and bagels. It felt good doing something other than planning the death and destruction of everyone implicated in Grace's death. A couple of weeks in Jackson Creek would certainly change the pace.

The fourteen-hour drive went quickly. We drove straight through, each of us taking a break at different rest stops. Maggie and I had not yet talked about our previous relationship and we knew it was best to let that sleeping dog lay. Right now we were partners – and nothing more was anticipated.

We arrived at Drema Sue's in time for a late lunch. Didn't really matter what time it was, Drema Sue always had something cooking and her kitchen always smelled good, homey, inviting and peaceful.

It was the way with southern women. They ruled their homes with a velvet hammer. They never had to raise their voice, shout at neighbor kids or throw dishes in the sink. But they could stop cold, any impure talk, jokes, or bad behavior with a subtle look of disdain and a slowly spoken, "Bless your little heart darlin', but that wasn't real nice to say to your sister now was it?"

After her point was made, all involved retired to the kitchen for homemade cornbread, pinto beans and collards boiled in apple cider vinegar. The South was different.

As we pulled into the driveway Drema Sue was on the front porch wiping her hands on her apron and waving wildly as we approached the steps.

"Simon baby, I have missed you so. Me, Pastor Bobby and the church been prayin' for you since we heard about Grace. We know she is with your momma at the Lord's Table and is at peace. And Maggie! Why you have grown into a beautiful woman – your momma was a real beauty in her younger days and you do favor her with that mahogany hair and green eyes. She was always beautiful till she married that Boyette fella and he hurt her bad. She was…"

Maggie interrupted with, "Drema Sue, how nice to see you again. Yes, it has been years since we shared time together and thank you for your prayers for Grace. Do you have any coffee made?"

Whoa, Maggie was good at this. I thought we were in for a thirty-minute rendition of past lives in Jackson Creek. We got into the house and Drema Sue had set up both bedrooms for us.

60 – The Confession

We dropped our luggage and immediately met in the kitchen. Drema Sue had the most comforting kitchen in the county - good smells, good food and good company. You just felt safe in her kitchen.

The good aqua melamine was on the table and Drema Sue put out a platter of pot roast and large bowl filled with baby carrots, dumplings and gravy. Baby peas and scratch biscuits with real butter filled the table.

We finished dinner, cleaned the dishes then settled back at the table for coffee, homemade pound cake and fresh churned peach ice cream. I should never have left her house. This woman could cook.

Over dessert, conversation went to the way back time in Jackson Creek. Drema Sue spoke about my parents, how they met, my birth and my grandmother Anastas. She was my daddy's momma and never did get along real well with my mother. Not bad blood – just, different people with different thoughts about family and about raising children.

I had not thought about Anastas in a long time. She lived with us till I was about eight years old. That's when daddy's drinking got really bad and my home life fell apart. Daddy took Anastas back to her home in Europe. I think it was Budapest. He stayed there for a few months and when he got home it was never the same. His drinking got worse and then he was killed in the mines. Momma didn't speak about Anastas ever again.

We sat at the table and talked and cried for a long time. Drema Sue did most of the talking. Maggie and I could tell she needed to let off steam, so we sat and listened. She so missed Wesley and prayed for his soul every day. And Sheriff Buck made sure Trevor stopped by at least twice a week to take care of anything that needed fixin'. He mowed the grass, did any repairs and even went to fetch groceries on days she was not feelin' up to snuff. She made sure Trevor had his dinner on those nights and always sent him home with leftovers.

We ended the evening with hugs and looked forward to a peaceful night's sleep on Drema Sue's crisp linens and in her calm house.

As I snuggled under the comforter, I thought about my childhood. I remembered sitting with Anastas on the sofa.

She would smooth my hair telling me I was so handsome. How I looked just like her Nicolae, my grandfather, when he was my age. She was so proud of my almost black eyes – just like hers and just like her Anya's. Just like all the beautiful children from her village.

This woman who I remembered as a child said I was her sweet little traveler and she always called me Gael while she told me frightening stories. I loved hearing how the hero would kill off all the monsters and save the village and rescue a princess. My mother was not happy that her mother-in-law took these liberties with me. Anastas said it was my destiny to be a monster killer so we kept those stories a special secret just between us.

She told me I could do anything especially if I thought about it long enough. If I practiced what she taught me, I could make things happen. I was so excited.

"Could I make a bike appear in the yard, Anastas?" She just smiled, hugged me tight and told me I would learn about the important things as I grew into a man and bikes were not important. Anastas said she had many lessons to share and because I was her most favorite boy we would have many special times.

She said she loved my daddy, but he was a disappointment so many times. He could not handle the tasks put before him. But, Anastas knew her blood ran through my veins and I was special. She would always be there to help me even when I didn't know she was around. I didn't even have to ask. And she knew I would make her proud.

I fell asleep quickly and when I woke I was fully relaxed and refreshed. The window was partially open and the cool night air had filled the room. It was kissing November and though not cold it did chill the autumn evening. It was 7:30 a.m. and I hadn't slept this late in many weeks.

I felt pretty good and there was the smell of sausage gravy coming from the kitchen. This was terrific.

Maggie passed me in the hallway going for the bathroom. She smiled contently and I knew she had to feel as rested as me. Being here was peaceful for both of our souls.

We sat for breakfast and Drema Sue had again outdone herself. Biscuits, eggs, sausage gravy and grits. Real grits with butter and cheddar cheese, not those wannabe instant grits they sell up north. We sat and enjoyed a most leisurely meal and lingered over coffee.

It was just like the last meal I had shared with Grace in Drema Sue's kitchen. For a brief moment a shadow covered my heart, but I chose to make it pass quickly. There would be plenty of time to revisit that sadness when her tormentors were kneeling in front of me begging for mercy. Screaming for their wretched lives.

61 – The Trunk

I asked Drema Sue if she remembered anything about Anastas. If she knew where she went to live. Drema Sue said she wasn't sure where she lived. It was one of those foreign countries in Europe.

She said my momma was never real clear about my daddy's kin. Though Anastas was always nice to Drema Sue, they just didn't have anything in common. And since she was not overly fond of my momma, Drema Sue felt it best to keep her distance.

Drema Sue said she had a bunch of my daddy's old paperwork and letters. When momma and me came to live with her and Wesley, she had Wesley put a couple of momma's trunks in the attic. They were still up there. They weren't taking up space that she needed and she hadn't thought about them in a long time. If I wanted, she said I could take whatever interested me.

Maggie and I could not wait to get up to the attic. We rushed cleaning the kitchen and headed for the pull down steps in the front parlor. Creeping up the steps I found the string to the bare bulb light in the attic. It was a treasure trove of stuff. Chairs, Christmas decorations, baby carriage and lots of old mirrors and chests. There on the far wall were two old trunks, collecting dust and waiting for someone to find the treasures inside.

Like two kids opening Christmas presents, we opened the first trunk and there were baby clothes I must have worn when I was two years old: a christening outfit, tiny white shoes, cowboy boots, a plastic guitar and all manner and sort of toys. I had to blurt out, "Why do mothers keep this crap? What purpose does it serve?"

Maggie smiled "Simon, I will likely do the same thing should I ever be blessed with a child."

62 – The Discovery

Digging deeper exposed children's books, crayon-colored papers of houses and stick dogs, and finger painted sheets that were unrecognizable. We had enough of those memories and went for the second trunk.

This appeared far more interesting. Some of my daddy's clothing, his "id" bracelet, DD214 separation papers from the Army, birth certificates and several bank account books – all with a zero balance. Sitting silently on the bottom of the trunk was a "Baby Book" along with a small lozenge tin.

We gathered the paperwork and the tin and left the rest of the items. These would be a good read with a cup of coffee or possibly a single malt. But that would not be in Drema Sue's house. Figured we could find a bar in town that offered a quiet back table and decent scotch.

My baby book was the oddest compilation of information I had ever seen. Looked like my momma had started it off real nice – then it went a bit crazy. I was born on a hot, hot day in August, on the 9th. I had all my fingers and toes and weighed in at 8 pounds 12 ounces. A *biggin'* was noted next to the entry. My hair was black and so were my eyes. Momma wrote that she hoped they turned a dark blue like hers.

My only aunt was Drema Sue and uncle was Yancy Dunn "that man of the Lord that was now in heaven." My grandparents from momma's side were Merlee and Delmar Benoit. Grandparents from daddy's side were Anastas and Nicolae Vasile. Vasile? My last name was Gautreaux.

I guess I had never heard my grandmother's last name and I did not remember my grandfather Nicolae. A bit more investigation would be needed to explain this oddity.

Looking at daddy's DD214 papers from the Army, the same last name appeared - Niko Vasile. What the hell? The other envelope held passports. One for me and one for Niko Vasile.

I was almost afraid to open the dented lozenge tin, but did so quickly. Old cotton batting covered whatever treasures were beneath. Dog tags with Niko Vasile emblazoned on the aluminum plates, a small lock of red hair, a gold charm, and a small pouch with some sort of grain and a signet ring.

The ring appeared to be solid gold and had several markings that were unfamiliar to me. I instantly removed it from the tin and tried to put it on my ring finger. A bit too small, but I would have it made larger. I tucked in into my pocket.

Maggie and I looked at each other. We decided it was time to corner Drema Sue.

63 – The Surprise

"Drema Sue, the passport has my last name as Vasile and my father's name as Niko Vasile. What is that all about?"

"Well, Simon, I remember when they got you that passport, but I never did see it up close. I don't know why the name is changed. You were just a bit over two years old and your Daddy wanted to show you off to his momma and daddy. They lived some place in Europe. He wanted you to have some connection with his family.

"Your momma stayed here – she wasn't up to a long trip and you and your daddy stayed away for I guess it was near on five months. Your momma was very upset about that. Then, when you came home, Anastas was with you. And that didn't make your momma happy at all.

"Your grandma was nice enough to everyone, but she was just different. She fussed over you all the time. Your momma didn't get much alone time with you cause Anastas was always at your side."

"Drema Sue, I really want to know about the passport names. First, who is Niko Vasile and second, how did my daddy get here if his parents were in Europe? I thought his kin were Cajun?"

"Darlin', it just never was important to bring up all that stuff, so we all let it be. Suspect it's time you got answers, now that you got questions.

"I kinda remember his family was here for some kind of reunion in Virginia or West Virginia. Your daddy got in some sort of ruckus with his cousins and, as I hear tell, he ran away. He changed his name and ended up in New Orleans where he met your momma and they moved here.

"Wasn't no reason to have all that family stuff spoken about in town so we just let things be quiet. Your daddy was a nice man in the beginning. It was after he come back with you and Anastas that he started drinkin' so bad.

"He was a changed man and nothing seemed to help. We had him in prayers till he died in the mines. I pray his soul is safe now."

64 – The Question

Now that I had Drema Sue talking I wondered just how many other secrets were in the attic.

"What else should I know about the family Drema Sue? Really, I need to know."

"Well, it isn't important now, but I guess you should know. Wesley was my son, but not my flesh and blood. Yancy and I adopted him. I believe the Lord knew he'd be needing a strong hand to guide him, so when Wesley was an infant and was left at the church, Yancy brought him home. We never thought it was important to tell anyone any different."

"Do you have any paperwork that might help me find Anastas? Do you remember anything about where she may have lived? Does Budapest sound familiar?"

Drema Sue pondered a bit, but thought Budapest was likely right. Maggie suggested we use the Internet to try and track down some of the names we had found on the paperwork.

"I think we should go over there and check things out firsthand. We would probably find relatives still living. Maybe even Anastas. Yeah, definitely we should get on a plane and go."

Maggie turned toward me with a look of surprise and Drema Sue slowly shook her head.

I felt an intense compulsion to find Anastas and maybe something of my background and why my father left his country. Still trying to heal from the past few months of horror and grief, this trip seemed to be a gift.

I tried to arrange my thoughts to assemble a clearer picture of what had happened, but there was no clear explanation. Nothing that had transpired was reasonable. Regardless of what my reality now encompassed, there was right and there was wrong. And I knew where I stood.

Slaying them, each and every putrid minion of hell responsible for taking Grace from my life, would be a service to the community. Revenge would be a truly satisfying achievement when I took them down. And I would get each and every one.

It would take time, likely a long time. However, there was no other outcome remotely viable. My destiny had been assigned in a long ago time. My revenge would be but a lovely perk – evil against my blood would not be accepted or ignored.

65 – The Trip

Once we made the decision to travel, nothing stopped us. We had passports, granted mine had to be updated, but there were no real difficulties. I made first class reservations; it was time to enjoy a little comfort after the ordeal.

We left Dulles Airport and prepared for our eight-hour trip. Usually cranky at long travel times, I had to admit First Class certainly tempered my annoyance factor.

Arriving at Heathrow, we went through the myriad of security procedures. I pulled my change, keys and gold signet ring from my pocket and placed them into the plastic bowl. The guard overseeing this operation gave me an odd look. Successfully passing through the metal detector, I was given back my items.

He then mentioned, "Sir, you may want to wear that beautiful ring. It could be easily stolen by a pickpocket. Unfortunately, we have a lot of that around the airport."

Appreciating his advice I said, "Thanks for the tip. Guess it'll be my pinky ring." I slipped it on my right hand and admitted to myself it looked quite nice. Heavy gold and quite interesting markings on the top.

We looked at the hordes of people in the airport and decided to relax in a restaurant before starting our odyssey. The Plane Food Restaurant beckoned. Chef Gordon Ramsey had opened this high-end eatery recently, but the Bridge Bar was closer and less crowded. We opted for being able to hear each other speak.

The waiter was accommodating in that brisk British way. As I raised my hand holding the menu, he commented on my ring. "Sir, that is a very smart ring. You must be quite proud to wear it, Sir."

A bit surprised at this second comment, I looked first at the ring, then the waiter, replying, "Well, yes I am. It was my father's and I have recently inherited it. Thank you for your comment." We had dinner and a few drinks then headed for the hotel.

We decided to stay outside of London for a couple of days trying to beat the jet lag. The Sheraton was a dozen miles away and afforded some calm and quiet in the surrounding area. We used the time to do more Internet investigation on the name Vasile. There appeared to be several Vasile relatives living in a small town outside of Budapest so we figured it was the best place to start. I truly hoped Anastas was still alive.

I wanted to rent a car and plunge onward to Budapest. It was seventeen hours and I thought we could stop and maybe investigate any small leads that might arise. I was anxious that we drive, but Maggie talked me into taking the train. The rail system there was far superior to our rails, and if we closed our eyes, it could be the Orient Express.

66 – *The Train*

After a restful night in the hotel, we enjoyed a relaxing breakfast and then headed for the train station. We purchased a European Rail pass. On the Paris to Munich leg of the trip, we booked passage on the high speed TGV train that had recently been redecorated by designer Christian Lacroix. It was twenty-four hours to Budapest, but we had a sleeper car and the café car got good reviews.

Maggie said, "I haven't felt this excited in years. What a wonderful way to travel. Aren't you excited, Simon?"

I had to agree. It was so much more relaxing than traveling by train in the States and much more than I had expected. It fully satiated my soul.

We boarded our train and life immediately changed. We opted for First Class on every leg of the trip where it was available. Personal stewards for passengers walked up and down the aisles offering drinks, food, whatever would make the trip more enjoyable. We were shown to our sleeper car and as I turned to tip the steward he said, "Sir, your pinky ring is handsome and looks quite old. Is that your family crest?"

This was the third time since we landed that someone commented on my ring. I hadn't paid much attention, but now it got me to thinking. If it is my family crest, maybe I can look it up on the Internet and find information.

We left the sleeper compartment and headed for dinner at the cafe car. White tablecloths, glasses and silver – Maggie was impressed. I didn't let on, but I was too. We sat, ordered drinks and looked over the menu. Our steward came by and stared at my ring, again.

"Steward, why does my ring fascinate you?"

"Forgive me sir, I did not mean to stare or make you uncomfortable. Simply, I have seen that particular crest several times previously.

"It is an important crest, sir. You will see that crest design in the stonework on buildings and cathedrals, especially in Hungary and the Czech Republic. I personally do a lot of traveling and am fond of looking at old stonework. Many churches and buildings incorporate different crests in their stonework, but there are only a few specific crests that are in prominent positions."

I sat quietly for a moment before responding, "I recently inherited this ring from my father and don't know anything about it. I am trying to find relatives that I believe are located around Budapest. Do you know anymore about the crest?"

"Sir, all I do know is I have seen it more often than others. May I suggest you try the local libraries and churches?"

"Thanks much for the information. I will do what you suggested." Maggie raised her eyebrows and put her hand on mine. She rubbed her finger on the top of the ring and stared out the window.

"Simon, this may be the break we're looking for in trying to find your bloodline. We've got wifi on the train and I think we should finish dinner, order drinks and set up the laptop. I'll bet we find something."

Maybe the ring was the key to unlocking my family history. I could not wait to finish dinner.

67 – The Crest

After my intensive investigative efforts tracking down vampires and werewolves, I was sure we would find answers now. Maggie pulled up several sites containing family crests. She typed in Vasile and numerous links showed up. Several had different spellings, all dependant upon their country of origin. There were many names to research so we settled in for a long evening.

Three hours into our search we hit pay dirt. Front and center on the computer screen was a picture of a crest that exactly matched my ring. Maggie and I looked at each other as if we had located the holy grail. I thought I would have all the answers with one Internet page. It was a start, but there was no way I had all the answers.

There were bits and pieces and that was terrific. It was a good starting place. Many of the links offered in-depth histories, colored crests both framed and unframed, extra deep background information all for a price. This was not what we needed. I wanted the quiet sites, those not offering a ten part family series for $19.95 and free shipping. I needed accurate and specific information.

We continued our search into the early morning and then agreed to a day of relaxing in our compartments. I was tired, but not enough to sleep. I sat quietly for an hour and then decided to relax in the bar.

We finished the trip in the touring section of the train. The large glass panels were wonderful, allowing an unhindered view of the countryside. I could not believe it was already January. It seemed like a week ago that I was holding Grace close to me and breathing in the smell of her hair.

It was painful thinking about Grace. My initial anger had turned into overwhelming grief. It was a battle I fought each and every day.

But, Maggie was right. This trip was the best thing we could have done. Hopefully, there would be answers. Enough to keep me sane and resolve some of the chaos that was resident in my being.

An answer that would help me understand why Grace was taken from me.

An answer that would soothe my soul.

An answer that would mend my heart.

An answer that would equip me for revenge.

For there would be retribution.

G G G

Journal #7 - Grace
Entries 68 – 71

68 - THE BARON

We arrived in Budapest early on Thursday morning. It was cold but clear and sunny. I was thankful for the brisk air. It cleared my head. Maggie had made reservations at the Kempinski Hotel Corvinus. We grabbed a taxi and upon our arrival it was clear it was not your average bed and breakfast. "Maggie, I knew we said first class, but this looks like we should be royalty."

"Simon, I got the inexpensive rooms. Don't worry."

Checking into the hotel, I picked up the pen to register. The desk clerk looked at me, "Baron Vasile, your room is ready sir. I'll have your bags sent up. Shall I…"

"Baron Vasile? My name is Simon Gautreaux."

"Sir, I beg your pardon. I am so sorry. We had been alerted that you, well, uh, Baron Vasile would be arriving and when I saw your ring I assumed you were the Baron."

Maggie gently cupped my elbow and guided me a few steps to the side. "Simon, you are a Vasile – not Gautreaux – your passport confirms it. I don't know how anyone knew we were coming, but since you put on that ring people are treating you differently. Let's just go with it and see what happens." I thought about it for a second and agreed with her advice. Why not see where this takes me?

I turned back to the desk clerk and "Sorry, it's fine. It's been a long trip and I am tired. I'll take the room you designated for me, but will need an adjacent room for my companion."

"Absolutely Baron. Please have coffee or a cocktail in our lounge and I will have the houseman take you to your room shortly."

Maggie and I walked into the lounge, somewhat bewildered about what had just transpired. As we sat down, a waiter immediately appeared at our table with sparkling water, a plate of fresh sliced fruit and warm towels with lemon wedges so we could freshen before eating. Maggie looked at me, "Baron? Well, you do know how to treat a lady. I must say I am very impressed."

I sat and stared, unable to gather my thoughts. Looking at Maggie, "Just what the hell is happening? Some guy at Heathrow sees my ring and all of a sudden I'm Baron Vasile? And, who knows I'm here? Or that we were coming to this hotel? I really don't like this Maggie. Feels like someone else is in control of my life. I don't like this at all."

"Simon, take it easy. If someone meant us harm, I believe the deed would already have been accomplished. I think we are very lucky. The crest on the ring is obviously important. If it belongs to the Vasile family and they have notability in these parts, it makes sense that you would be known – at least by the ring. Let's take it slowly. This trip gets more interesting by the day."

The houseman alerted us that the suite was ready. I looked at Maggie with a questioning face and she replied, "I reserved the least expensive – I promise."

We followed our steward to the top floor and were shown into the Presidential suite. He said, "Baron, there is an adjacent suite for your companion. We have taken the liberty of unpacking yours and madam's luggage. They are arranged in your closet and toiletries in the bath. Your footwear has been sent to the cleaners for polishing and your clothing is being steamed and pressed. If you need anything sir, the staff is available 24 hours a day. Please call the desk at any time for any reason."

He placed the keys on the entry table, showed us the fruit, wine and cheese that had been set out on sterling trays, and the crystal champagne flutes chilling by the champagne. "Please enjoy your stay with us, Baron and Madame." He quietly excused himself and shut the door.

"Simon, this is unreal, but this is fabulous."

"Maggie, my gut is starting to ache – I've got a feeling about all of this and I'm not sure it's a good one."

69 - THE NEWS

We spent the night resting and enjoying the beautiful views from the balcony windows - too cold to sit outside and enjoy coffee or wine, but stunning with the insulated glass between the cold and me.

It was curious, yet comforting, that Maggie and I had grown into a deep friendship instead of revisiting the chaotic physical times we experienced as teenagers. Our love for Grace had settled our souls and directed our future.

I awoke with Maggie calling me about brunch. We dressed and headed for the restaurant. As we passed the front desk, a small TV had on international news and we stopped in our tracks and stared at the screen.

Washington, DC: CNN, MSNBC and Fox News all reporting: "On their way to a business dinner, three dignitaries were viciously attacked and mauled by a pack of feral animals. They were walking from the parking lot to an upscale restaurant in Middleburg, Virginia, when the attack occurred. Martin Brownsten, US ambassador to Turkey, Reverend Aldo Marisone, Emissary from the Holy See of the Vatican, and his honor Judge Geoffrey M. Willows from the 9th Circuit Court of Appeals were about 200 feet from the front door when approximately nine animals surrounded them and attacked. Reverend Marisone is dead; Ambassador Brownsten and Judge Willows are in critical condition. Ambassador Brownsten has lost his right hand and sight in both eyes as well as significant facial wounds. This is another, in a lengthening list of deaths, involving feral animals.

Thus far, the administration has kept a low profile on these deaths. However, since it now involves key dignitaries it is assumed the White House will have a statement.

"Bill Rousch, Chief, Special Assignments Task Force, confirms the attacks were made by animals." Several witnesses in the restaurant parking lot that had taken refuge in their cars reported the horrific scene. They were unanimous that the attackers were animals but the eyewitness reports vary significantly on what kind. Some report large pit bulls; others describe bear-like dogs while others insist they were wolves – extremely large wolves.

We will keep you updated as new information is released."

Maggie and I stared at each other. There were likely other attacks, but since these were notable people, they had to be reported. I made a mental note to call Bill Rousch as soon as we finished our meal.

We stopped at the front desk to arrange for a rental car for the day. I put down my credit card and the concierge stepped forward with, "Baron, I have your itinerary prepared. If you would allow me?

There is no need for your card. Your statement has been fully settled, your car and driver are available at all times and your dinner engagement this evening starts at 8:00 p.m. here in the hotel in one of our private rooms. I took the liberty of having several dinner outfits sent over for you and madam to review. If any interest you, please make a choice at your convenience."

I could not contain myself, "Exactly who asked you to do all of this? I had no intention...."

"Baron, please forgive me. Contessa Vasile formally requested the arrangements. Madame spoke with our manager last night with quite explicit requests. If I have overstepped..."

"Contessa Vasile? Contessa Anastas Vasile? Wait a minute."

Maggie touched my arm and gave me her "keep your mouth shut and go with the conversation" look. I was becoming quite familiar with that look. "Simon, these guys have no idea what is going on. Just accept their assistance and we will find out later."

I shut my mouth. I was remembering the last time I didn't ask enough questions.

70 - THE WAIT

I simply gave up and let Maggie lead the way. We walked into the restaurant and if ever I needed a drink, now was the moment. We sat and Maggie was the first to speak. "Simon, this is really a gift. Your family has sought you out. We're meeting them this evening. All your questions will be answered. You must be excited?"

"Maggie, this whole trip has been fast and loose. From the moment we landed in London it's been a roller coaster. How did anyone know we were coming? When you made the hotel reservations did you use my name?"

"No, I used my name for both the rail passes and the hotel to correspond with the credit card. But, you used your passport for the flight and at customs. Perhaps the name Vasile is flagged for some reason. Who knows? Guess we will find out this evening."

We ate lightly and then returned to our rooms. I could not deal with visiting historic churches or libraries. I needed down time more now than ever before.

It was an uneasy feeling waiting for dinner. I had not seen Anastas for almost twenty years and had no idea if any other family members would be with her. As I walked around my room, I could hear Maggie moaning joyfully about the beautiful dresses sent over for her to view and I had to decide on a tux. There was open champagne on the table.

It reminded me of my last day with Grace. I only hoped it ended better.

71 - THE DINNER

Time was nearing for dinner. I girded my loins then knocked on Maggie's door. She walked out of her room and almost took my breath away. Her gown was beautiful. She was excited saying, "I cannot believe this! Look at this gown. And the other five inside are just as beautiful. Simon, this dress is completely hand stitched. It fits as if I modeled for it. Look at this bracelet! There's an assortment of jewelry on the dressing table that looks like a showcase from Harry Winston."

"You are gorgeous Maggie and the dress isn't bad either."

"Simon, you certainly have grown since we arrived in Budapest. I like it. I like it a lot."

Walking to the elevator my mood had already changed for the positive.

We exited in the lobby and slowly walked toward the dining room when the matire'd aptly escorted us to the private room. He said our guests had already arrived. I asked him to send in a bottle of his best single malt, but he noted one was already in the room. Madame Vasile preferred the same liquor. He opened the door and we entered. Maggie actually squeezed my hand.

I could barely breathe. From my right side I felt a hand on my arm and the lightest of touch pulled it slightly downward. In a whisper I heard "My Gael, my Gael, finally you have come home."

Gael was the secret name Anastas had given to me as a child. "Anastas, is it really you Anastas?"

"My sweet it is. I have missed you for so very long. My heart is mended now that you are here. I knew you would come home."

"Anastas, this is Maggie Benoit. She lived in Jackson Creek not far from our home."

Looking at Maggie she said, "I know of you child. I remember you as a young girl. You had a sister - Grace?"

"Yes, that was her name. I'm sorry, I don't remember meeting you, Madame Vasile."

"Oh, that is not important. I do remember you though. Please, let me introduce both of you to Allya. Nicolae, please greet your sister."

If ever I wanted to down a drink, this was the moment. I tried looking at this beautiful young woman and understand what Anastas was saying. "My sister? Anastas, how…"

"Simon, let us sit and I will explain all to you. Please, we shall have a welcome drink and get to know each other."

Sitting was good; I could barely keep my knees from folding. It was a round table allowing for intimate conversation. Anastas sat on my right, Maggie on my left and Allya across from me. It was a hormone-driven table.

"Simon let me try to explain just a bit. Do you remember when your father came back to visit me when you were eight years old?"

"Yes, he was gone for several months. I didn't know if he was coming back home."

"Well, your father Niko was not a proper father and he could not hold his liquor. He had an affair with Allya's mother while he was here with us. When Niko left, Allya's mother was left to carry the baby and fend for herself. Unfortunately, she died in childbirth. We have raised Allya all these years."

Allya sat across from me and I could sense a great tenderness about her. I kept staring and she said, "My big brother. It is satisfying to finally meet you. I have waited many years and I am not disappointed. Anastas has told me so much about you and your father. I feel as though we have been together forever."

Maggie sat silent knowing she would not be a participant this evening. She settled into a role as an onlooker.

Anastas continued, "Simon, I have been waiting so long for this moment, for you to come home. Your true home."

"Anastas, I am without words. My mind is racing trying to put all the pieces in place. I have so many questions, but I cannot get one out of my mouth quite yet."

"All in good time Simon, all in good time. You are here and we will have all the time we need for conversation and questions. All the time we need.

"I see you are wearing your grandfather's ring. I am proud you have chosen to wear it. Your father never would. From the moment of your birth I knew you were a gift and would be special. I am not wrong."

Allya shared, "Anastas, you never are wrong. You always know what is right and what is best for us."

The waiter entered and poured Anastas and me a scotch. Allya and Maggie chose champagne and became involved in conversation over some designer. I drank deeply before putting the glass back on the table.

Anastas put her hand on my arm, "Simon, I know this is a trying time. You have so many questions and many things have happened to you that are beyond your understanding. Please, for your Anastas, let us have a quiet dinner and learn to enjoy each other's company once again. We shall have much time to exchange information. Tonight we must simply be family and break bread and of course, enjoy more scotch."

I could only agree with her. I was too tired to form words let alone question the last twenty years. I gave up, let my shoulders relax and tried to determine my dinner menu. That was difficult enough.

The evening proceeded and I remembered little of the conversations. It was not so much the scotch as the intensity of emotion and flooding of old memories that clouded my every sense.

GGG

Journal #7 - Grace
Entries 72 - 80

72 - THE AFTERMATH

I awoke at daybreak, safe and warm under the down comforter. I don't remember much of last evening, but it wasn't the drinks. Though I enjoyed my scotch I had not enough to cause this terrific void in my head.

As I stumbled toward the bathroom I picked up the phone and ordered a pot of coffee and sweet rolls. It was satisfying standing under the shower for twenty minutes then wrapping myself in the luxury bathrobe hanging on the door.

As I stepped out, Maggie had already entered my room, poured the coffee and started on a sweet roll. We sat silently across the table for several minutes and she was the first to speak.

"Simon, or should I call you Nicolae? I cannot believe last night happened. It is a blur. I have no idea where to start putting all the pieces. You have a sister and she is beautiful and very smart. I had a great conversation with her. And Anastas is perfect, isn't she? I barely spoke with her, but you and she spent the entire evening with your heads together as if it were a strategy session. What's with that?"

"Maggie, give me a break, will you? Just let me finish this cup of coffee and then we can move around the puzzle pieces. Okay?"

"Well Baron, attitude will get you everything! I'm going to change. I'll be back in fifteen minutes. Hope you're finished your coffee by then."

I was being pretty bitchy to her. Changing my attitude is crucial. Maggie is a friend, not a whipping post. By the time she returned I had ingested sufficient caffeine to be reasonable. When she walked into the room, "Maggie, I am sorry. Am just out of sorts today."

"Don't worry Simon. I really do understand. We need to try and reason out last night's revelations. Let's go downstairs, get some real food and play with the puzzle pieces."

73 - THE PUZZLE
Finishing her cup of coffee, Maggie turned on the TV and accessed CNN. Life had not stopped because we left the States. The deadly attacks were continuing to be newsworthy.

The White House press secretary had issued a statement indicating, "The attacks may be related to recent terrorist threats. Several high level informants confirmed the animals were specially bred attack animals - they were not dogs – they were not even wolves. They had been the result of a collaborative stem cell research experiment in Greece and Iran. Informants said the animals are being raised and trained in the States.

"The White House promised the full support of its agencies in support of the investigation. It would be headed up by Secretary Bobbie McClintock, head of the Department of Homeland Security. She was scheduled to speak from the White House this evening."

Maggie and I sighed in unison. She turned off the TV and we headed for the restaurant. I actually had an appetite.

We took a corner table, ordered breakfast and a couple of Bloody Marys. Good way to start our puzzle odyssey.

I needed to accept the fact that I was now Baron Simon Nicolae Vasile. My Anastas was alive, I had a sister, my grandfather was alive, but on a trip to Oradea on the Romania/Hungry border, and my father had a lot of unresolved issues. There were more relatives in the area that I should meet at some point and, most importantly, Anastas wanted me and Maggie to stay with her during our time in Budapest.

Enjoying my first sip of the Bloody Mary I looked at Maggie, "Anastas is a force to be reckoned with, like it or not. She is a key, but I don't yet understand."

"We have to stay with Anastas. I don't believe we will find out anything of substance unless we do. This entire trip has been surreal."

"Simon, do you think Anastas knows anything about Mel or Daphne?"

"Maggie, my gut tells me she knows everything. I came here looking for my grandmother and dammit I don't know what we've found. Sitting here trying to connect the dots is useless. We need to pack and go to her house. Today!"

The moment the words left my mouth my phone beeped. It was Bill Rousch. Considering it was 10:00 a.m. in Budapest he was calling me at 5:00 a.m. DC time.

"Simon I've been trying to get hold of you. Things are crapping up around here. We've had dignitaries killed and now Homeland Security is involved. My hands are being tied at every turn. I'm even using a disposable cell to call you. When are you coming back?"

"Bill, things are just starting to unfold here. I'm going to need some time. Please, let me know what is going on whenever you can."

"Simon, I found a hacker that was able to break Zoe's password protected flash drive. He was supposed to meet me at my house last night. They just found his body, or the parts that were left, off of Connecticut Avenue. The flash drive I gave him is gone, but I still have the other one you gave me. I don't know if they – whoever they are – know about it. I'm sending my wife and boys to visit relatives. I have a bad feeling Simon, a very bad feeling."

"Bill, listen to me. Send your wife away but do not send your boys with her. I can't go into it now, but your boys are involved with Mel. It is all connected to his West Virginia camp. Bill, trust me, please. Send your wife, but leave the boys at home. And keep any information you have to yourself! I will get back as soon as possible.

"Maggie, Bill Rousch said things are getting really intense. Crazy enough that he is sending his wife out of town. We have to get to Anastas now."

74 - THE MOVE

I called the desk and had them have our car and driver ready. We threw our things together quickly and went to the lobby. The driver knew exactly where to take us. Maggie and I sat silent as we drove the thirty minutes to Anastas' home.

Her home was in the mountains. When we approached the structure I was speechless and Maggie sat wide-eyed. The stone structure was Gothic and imposing, but tasteful. There were several turrets with glistening windows, some with bars, and it appeared to be two stories. It was backed into a mountain that appeared to be part of the house. The landscaping was beautiful, but simple. No flowers, but shrubs and many trees that sheltered the stone steps to the house as well as creating a natural fence for the property.

Allya met us at the door and almost immediately whisked Maggie away to another part of the house. Anastas entered and hugged me. "My Simon, you are here. I am so happy. Now, shall we sit together in the library? We have so very much to discuss."

"Sure, but where is Maggie?"

"She is with your sister. They are having a good time together and are getting along just fine. Now, follow me."

The inside of the home was overwhelming. Though I could not put my finger on exactly what I felt, the intensity of strength that emanated was palpable. Anastas held my hand, lovingly, and guided me down a stone hallway decorated with a silk carpet and some of the most stunning furniture I had ever seen.

We entered the library, a fireplace was warming the room and we settled in on a comfortable sofa. Anastas sat at the end nestling into the corner holding one of her three cats. On the table stood a bottle of a 30-year old single malt flanked by two crystal glasses. Anastas had class.

I poured each of us a drink and then waited for her to speak.

"Simon, I am about to tell you many things you may find difficult to absorb at this moment. As you reflect on my words, you will realize that you have known these statements to be true, but you have not had the need to access this enlightenment.

"You possess a long, proud and extremely powerful legacy. My Niko, your father, was to ascend to the role of overseer, but he refused to accept his noble responsibilities. Simon, you must listen to me carefully. When you reflect on our conversation you will realize that you know all I tell you is true.

"My sweet Gael, the name I gave you when you were born, you are special in so many ways. You are a Lycan and you are a powerful soul."

"Lycan? Do you mean werewolf? That can't be true. I, I…"

"Listen to me. You are a Lycan, as am I and all of your family. Your father was to take his place as overseer of our community, but he would not accept his role or responsibilities. He was weak and he fell into a pit of fear and despair.

"We had gone to Virginia to host and participate in a festival that would announce your father's ascendancy to power. There were many of us in attendance, as well as other entities. Yes, vampires, skin walkers, shape shifters and many others. My sweet, they all exist, but not as written in books and newspapers. As there are good and bad in humans there exist the same levels of good and depravity in our worlds."

"Anastas, you must give me a few moments. I think I am dreaming."

"Simon, you are not dreaming. You must let your heart and mind open and listen to all I have to say."

"Am I going to turn into a werewolf?"

"Only if you choose to do so. You have a familiar with you at all times and she will do your bidding. But, should you want to change, you may will yourself to do so."

"A familiar?"

"Yes, a familiar spirit that is always with you and mandated to complete any deed you may need accomplished. Have you never felt a presence by you?"

"Anastas, I remember walking home from Becketts one evening and felt a shadow following me. And the night in Dupont Circle when the mugger was attacked, I knew something was by me, but I thought it was one of the animals.

"Please help me understand – my head is hurting."

"I know, Simon. There is much more to tell you. Let me speak, we shall then take time to relax and let things clarify in your mind.

"You will be the overseer of a powerful family legacy and you are becoming an extremely commanding individual. This is part of the reason your enemies have never physically attacked you. Your adversaries will torment you by hurting those around you, people you love and those you protect, but they will never touch you."

"How have I been protected before this?"

"Simon, my Gael, I told you I would take care of you and always be with you. The torments of hell would reign upon those that overstep their boundaries concerning you."

"Anastas, do you know about Mel? And Daphne?"

"I know them both, very well. We have been on competing sides for many, many years. Mel's followers are many, especially in the Washington, DC area. And, Daphne Cosic Delaine. Yes, I know her quite well. We had business dealings many years ago. I would say we are on cordial terms.

"Simon, neither Mel nor Daphne will ever attempt to attack you physically. For that transgression they would answer to me, and of course, your grandfather. That is not a line either of them would wish to cross.

"Mel and Daphne have clashed many times. They are currently in a struggle to control as many US politicians as possible. Their ultimate goal is to manipulate your Congress. When that is accomplished your White House will follow suit. Both want to direct the voting blocks that will determine quotas on Eastern European immigration, stem cell research and a new, and yet unannounced, series of in-depth blood testing research scheduled by your National Institutes of Health.

"Mel and Daphne choose to use their abilities for personal gain and political power. Daphne is a formidable force and her bloodline emanates from Greece and Turkey. Mel has bloodlines that flow from Odessa and Cyprus.

"Simon, you look tired my child. I think it is time you rest. I have told you many things and you may think them stories you read in fantasy books or movies you watch on television. However, all are true and bear upon your destiny.

"You will understand and accept these things more quickly than you may have thought possible; your power, the responsibilities that will sit upon your shoulders and the enormity of your legacy.

"Let me walk you to your room. Please sleep well this evening. Tomorrow we will talk again. And, your grandfather will arrive tomorrow in time for dinner."

75 - THE REALITY

Anastas kissed my cheek and bid me a restful goodnight. She said Maggie was just fine and her room was down the hallway. The servants would prepare a grand breakfast in the morning.

The houseman had unpacked my clothing, arranged the toiletries and turned down the bed, which was the most amazing, welcoming bed I believe I had ever seen. My head told me to find Maggie and talk to her about the past three hours with Anastas, but my body was drained of all energy.

It was satisfying to simply drop my clothing on the floor and crawl into a bed with big, soft pillows and thick comforter. Lying down, I wanted to go over things in my mind about the evening's conversation, but I don't remember anything after putting my head on the pillow. I simply collapsed from the emotion and overload of information that now filled my head. One of Anastas' cats lightly jumped on my bed and lay next to me. I was not fond of cats, but I was too tired to care.

Morning arrived all too quickly, but I felt rested and relaxed. The sun filtering through the drapes felt warm on my arm and face. After a hot shower, I dressed quickly, anxious to again see Anastas and continue the conversation. As I shaved, I could not help but look deeply at my face and see if there were any telltale sign of my bloodline starting to appear. Thankfully, there was nothing different.

My mind alternated between disbelief, the possibility of a mental breakdown and the thought that everything Anastas said was true. And if it were, my life had dramatically changed and I was unsure of my next steps.

This newfound knowledge is starting to unhinge me. Silly though it was, while putting on my shoes, I looked around to see if I could find my familiar, maybe scurrying around the floor. Did it have a name? I wondered what it might look like or how I contact it? I hoped it wasn't the cat. Time for a reality check. I really needed coffee and a friend to listen.

Knocking on the other hallway door, I waited for Maggie to answer. It was silent, so I figured she was already enjoying a cup of dark roast with Allya. I didn't remember my walk to my room last night and there appeared several hallways off what I perceived as the main hallway. There were a lot of rooms in this place. I wondered if Anastas did a lot of overnight entertaining.

I turned left at the end of the hall and saw the stairs to the foyer. Impressive home with its silk carpeted stone floors and polished wood railings. A lot nicer than my condo. Reaching the bottom step, I heard laughing and had to admit it was a nice sound. It had been a long time since laughing touched my soul.

The ladies were already enjoying breakfast and deep into conversation. Maggie, Allya and Anastas were having an animated conversation about some designer. I never did understand all the fuss over designers. Like buying my tux, you walk into the store, try on a few suits and buy one. Discussion about the torrid love life of some guy making dresses totally escaped me.

As I sat at the table they turned their gaze toward me. It was odd really. It felt like a person of importance had entered the room and they were acknowledging his entrance. I looked at each and smiled. What beautiful women surrounded me.

Maggie, with mahogany hair and green eyes was drop dead gorgeous, and Allya with dark eyes, jet hair and creamy skin took your breath away. Anastas, the matriarch, was still an attractive woman.

Her skin appeared soft and void of wrinkles, her black eyes were clear and bright and her hair, jet like Allya with a few carefully placed strands of white. Her quiet presence commanded attention.

"Good morning ladies. How about today we…"

Allya interrupted, "Simon, Maggie is mine today. We have decided to see some of the boutiques downtown. Maybe we will buy something, maybe not."

"Somehow Maggie, I think you will find something to buy. Take care of each other. Will we see you later for dinner?"

Maggie rolled her eyes, "Simon, you are already getting overprotective. Lighten up. We'll get back when we're done. This is the first time I've had fun in a long while. I'm up for whatever Allya is willing to show me."

Allya grabbed Maggie's arm, "Let's go. We can have a quick lunch downtown. They opened a new Max Mara and Hugo Boss. Perhaps we can find a gift for my brother, the Baron."

Anastas looked gently at Maggie and Allya. "May I ask you to be careful, for me?" Allya turned, "Oh, Anastas. You know we will not be bothered. Don't worry."

"Allya, you will listen to what I ask of you?"

Allya stood still, turned and met Anastas' gaze, "Of course my Anastas. Please forgive my rude answer to your request. I am sorry. I would never mean to offend you."

"I know that my child. Both of you go and have a lovely day. When you return your grandfather should be here. We will have a family dinner and relax and enjoy each other's company. Biztonságos."

"Biztonságos, my Simon, means *be safe*. I know Allya will listen. She is a little headstrong, but she is mature for her age. Now, after you finish your breakfast, we will walk and I will answer your questions and continue to fill in your family history. Is that something you would like to do today?"

"I would love to do whatever you have planned. I am yours today."

"Simon, you have always been mine."

76 - THE WALK

I took my time enjoying breakfast and was becoming more comfortable with my surroundings. We grabbed our coats and Anastas led me to a beautiful stand of trees at the edge of a forest. We slowly followed a path that seemed to have been walked many, many times. I wondered if it had been her that spent time in these beautiful woods. We continued silently for twenty or so minutes then came into a slight clearing. There was a small pool of water and a natural stone bench to the side. We sat and remained quiet for some time.

"Simon, I have waited all this time for you to sit here with me and I am not disappointed. My dream has been fulfilled and your destiny is now in place. I realize all that I have told you may be overwhelming, yet I believe you are accepting this new role in a way your father never could. You should take a few days of walking in these woods and reflect on all that has transpired. When your grandfather arrives this evening he will want to spend some time with you."

"Anastas, what is my destiny? I don't see a clear path. What am I supposed to do when I return to DC? What about Mel and Daphne?"

Before she could answer a crackling of dry wood in the distance took our attention. Suddenly her neck arched. She stared toward the noise, seemed to smell the air several times and I saw her facial muscles contort ever so slightly. I was not afraid, but I was very curious. I had seen that facial movement before and it was not a good thing.

"Simon, for the interim, you need only become comfortable with your legacy. You have no immediate responsibilities as overseer. But you will. And when you are ready we will be here to guide you. As for Mel and Daphne, things will be very different when you return.

"You are a peer. Actually you are a bit higher on the scale than either of them. But do not deceive yourself. They are very powerful and if they determine you are an active enemy it will be burdensome for you. When you deal with them you will speak as an equal. They will not order you around. They will ask for your input. I believe they thought you would be weak like your father.

"They will discuss with you any plans that might affect or involve your clan. And, you do have a clan. Right now, those that do not belong to Daphne are roaming about with no direction. They are likely part of Mel's Lycan group, but they belong to you. When you speak with them there will be no doubt in their mind and they will welcome your direction and discipline.

"It is likely that since our clan has had no local leadership, Mel has gained control. And you must stop him. When you fulfill your goal of gathering your people, the useless killings will stop.

Mel directs, and delights, in that kind of violence. Daphne is smarter and has never appeared to enjoy random violence. She would not draw this much attention for such little benefit."

"Anastas, in so many ways, my time with you has answered questions and emotions I have had all my life. It is not possible for me to digest all what you have presented, but I will defend my legacy. I will do my best to ensure there is peace. I will not fail the tasks assigned to me."

"You lighten my heart Gael, you are the answer I sought these many years. You have fulfilled my quest.

"You and Maggie should leave in a few days and I want Allya to go with you. She needs the guidance of a strong man and who better than her brother. She is not wild, but she needs a strong hand and guidance. If problems arise I expect you to stop them immediately."

"Anastas, you have my word. Nothing will happen to her. I will find a new home and she will live with me until we discuss other arrangements. Maggie will be a steadying influence for her as well."

"Simon, you need not work. You will have no issues concerning money. Your grandfather has taken care of your finances at Credit Suisse. You will not encounter any financial difficulties. Now, let us return and prepare for your grandfather's arrival. We must freshen up before dinner. And please remember, we always dress for dinner in this home."

77 - THE MEAL

I welcomed a few hours alone to go over the information in my head. I cleaned up in my room and decided to explore the rest of the house. It was warm in the house, despite stone that made up the walls and floors. I looked at the portraits that covered the walls. Each was a magnificent oil painting and I assumed they were all relatives.

One portrait caught my eye. The brass nameplate read "Baroness Erzsebet Bathory – 1560–1614." The portrait was of a desirable young woman with milky skin, raven hair and amber eyes. She was gorgeous and somehow terrifying at the same time. I wondered just how we were related. Other portraits were provocative, as well as formidable.

I opened door upon door along the different hallways. Each contained a beautiful room, perfectly kept and nicely decorated. I thought Anastas must entertain on a huge scale. At the end of one hallway was a large, commanding, wooden door. I attempted to open it, but it was locked. I'd ask about the door later. It was not crucial at this very moment. I continued surveying the walls, furniture, windows and carpet. I tried to absorb everything I could before I had to leave.

When I returned to my room I could hear Maggie and Allya laughing. This was becoming a sound I wanted to hear more often. I put on my tux without questioning its necessity. Anastas had made it clear that dressing for dinner was not optional. It actually felt good. I started to like the formality.

The houseman called us to dinner. As I entered the dining room through the carved, wooden archway I stood quite still. Maggie and Allya were flanking a tall and quite handsome older gentlemen. Anastas said, "Simon, this is your grandfather, Count Nicolae Vasile. And Nicolae, this is your grandson, Baron Simon Nicolae Vasile."

I walked toward him extending my hand, "Sir, I am happy to meet you."

He looked me in the eye and then extended his hand. "Simon, I am glad we have finally come together. Destiny sometimes takes longer to reveal itself than we might prefer. Do you not agree?"

Maggie let go of his arm and cupped mine with both her hands, slowly guiding me toward the table. Allya took the Count's arm and walked with him. Anastas took her seat next to the Count and said, "Our circle is complete and our blood now flows together at long last. We are a completed family, we must be thankful, embrace and trust each other and allow no one or any thing to come between us. We are now as one."

We enjoyed an intimate and relaxing dinner. It felt as though I had never been away from Anastas and I was now questioning my need to return to the States. When dinner ended, Maggie, Allya and Anastas went to the living room.

The Count and I retired to his library. He poured a healthy snifter of brandy for each of us and we settled in front of the fireplace.

78 - THE CONVERSATION

"Simon, my grandson, my namesake, my legacy. Finally I am able to sit across from you as a grown man. Our first and only visit occurred when you were a few months old. I held you and would tell you stories before your grandmother would take you from me and put you to bed. Now we will sit and speak as men and enjoy each other's company with no worry Anastas will whisk you away to a cradle.

"I am very proud of you Simon. You have handled many pressures and trials and you have come through it as a man. I was disillusioned with your father. Sometimes courage and commitment are lost in a generation, but you have proven it is not lost forever."

"Count, please tell me, do you know how my father died?"

"Simon, it was told to us he was killed in the gold mines in your hometown. That does not mean his death was a mining accident. It is just the geography where the deed occurred. His body was not found, so it is unclear exactly what happened. Anastas will uncover the truth and it is not pleasant when she shows her anger.

"I know Anastas has given you some family history, but you should ask me those questions which sit heavy upon your heart."

"Count, does our Lycan heritage go all the way back to your family beginnings?"

"No, I am only the twelfth in my line. The extensive lineage is from Anastas side of our family. Her ancestry goes back well before the 8th century. Though she is not proud that Baroness Bathory is in her lineage."

"I did see her portrait on the wall. Who is she?"

"She is known as the Blood Baroness. You should research her sometime, but I would suggest not asking Anastas for information.

"Simon, I will tell you I am available whenever you need counsel. You will realize that you will now understand things as they happen to you. You will learn to use your senses and your intellect when you settle disputes, make decisions or defend your line.

As you have slowly accepted what is happening, you have allowed your mind to open to extensive knowledge. It will unfold each day and you will only realize it when answers are apparent before you think about a question.

"I would advise you think seriously before allowing yourself to *turn* into another form. Use your *familiar* for those needs. There are some like us that become too fond of *turning* and that may cause you problems. Although, when necessary, it is a powerful position you may wield."

"Count, how do I use my familiar? I don't even know how to find it."

"Simon, you need only sit quietly and concentrate. Your familiar will know exactly what you want done. As you grow in strength and become confident in your inner spirit you will need only to think about a task and it will happen.

"I do suspect, however, that Anastas will send you home with one of her favorite carriers. They have been with her for many years. Though you have and always have had a familiar, you have not acknowledged nor interacted with it in any way. You have never asked it for any help nor given it any task to complete. It has been a temporary, protective force that has followed you.

"I have no doubt Anastas will give your familiar a pleasing form that you will recognize and come to depend upon.

"For your future needs, I have taken care of your finances. I have arranged with Credit Suisse for a

Centurion Black credit card for you. You will not be bothered with a monthly bill. Use this for anything you need, or, for that matter, anything you want. Allya has her own financial needs met with a different card that ensures her immaturity does not get in the way of reason.

"May I suggest you wear your ring at all times. It will confirm your stature and influence. The crest is well known and respected and will grant you access to places that would not normally be open to you. It will also reaffirm your position of leadership and power.

"Simon, I so wish you had been brought up as Nicolae, but I digress. Though your beginnings were difficult and you had neither guidance nor information about your heritage, you have matured into a man. A powerful, knowledgeable and formidable man, that commands attention and respect.

"You must let your old, fearful ways fall to the side and accept your inheritance. You will no longer be at the beck and call of others that only wish for power or monetary gain. You are an equal participant in all future discussions and decisions that touch your bloodline. It will, most assuredly, be a burden for you to ensure that our legacy, our future, our integrity is maintained at the highest level.

"Simon, you are now our overseer, our *new* blood, and our new force with which we will move forward. With your leadership you will determine the future of not only our bloodline, but the future of your country. There is much for you to learn, to absorb, and to reconcile, but you are the chosen among us. It will be a difficult and arduous road, but you will succeed.

"Anastas will not allow anything less than your complete success. She is an unrelenting taskmaster and has failed but one time. That one time was Niko. Simon, you are her grandson, the spawn of a son that never fulfilled his appointed destiny. She will not permit your failure. Nor will I.

"Now, we will speak again before you leave, but for the rest of this evening why don't you relax and enjoy a late evening walk or some quiet moments here to reflect."

With that said the Count left the room. I relaxed in front of the fire enjoying the last of my brandy.

79 - MIRA

I was unsure of all that had transpired during this short visit, but I was not at all concerned with unanswered questions. In fact, things were pretty amazing. It's as if I've been transformed from a bottom-rung piece of humanity to an accepted and sought after companion.

I had grown and left my sad immaturity behind. A long ago memorized verse came to mind "...but when I became a man I put away childish things." The world was different and I liked the way it looked. I liked the way I felt. I liked every bit of it.

After enjoying the last embers of the fire I went to my room. The house was quiet and I looked forward to another good night's sleep. Here I had enjoyed more rest and relaxation than I had experienced in a very long time. As I crawled into bed, one of the cats jumped on the bed and lay beside me. I again wondered if this was my familiar. Ummm...cat hair – terrific!

In the morning, I found myself walking the path Anastas and I had traveled a day earlier. The sun had just risen and the crisp air let me see my breath each time I exhaled. After a few minutes I found the clearing and small pond where we had relaxed.

As I sat on the stone bench, a dog emerged from the woods across the pond. It had a rusty, red coat and bright amber eyes. I half whistled and patted my knee and the dog immediately came to me. She sat at my feet and stared up at me. I started rubbing her neck and she put her head on my knee, obviously enjoying the attention. There was no tag or collar and I wondered where her owners lived. She seemed too well cared for to be a stray.

For a long time I sat thinking about my new life while rubbing the dog's head. It was peaceful here and I hated the thought of leaving. I knew it had to be, but I had come to enjoy the stillness and internal quiet that filled me each day. After arriving in DC it seemed like hell had opened its gates and allowed its minions to invade all of my existence. I sighed heavily and headed for the house, the dog following close behind.

As I entered the, foyer the dog was close on my heels. I turned to scoot her away as Anastas walked in, "Simon, I see you have met Mira. Isn't she beautiful?"

"Oh, you know this dog? She was at the pond and followed me home."

"Yes, I know Mira very well. I named her after a beautiful red star that shines in the constellation Cetus. Her name means "the amazing one" and she is a Viszla. They are a very old breed originating in Hungary and are well known for their superb hunting skills. They are fearless and protective of their owners."

"I didn't realize you liked dogs. I have only seen cats about the house."

"I love dogs. It is just that my cats have been with me for so long and are more attuned to females. Simon, Mira is your dog now. She is your familiar."

"Mine? But, I've never seen her before. I thought my familiar was just a shadow? Just a thought."

"It was for a long time, but now that you have matured your familiar will be with you at all times and take whatever form is required. However, I think Mira is beautiful just as she is now."

"I agree. She is beautiful and I thank you for her. I will care for her well."

"Simon, she is there for you. Depend upon her. You alone are her master. Remember that."

80 - THE ARRANGEMENTS

I escorted Anastas to breakfast. Maggie, Allya and the Count had just seated themselves and Mira followed me and lay at my feet. Breakfast was enjoyable and the conversation eventually turned to our leaving Budapest.

The Count said, "Credit Suisse is going to messenger your card to the house tomorrow morning. The Centurion card has an extremely capable concierge service so please make use of them. They ensure first class accommodations for any service you might need. Also, they will ensure Mira is welcomed wherever you go."

Anastas added, "Oh Simon, please leave those detail discussions for later. Let's enjoy our meal and the last day or so we have together. "

"I really don't want to go, but I know it is necessary. We will leave tomorrow afternoon for London. I expect Maggie and Allya will need today for some shopping before we depart."

Both of them laughed at my comment, but acknowledged they had already planned for shopping later in the day. The Count and Anastas smiled knowingly.

We finished our meal and I started to prepare for the trip home. Maggie and Allya had decided they would share a townhouse. Both seemed excited about searching for a new home that was not too close to me. Their conversations were about color schemes, furniture, drapes and many other items that held no interest for me. I was happy Maggie seemed to have made a turn in dealing with the past few months of despair. She had a smile on her face and we rarely spoke about anything to do with DC.

A call to Bill Rousch was essential. I decided to take Mira to the pond and get that call out of the way.

G G G

Journal #7 - Grace
Entries 81 - 88

81 - THE PREPARATIONS

I called Bill the moment I arrived at the pond. I had not taken into consideration the time difference and had interrupted the treasured bit of sleep that he was getting lately.

"Bill, how are things going? Any new deaths or assaults?"

Yawning into the phone Bill said, "Thankfully no. Things are at a standstill for the moment. Believe me, I need the rest. The politics are still a big issue. My hands are tied each time I try to investigate anything with the attacks in Middleburg. The White House and Homeland Security have been strangely quiet and I know something is wrong.

"My wife is at her sisters and I need you to tell me why my boys are an issue. Has that bastard Mel done something to them? I can barely hold a conversation with them without looking guilty. What the hell am I supposed to do? When are you coming back?"

"Bill, take it easy. I'm scheduled to leave for London tomorrow afternoon and then depart Heathrow the day after. We should be in DC on Friday afternoon. We can meet then."

"Simon, the jet lag is gonna kill you."

"I'll be fine. Am anxious to speak with you and discuss all that has happened in my absence. Do you still have Zoe's flash drive?"

"Yes, and I haven't tried to hire anyone else to attempt breaking the password code. Not after the last techy that touched her computer was found in pieces. I can't put anyone else in harm's way. I figured you might know someone outside of DC that could help."

"Bill, I'm sure we can resolve it when I return. Maggie is coming with me and I have found that I have a beautiful half sister, Allya that will also be returning with me. Don't attempt to investigate anything further until we meet. As far as Mel is concerned, ignore anything that happens with your sons. Trust me on this, things will smooth out soon."

"Simon, I do trust you. I have to say you sound a lot different than you did before you left for Budapest. Has something happened?"

"Bill, it has been a relaxing and very energizing trip. My mind is clearer now, more than ever. I know that between the two of us we will be able to sort out the troubles plaguing the city. Take care of yourself and the boys. Have your wife return on the weekend. I'm sure she will be fine at that time."

"Thanks Simon. Gotta say, your confident approach has calmed the three nerves I have left in my body. Have a safe trip. Call me if anything happens."

"Thanks, Bill. See you Friday evening."

My life had changed dramatically since arriving in Budapest. It sometimes felt like a dream, but I knew in my soul it was reality. A reality that, going forward, would change my life.

Thinking about Mel and Daphne at this moment did not cause me the violent reactions I had after Grace was killed. I thought about them in an entirely new way. I relished the thought of our first meeting when I returned to DC. Perhaps I would ask them to join me for dinner or drinks.

They would remember me as gullible, inexperienced and socially unsophisticated. An innocent fool that jumped at their commands and tried to please their wretched appetites for terror and fear.

Knowing my background before I did, they must have had many good laughs about me. Did they not think I would ever find out? That I would never realize or accept my legacy?

The game may be the same, but the players have changed. And they will find the change to be dramatic. Mira started rubbing her head on my leg as if she knew what I was thinking. I enjoyed this new companionship.

I decided to let the Centurion people handle the remaining arrangements for our trip. Today I would relax, finish my visit with Nicolae and Anastas and enjoy our final meal before leaving.

I wondered if I should send Mel a bottle of single malt and Daphne her favorite rose and peony bouquet, to announce my return?

82 - THE RETURN

The trip back to DC went smoothly albeit long; however, First Class does make travel far more palatable. There was no issue at all with Mira on the train or plane. She sat in first class with us – enjoying the wide floor under her own seat. Mira was a perfect companion, sitting by my side and not stirring. Occasionally, she raised her head to look at someone passing, but relaxed again and lay back down.

Maggie and Allya were like old souls reuniting after many years. Both were anxious to return to DC and find a new home. Maggie was taken with a Georgetown address she had spotted on the web and could not wait to show Allya the variety of homes available.

I thought instantly of Daphne. Perhaps I should suggest that Maggie give her a call for recommendations? I let out a small laugh thinking about how that call might go.

We landed at Dulles right after 4:00 p.m. on Friday. The car was waiting and my driver ensured the decanter was filled with my preferred single malt.

The Count had insisted I use his permanent suite at The Willard so I would not have to revisit my condo. He said his personal concierge, Nigel, would arrange to have my things moved to the suite and take care of any needs I might encounter.

After a ride home in Friday, rush-hour traffic I was ready to relax, but I had promised to meet Bill Rousch. Allya and Maggie would spend tonight at The Willard and leave on Saturday for Maggie's house in Chevy Chase.

When the girls opened the door to their suite, they were greeted by the white roses I had ordered and the champagne and fresh fruit on the table. They turned a simply hugged me.

Mira walked around checking every square inch of space. She seemed to like the balcony outside my bedroom and she made herself comfortable on the corner of my bed. It was apparent she had staked out her claim to space.

I encouraged the girls to order in and relax for the balance of the evening. After phoning Bill, we arranged to meet at the Off The Record Bar in the Hay Adams Hotel.

Allya's promise to properly dress me before leaving Budapest had been accomplished. They had gone to the Hugo Boss shop and purchased suits, slacks and shirts. They threatened me with bodily harm if I returned to my jeans and button down shirts.

I dressed in a Boss Black suit over a black turtleneck. I checked myself in the mirror and realized I was becoming quite taken with my appearance. That self-indulgent attitude reminded me of Leslie, that stinking slime. I thought about slapping myself then simply laughed in the mirror, shook my head and went to find my matching black leather belt. I needed to get down to business.

Entering the St. Regis, I saw Bill had already arrived and was sitting in the lounge. I barely got to the table when Bill said, "Whoa, Simon. You look different. What the hell happened in Budapest?"

"Rest and relaxation Bill. I hate to use that tired old expression, but I found myself."

"Well, finding yourself really made a difference. You look great."

We ordered drinks and appetizers and settled in for a lengthy conversation. The bar was relatively quiet for a Friday night and the dinner crowd was light.

Bill started, "Simon, you have to tell me what is going on with my boys. I've been a worried sick since we spoke and I can barely look them in the eyes. Please, tell me what has happened?"

"I did not mean to scare you Bill, but wanted to ensure you took proper precautions to protect you and your family. I've learned a lot about what's been happening around here. You need to keep an open mind about what I tell you right now. You cannot react with unleashed emotions.

"Mel is a pretty dark and powerful character; definitely not what he appears. What has been happening in DC is a power struggle between vampires and werewolves. Mel and Daphne Cosic Delaine are the mongers causing the trouble...."

Bill's face had turned ashen and he was hanging on my every word.

"What? What are you telling me?"

"Bill, take some deep breaths, a sip of your drink and wait a moment. You and I spoke briefly about a werewolf connection with the slaughters happening in town. I know that Mel has been behind the killings. He has a cadre of werewolves at his West Virginia camp. Your sons have been to his camp and I am not sure what their disposition is right now. But, I will find out and take care of things."

"This is insanity. I listened to your werewolf idea and thought you were pulling my leg. No way I believe my kids are werewolves, or vampires or whatever the hell else cannot be explained right now. If Mel has anything to do with hurting my kids....I'll kill Mel...I'll kill all..."

"At this point Bill, there is nothing you can do except keep calm. I don't know exactly what has happened. I realize everything you have heard and seen lately is outright insanity, but you have to keep calm. Anything within my power that will keep your boys safe, please know I will do - without question."

"I don't understand Simon. How can you do this?"

"Trust me on this, Bill. Let me have some time and see what I can do."

"I will, Simon, I will. Please let me know the minute you find out anything about my sons. There must be something I can do about Mel? Tell me what."

"No, it is more important for you to keep the media placated and your police force calm. Bill, listen, things are likely to become intense here for a while. There are two factions trying to control parts of Congress and..."

"What? What the hell is going on? Yesterday three Vatican representatives arrived in town to take home the body of Monsignor Darica who was killed in the Middleburg attacks. The city has been swarming with reporters, cameras and a lot of black SUVs with tinted windows. I cannot get any information from my superiors. I feel like a spectator in my own city."

"Listen, the best thing you can do is not ask questions from your superiors. Let's have another drink and talk about our next steps."

"One last thing Simon, here's the flash drive you gave me. After the kid I hired to break the computer password was killed, I don't want to chance making another twenty-something a statistic. One more thing, there was a witness at Zoe's apartment. A women across the hall said she heard a lot of banging and glass breaking. When she looked out her window she saw three men get into a black Suburban with tinted windows. She's positive it had government plates but couldn't see the numbers. Just the "G" on the plate."

"Bill, leave the flash drive to me. I am sure I will be able to find someone who can assist and won't be in danger. Look, get on home and take it easy."

We parted twenty minutes later and arranged for a dinner the following week. Keeping Bill on track was going to be difficult, but I understood and believed I could keep him in line for the interim.

I walked slowly back to the Willard, thinking how nice it would be to have a few moments of solitude to enjoy the spectacular views, a glass of wine and Mira by my side.

As I entered the suite the only thing stirring was Mira who seemed excited to see me. The girls were settled in their room and a bottle of Clois du Bois Cabernet was left open to breathe on the living room table. There seemed no reason to let it sit overnight.

February was a cold, dreary month in DC, but I thought about Grace and how much we loved sitting on the balcony with a glass of wine and some cheese. I could feel her presence and almost smell her perfume. I missed her so, but there would be recompense for her death. However I may have failed her in life, I would make up for it now. And, as never before, I would revel in the task.

82 - THE UNDERTAKING

I slept quite well with Mira at my feet. Allya and Maggie had entered the suite so I grabbed my robe and went looking for a cup of French Roast. Thankfully, Maggie had started brewing a pot and Allya had ordered up some rolls. It was early, but they wanted to start looking for new homes.

Maggie had called a friend and gotten a recommendation for a realtor. They were meeting at two and wanted to concentrate on the Georgetown area, but were open to something up Connecticut Avenue. My only caution was to keep them away from Embassy Row. After they both rolled their eyes, I decided to stop sharing suggestions.

I finished my coffee and realized Mira would want a brisk walk, so I dressed and we left for Dupont Circle. A little exercise would be good for me as well as Mira.

Saturday is always busy in the Circle. Still, it was not all that cold, but a brisk breeze would start up occasionally and that kept visitors to a minimum. It felt like springtime in comparison to Budapest.

We took a slow walk around the Circle then sat and did some people-watching. Mira sat by me and looked over the joggers and the die-hard marathoners running the concrete.

I thought about my meeting with Mel and Daphne. Though anxious for it to take place, I wanted my proverbial "ducks in a row" before sitting across from them. After spending an hour or so enjoying the brisk air, I decided a dinner with both of them was best. However, I would invite them separately. I did not want them chatting prior to our meeting.

As we started for home, I heard Mira growl. It was the first time I had heard her utter that sound. She stopped dead in her tracks and would not move.

I looked in the same direction as Mira and there was Leslie, bouncing across the Circle with some unsuspecting rube who probably admired Leslie's long, slim fingers. Mira kept her eyes on them until Leslie disappeared onto Connecticut Avenue. She definitely had great instincts.

When I returned to the hotel, I stopped to see Nigel my concierge. Nigel knew everything and everybody.

He had held the concierge position at the Hay Adams and Willard Hotel for many years. His last tenure at the White House bridged both Presidents Clinton and Bush. He then became a personal assistant to elite personnel, maintaining an office at the Willard for the convenience of his benefactors. If Nigel could not assist, no one could.

While putting out my hand to shake his, he immediately focused on my ring. Without missing a beat he asked, "Would you prefer I address you as Baron or Count, sir?"

I looked at him with a questioning expression. "Sir, I know the crest on your ring. It is well known."

"Well known? Even here in the States?"

"Yes sir, however coming from England as I did, I had a lot more exposure to those wearing that particular crest. You may be surprised at the amount of people in DC that are familiar with your family."

"Excellent. And no, please do not address me as either Baron or Count. Would you secure reservations for three at Citronelle for tomorrow evening at 8:00 p.m?"

"Sir, I will make the reservations."

"Nigel, will you call me with the confirmation?"

"No, sir. There will be no problem with your confirmation. Consider it confirmed now. May I assist you with anything else? Will you be traveling to dinner alone? Shall I arrange for flowers for a lady friend or…"

"Not right now, Nigel. Thanks for your help."

"Sir, I am available whenever you may need. Please don't hesitate to let me know your requirements at any time."

I was ready to make the calls and extend dinner invitations. I smiled anticipating their reaction.

83 - THE PROVACATION
I wanted to walk into Becketts and smile knowingly at Mel, but rethought that avenue. Meeting Daphne and Mel

at dinner would more than satisfy my longing for surprise.

I was actually quite calm when placing the calls. My first thoughts were wondering if I could keep my temper under control. And, I did. It was surprising to me how my emotions were now easier to restrain. This was definitely a better way to manage my passions.

Picking up the phone, Daphne was my first call. Sophia answered and Daphne was actually free to speak with me.

"Simon, is that really you? You've been out of touch for so long. I hope you're well."

"I'm just fine, Daphne. Quite rested and relaxed, actually. Getting away helped me focus and clarify many items."

"Simon dear, so nice that you have found some peace. What is it that's on your mind?"

"I thought a quiet dinner at Citronelle would be a nice way to celebrate my return to DC. Would you join me tomorrow evening at 8:00 p.m?"

"How nice of you to think of me. I would love to join you. I'll make sure Sophia clears my calendar for your dinner. Since you are inviting me to break bread am I to assume there are no hard feelings about Grace?"

I felt my jaw tighten and my knees lock. Maintaining composure I replied, "Daphne, I thought this would be a good way for us to start anew. Perhaps get to know each other a bit better, maybe talk about some ground rules?"

"Oh sweetie, where did you go these past few months? Did you take a course on how to play nice with others? You're suggesting ground rules and knowing each other better – as if we are on equal footing. How cute you can be at times. That's probably why I always liked you, Simon. Your sense of humor is fabulous. I can't wait for dinner. See you tomorrow."

That conversation encouraged me to change from French Roast to single malt. Any man who was able to hold his or her own while speaking with that particular spawn of hell deserved the best scotch money could buy. Finishing my drink was critical before I placed my call to Mel.

Before I could again pick up the phone, Maggie and Allya exploded into the room. Maggie started first, "You will not believe the house we found. It is unbelievable and it's in Georgetown. It's just terrific, but a little expensive. I didn't think I could qualify for the mortgage, but Allya is buying it – as an investment."

Looking over at Allya I asked, "An investment? You decided to invest?"

"Oh, Simon. Don't be so strict. When I tell Anastas and the Count it is an investment, as well as living space, they will be proud of me. Aren't you proud of me?"

"Okay, I'll give you this investment thing and only because of Anastas, but from now on no major expenditures without talking to our big brother first. Understand?"

"Yes, yes. I promise. Oh Maggie, we can move in. We have to go furniture shopping. Where should we start? Is Georgetown good for furniture shopping?"

I looked at them both with my best parental frown. "Maggie, you are responsible for keeping the costs down. Allya, if you aren't acting responsibly, Anastas will shut down your spending card."

"I know, I really do. I will not go crazy. Maggie let's leave. We have a lot to do."

The phone rang and it was Bill stating the memorial service for the victims killed in Middleberg was scheduled for this evening at 6:00 p.m. at the National Cathedral. He thought we should both attend and I agreed indicating I would pick him up at his office at 5:30 p.m. and travel there together.

I prepared myself mentally for calling Mel. I finished my drink, sat on the sofa and stared for just a few minutes through the balcony windows.

Letting out a long sigh, I picked up the phone and dialed Becketts. When the phone was answered I asked for Mel. They asked my name and put me on hold.

As I was reaching for the scotch to refill my glass I heard, "Well, well Simon. When did you come back to DC? I've missed seeing you. I thought you moved to Jackson Creek."

"And how wrong you were, Mel."

"Simon, you found a backbone on your trip to Georgia, didn't you. However, I would caution you to watch your tone."

My teeth started to grind and the muscles in my back were starting to spasm at lightening speed, yet I knew I had to control myself. Watching them at dinner was going to be so fulfilling.

"Mel, I wondered if you would have dinner with me at Citronelle tomorrow evening. Say 8:00 p.m.? We can discuss my tone then."

"Simon, I'd like to join you. I'll see you at 8:00 p.m."

Well, that wasn't so bad. Having made both calls I felt strangely calm. I had promised to meet Bill soon, so I made a quick sandwich then got into the shower.

84 – THE INVITATION

Grace had always reminded me about being on time. I thought I should follow her guideline. Mira would come along, but I would leave her in the car. Her appearance at the cathedral might cause disruption.

We picked up Bill, and as we got close to the cathedral, I was thankful for my driver. The traffic was terrible and we got off at the corner of Wisconsin and Woodley Roads, NW and walked the rest of the way. The security was intense. As I looked at all the black

Suburbans, I wondered why the government picked vehicles that were so identifiable? Why not a Prius or Ford truck? They could be armored and have their windows tinted. If only they would review how Israel handled security issues.

As Bill and I walked toward the sanctuary, we had to go through a metal detector. This was new at the Washington National Cathedral. It made me wonder what security level DC was at now.

The church was packed and the cameras rolling. A contingent of Vatican members caught my eye as we entered. The President, assorted White House representatives, members of Congress and State and foreign dignitaries peppered the rest of the audience. Bill was my ticket in and we sat midway at the end of the pew.

The President spoke quite fondly of Monsignor Darica – unexpected from my perspective considering their religions differed on so many levels. But, Darica was a close aide to the Pope and the President wanted to encourage a closer relationship with the Vatican.

Thankfully, the service was not as long as I expected. The crowd had swelled, but leaving the church was quite orderly. The first ten rows of pews were ushered out by security while the rest of us followed in a systematic fashion.

Bill and I stood off to the side on the steps watching the parade of self-important clowns chattering as they flooded the lawn. Politicians trying to get the arm of another with more political clout; those trying to impress the President; foreign heads of state puffing their chests to display their perceived power and the army of security guards trying to keep all under control.

In the distance, we heard what appeared to be screams that quickly brought the chatter to complete silence. The President was immediately hurried into his car and taken away. Suburbans were being jammed with dignitaries and security personnel were running to the street.

At the end of the block we saw flashing lights, heard sirens screaming, and ultimately distant gunshots.

Bill and I could do nothing except look at each other. We were not in danger, but the movement of security personnel pushed the crowd ever closer together. We found ourselves in the middle of the Vatican contingent. The Holy Fathers were a bit on the timid side. I expected more stoic behavior, but gunshots scare the hell out of anyone.

Whatever had happened, we were far enough away not to be in danger though security insisted we all stay put until the police had cleared the streets for safe passage. Being unable to get to our car until security let us leave, we were simply onlookers at a sea of bobbing heads.

A monsignor put his hand on my shoulder and offered comfort saying "My son, be not afraid, you are surrounded by God's couriers and…"

"Father, I'm fine. I do not need your attempt at comfort."

"Forgive me, it is reactive on my part to try and help during a crises. My name is Monsignor Delacroix."

"I am…Simon Nicolae Vasile."

Bill touched my arm with a quizzed look on his face. We had not discussed my changed name. I shot a "keep quiet" glance his way and continued with my conversation.

"Simon Nicolae Vasile? Seems I have heard of that name before. Do you have a relative in our brotherhood?"

"I think not Father, but stranger things have happened."

"You hail from what country? Romania or perhaps Hungry?"

"Yes, in that area. My family has very old roots in that region. They still maintain a quite active presence in their community. In fact, I just returned from a trip to Budapest where we spent time together."

"Yes, yes, I do believe I know of your family. Though my father, Emile Delacroix is from France, my mother hailed from Odessa so my background was quite varied and very rich in the history of Eastern Europe. I do wonder what has happened to cause all this furor?"

"I'm sure when the dust lifts we shall be told whatever the authorities feel we will believe. Don't you agree Father?"

The Monsignor smiled at me and then tried to introduce the rest of the contingent. Security was trying to get us out of sight and on our way home. As we parted company, the Monsignor asked, "Mr. Vasile, I wonder if you might be available for a brief meeting, perhaps on Monday around 2:00 p.m?"

"Actually, I would find that interesting. Where shall I meet you?"

"My son, we are staying at the Embassy of the Vatican on Massachusetts Avenue. I'm sure you will no trouble finding it. I bid you a safe evening, Simon Nicolae Vasile."

Bill and I pushed our way through the balance of the crowd looking for my car and driver. As we got to the sidewalk it was not difficult to see what had happened. Though bordered by ambulances and police cars, blood was filling the street, from several different locations. It looked as if more than two people had been disemboweled. This has got to end. It will stop and stop very soon. My discussion with Mel tomorrow evening would ensure his cooperation in stopping this carnage.

Bill rubbed his hand over his forehead. "I'm at a loss here, Simon. I just don't know how to stop any of this. The papers won't report this attack tonight and my superiors will disavow any knowledge of a disruption at the cathedral.

"And what is this with your new name? Vasile? Nicolae Vasile? Is that correct? And you're connected to the Vatican?"

"Yes, my name has changed, but it's just a minor blip in the scheme of life. I didn't realize my father had changed his name when he moved to Georgia. As far as this continuing bloody slaughter, give me until tomorrow evening. I'm sure things will calm down. As for the Vatican, I don't know any of them. My grandparents are still in Budapest and they may know people in Rome. The Vatican is an incestuous group anyway." Bill shook his head, but agreed to stay calm and quiet until we met for dinner during the week.

When we got into the car my driver said Mira had been very animated for the better part of the last hour. He was going to let her out then rethought that action. She completely calmed down when I got into the car.

Bill and I expected the news headlines in the morning to scream more about another impromptu slaying on the streets of DC – and this one, right outside where the President had been giving a eulogy.

After dropping Bill off I could not wait to get back to the hotel. The girls were likely still out looking at furnishings, so Mira and I were alone. I could not bear to turn on the TV. Silence was becoming a welcomed friend.

85 - THE NECESSITIES

Since returning to DC I was enjoying the most restful of sleep. Sleeping away from the memories of the condo allowed me to get up each morning relaxed and far more confident than I ever remember. The changes in my life were rapid and intense, and felt good.

Maggie and Allya wanted me to see their new place in Georgetown. Spending some time with them would be good, so I dressed quickly and promised them brunch if we got an early start. Mira, Allya and Maggie were at the elevator before I could lock the door.

We got to their new place by 9:30 a.m. and the two of them were acting like it was Christmas morning. I had to admit, it was a really nice house. One of the old brownstones in Georgetown, that offered beautiful wood work, built in bookshelves, high ceilings and gleaming wood floors. The kitchen had been remodeled into a cook's paradise and the fireplaces had been converted to gas. The house was pricey, but so was everything in Georgetown and this seemed more than worth the price. The yard had been professionally landscaped and it had an attached garage – always a perk in the DC area.

They dragged me through the entire house getting more excited with each room we entered. After their furniture shopping spree the previous day, they had decided what chairs and sofas would decorate each room. Mira, after checking out the entire house, decided to retire to a comfy spot by the kitchen fireplace.

I offered brunch at the Peacock Café on Prospect Street in Georgetown. Both of the girls smiled and were ready to leave and enjoy some crepes and champagne. I however, loved the smoked ham mac and cheese the café offered. Too early for scotch, but a Bloody Mary seemed respectable.

We sat at a front table and Mira lay quietly by the entrance to the eatery. The food was great and our conversation was completely geared to the new house and color palettes and furniture placement.

I had grabbed a Sunday paper at the corner stand. The front page was, as Bill Rousch had expected, devoid of any mention of the previous night's attacks. There was a story about a shooting involving a drug deal gone bad in an area close to the National Cathedral. That was it. Nothing about the bloody aftermath of the attacks, exactly what Bill said had been happening with the papers and his superiors.

We finished brunch and Maggie wanted to take Allya to her place in Chevy Chase. They were moving in today and tomorrow and wanted to get as much accomplished as possible. My driver dropped me at the hotel and then took them to Chevy Chase. I wanted to shower and relax a bit before my dinner with Daphne and Mel.

I started to dress early; something I remember Grace saying to me. As Anastas had advised, a tux was essential. Well dressed, relaxed and confident. It fit the entire bill.

As I grabbed the cummerbund from the closet, my .32 Walther fell to the floor. I had left it in the pocket made especially for that gun. There would be no further need for my .32 since Mira was with me. Perhaps it would be wise to give it to Maggie for her personal use. I let that thought stay in the back of my head for the interim.

I looked for the cufflinks Allya had given me. Expensive, gold and engraved with the word Védő on the front. She told me it meant protector, but knowing her playful spirit I thought I should look it up just to be sure. They were very nice. As I rummaged through my drawer looking for collar stays I saw a small box with an envelope alongside it. I opened the note and took in a deep breath; it was from Grace.

"Simon, you rescued me. You have been my love and taken care of me in so many ways. It is the initial "G" in an art nouveau style and quite old. When you wear this remember how much I love you. Grace."

Opening the box I saw the most elegant gift I had ever received. Grace was right; it was not easily distinguishable as a letter "G," but classy and appropriately sized for a man's lapel. I could not believe what I had just read. From the grave Grace had reached out and taken my heart.

Putting the pin in the palm of my hand, I held it tightly and then rubbed the smooth gold initial for several moments. Remembering my time with Grace brought me happiness and then the inevitable ache and longing in my heart. I immediately put the pin on my lapel. Small, elegant and unobtrusive. She had simple tastes and this was her best choice. I did not need this to remember her love, but I would never take it off.

This definitely set my mood for this evening's dinner.

86 - THE ATONEMENT

My driver dropped off me and Mira at the restaurant. Mira stayed outside close to the parking garage next door. Though I arrived early, I was immediately lead to a corner table allowing me to keep an eye on the entrance. Nigel had perfectly read my needs and I would remember to thank him.

I ordered my scotch and a bottle of champagne. Daphne would require her bubbly and, I suspected she would need it tonight. I people-watched for twenty minutes then the unmistakable laugh of a flirtatious redhead filled the dining room. Daphne Cosic Delaine had arrived. The maitre'd showed her to my table. I stood up as she was seated. That red hair, diamond choker and sable on her shoulders was nothing but a statement of "I am in control."

"Simon, my sweet, you look wonderful. Absolutely wonderful. I didn't realize they gave classes in appropriate dining attire in, what is the name of your little hometown? Oh, yes, Jackson Creek. Is that Georgia or Mississippi?"

"Daphne, you haven't changed. A bit more sarcastic perhaps, but you look stunning as usual. Any reason you have your colored contacts in this evening?"

"Ummm, Simon, are we playing games?"

"No, I am deadly serious Daphne."

The waiter brought the champagne and Daphne wasted no time in draining her glass. I ordered another scotch and sat silent. Daphne was about to speak when I looked up and saw the maitre'd escorting Mel to our table. As they approached, I rose to greet him and Daphne turned toward the door. When she realized it was Mel, the look on her face would remain in my psyche for, well, forever.

Mel hesitated, but continued to the table. Before he even sat down he ordered a double scotch neat. We looked at each other for a couple of seconds before Daphne spoke up.

"Mel, how are you this evening? I didn't realize you would be joining us. Simon never mentioned a word."

"You are looking lovely Daphne. I was also unaware that you were invited to this little dinner. Simon, was this your intent? To startle both of us, or did you just forget to mention it?"

"I didn't forget anything Mel. Absolutely nothing. I wanted the three of us to get together and layout some ground rules."

Mel quickly said, "Look Simon, you may have gotten your second wind while eating your fill at Drema Sue's kitchen table, but don't think for a minute you are here to take me to task."

"Or me." chimed in Daphne. She continued, "You may have changed your clothes and attitude, but you are still Simon, little gofer and wannabe reporter from Jackson Creek. Don't waste my time!"

Mel added, "Look Simon, I don't know what game you're playing and I really don't care. Your stubbornness got Grace killed. You refused to follow directions, questioned every single task given you and did not play on our team. Grace's death was inevitable."

I asked, "Tell me, both of you, why didn't you just kill me. Why Grace? If I was the irritant why not just dispense with me that night in Dupont Circle."

They were silent. Daphne was first to respond, "You may still have further use to us. You do have some talents that are viable while your silly little Grace was a nothing. A bit of distraction for you that did little to advance our goals."

Mel followed, "Grace was a flighty child that held you down. Interrupted your focus. What's the big deal? You can always find someone else. What about her sister? I understand she took care of you after your little pity party when Grace died."

I could feel the anger rising with every word out of their filthy mouths. I kept letting Anastas' words play over in my head. I would not lose my temper. I would stay in control. I would win.

Almost on cue the strained silence at the table was broken by loud screams and growling from the street. Daphne looked up. "My bodyguards are outside. They'll take care of whatever might be the issue."

Daphne began, "Listen Simon, there are a few things you can do for me. Why don't..."

"Daphne, why don't I help you and Mel in your next strategy session. Mel, why don't I take a day trip to your WV camp and speak to the group staying under your roof. Daphne, why don't I call Zarega and have him run me stats on Griffin Marino's financial dealings with the Vatican. Do you think the President or his new Czar would mind?"

With that said, I slowly raised my drink to my lips and took a long swallow. From the beginning, I had made a conscious effort to keep my left hand below the table. As I brought my glass down, I allowed my hand to rise to the table.

Mel and Daphne's eyes were frozen, staring at the ring.

"By the way Daphne, I just returned from Budapest and Anastas asked me to give you her regards. She hoped you and she would have the chance to meet sometime soon.

"And Mel, the Count asked if you needed any assistance with your banking problem in Iberia."

Neither of them replied. They simply stared at my hand.

Looking at them both, "Did you not think I would never find out about my heritage? That I would continue to run your silly little errands? That I would simply ignore your killing Grace and accept the horror both of you spew forth?

"No, things have changed. Simply welcome your new player to the table. From this moment forward I will be involved in all decisions that remotely impact common goals. You will keep me apprised of your plans and your ultimate plan to infiltrate Congress and the White House. You will leave nothing out.

"Mel, I will be visiting your camp in the next couple of days and speak to those that are of my clan. And understand me clearly, the slaughter stops. It stops now! You will instruct your wards that no running will be tolerated. Control your underlings and send them out on personal missions, however your current attitude of helter skelter to keep them occupied ends. Any deaths that ultimately cause problems for a common goal or that you allow for their amusement will not be tolerated.

"Mel, you must realize Daphne cares not about what you do because it will lead to your ultimate failure. Your actions assist in discrediting you and your goals. She is a far better strategist than you Mel. Think about that for a bit. Daphne, would you care to say anything?"

Her only comment was to order another bottle of Dom Pérignon. I suggested we continue our conversation over dinner, the champagne and, of course, scotch. The bit of downtime would allow them to reassess their choices in responding too quickly.

We gave the waiter our dinner orders and sat in silence until the entrees arrived. Mel said, "Simon you seem to have quickly assumed your new role. Are you sure you're ready for the burden it carries? Are you sure you have the guts to play?"

"I have not the first doubt that I will succeed. Why do you think I won't?"

Daphne interrupted, "Your father Niko fled his responsibilities. As his spawn, I thought you certainly would follow his cowardly lead."

"You really enjoy being cruel; enjoy provoking sadness and anger. Is that your intent, Daphne?"

"Absolutely not. As we all know, the truth can so often be hurtful. You asked me the question – I simply answered. I assumed Anastas told you about all that happened in Virginia those many years ago. The embarrassment for your family, the ensuing lack of leadership, Niko's juvenile actions as he threw his ring, that same ring you are wearing, into the lake. No, I do not think my question was out of place.

"And, tell me, how is the Count?"

"He is just fine. Actually he never inquired about you nor asked me to pass on his regards."

Daphne resumed slicing her rare rib eye and making quick work of the second bottle of Dom. Mel pushed the lobster around his plate, but was solidly into his third scotch.

The table was quiet, almost making me forget the reason for this dinner, but that thought was fleeting.

I was unsure they both accepted what was happening. As Anastas had cautioned, "They are formidable enemies and though they will not touch you, they will hurt those around you." Heeding her advice, I determined to end this dinner on as positive a note as possible.

As we finished our meal, coffee was brought to the table. We all knew it was time to redefine our roles without giving away one inch of perceived territory.

"Mel, Daphne, I think we have made headway this evening, but another meeting would probably be in all of our interest. Would you like me to make the arrangements?"

Daphne answered, "Simon, I think I'd like to host the small gathering at my Watergate condo. There are a few others we should consider inviting. Shall I send you both a list of possible guests?"

"Thanks Daphne, I would like to see it. Mel, have you anyone to add?"

"Not right now. I'll revisit my game plan and see if there is a recommendation missing. When is this meeting?"

"Mel, I can have the list to you and Simon on Tuesday and the meeting set for Saturday evening. Does that work for you both?"

We both nodded yes. Mel's demeanor had changed ever so slightly and Daphne appeared resolute. I felt progress had been made, although I did not trust either one.

The gauntlet had been thrown down and neither backed away. I knew they were already making plans to do away with my interference in their little kingdoms. Yet, from my perspective, any plans they hatched were doomed to fail.

After we finished dinner, we left the table to go back to our own protected spaces. Each of us needed time to go over this evening's revelations and the abrupt, but inevitable changes that had to be made in our futures. Walking out the door, we saw the street crowded with police and media. Onlookers explained that there had been another strange attack. Two men had been torn limb from limb. When Daphne's guards did not appear beside her, it became apparent that this attack was aimed at them.

Daphne turned quickly, her red hair swinging to the side. She stared at me, wanting answers. I had no intention of playing her game. She kept her eyes on mine as her lips curled into an evil smile of knowing, and apprehension.

Mel simply smirked and said, "I'm glad none of my people accompanied me this evening." He walked away with a swagger.

Daphne hailed a cab and left all alone.

When I got in my car, Mira put her head on my knee. As I rubbed her neck I ran my hand over my lapel pin.

I whispered into the night, "Grace, I will always remember you."

87 - FIRST VISIT

The next morning I realized Maggie and Allya had not returned home. They were likely celebrating late into the night at Maggie's apartment. I was glad they had things to keep them occupied. There was too much happening at the moment to keep watch over them.

Mira and I took our morning walk in Dupont Circle. I enjoyed walking there, however the morning traffic was noisy and unwelcoming. We cut our walk short and I decided to stop at Becketts for a coffee and bagel. Mira walked closely alongside me. I opted for an inside table, on the east side so I would be able to watch the crowd of mortals running to work. Mira sat at my feet.

A waiter brought over coffee and I ordered. Out of the corner of my eye I saw Leslie coming my way. Almost instantly Mira sat up, ears back and a slight growl started coming from her throat. I simply touched her neck with a silent command to be quiet. Mira obeyed, but continued sitting with her ears back.

As Leslie approached my table he stopped, his face turning a shade whiter than usual.

"Whoa Simon, what's with the attack dog?"

"What attack dog Leslie?"

"That, that thing by your feet."

"Leslie, you are being rude. Please meet Mira. She is my companion and goes with me everywhere. It is gracious of Mel to allow her to stay here with me."

He started to move to pet her, but she showed her teeth still not making a sound. He pulled back quickly and stood quite still.

"Oh, Leslie. Mira is just a pet. Do you not like dogs?"

"I like dogs well enough, but not her."

"Don't worry, I don't think she likes you either. Did you want something in particular Leslie?"

"I wanted to know if anything had happened last night. Mel is in a mood and snapping at everyone. Do you know if anything happened to piss him off?"

"Leslie, I've barely spoken to him since my return. You might want to ask him yourself."

"Nah, I don't think so. Sometimes it's just better to leave him alone. By the way, you look nice, Simon. Did you enjoy a vacation in someplace fabulous?"

"Yes Leslie. Someplace fabulous."

"Wow, give me your recommendation, I'd love to go and look as rested as you do."

"Leslie, leave me alone. Go out on the street and try to get hit by a car you annoying piece of refuse."

He raised his voice with, "No way to greet a friend Simon. That hurts me. I think you should…"

With his tone bordering on threatening, Mira stood up again bearing her teeth. Leslie took one look at her, turned and walked quickly to the other side of the café. Over his shoulder I could hear him saying, "Talk to you another time. Bye, Simon." I only wished I'd had Mira when I first met this lackey from hell. Mel never appeared and I was glad. At least I would enjoy my coffee and bagel in peace. I ordered a cinnamon raisin bagel for Mira. That appeared to be her favorite.

After enjoying coffee and browsing the paper we left for the condo. Passing Nigel in the lobby, I thanked him for his help with dinner at the Citronelle the previous evening. I told him I needed the driver by 1:30 p.m. for a meeting at the Embassy.

"May I be so bold as to ask whom you are meeting with sir? I know many of the delegates that frequented the White House and thought perhaps I might be able to share some background."

"Actually Nigel, I am meeting with Monsignor Delacroix."

"Oh, sir, I know him fairly well. He visited the White House many times in 2000, some additional visits during 2006 and, as I hear, more frequently with the new administration."

"Nigel, you are a font of information. Would you know the reason for his visit?"

"Sir, I was not privy to that particular information, however his meetings were not usually attended by the President."

"Then with whom did he meet?"

"Sir, there are many layers to our government. Different committees and projects. The monsignor appears to have influence with several groups, but he appears deeply involved with a rather unknown circle of officials. I believe the name I've overheard has been The Collective, but I am unsure of its' purpose. As for the monsignor, as I understand, is next in line to succeed the current Pope."

"Nigel, I may have to put you on a payroll."

"Sir, that is totally unnecessary. I am happy to be of service to you and your family. Don't hesitate to ask me on any item where you think I may have information. Is there anything else I can do for you?"

"No, you have been very helpful. Thank you."

"Very good sir, have a lovely afternoon."

It was evident Nigel was an excellent resource and appeared more than happy to be of service. I wondered the exact nature of his family tree. As Mira and I rode up in the elevator I could not help but remember my life three months ago and the 180° turn I had taken. It was as though I had been reborn, which if I asked Anastas, she would say was exactly what had happened.

88 - THE CONFESSIONAL

I showered and prepared for my meeting with the monsignor. I was curious as to his motive for inviting me since I had no knowledge of the Vatican or their dealings. But, if he knew my grandfather, something was bound to surface.

My driver was there at 1:30 p.m. Mira and I settled in the back seat for the drive up Embassy Row. As we passed the sumptuous buildings, the Naval Observatory and whatever other covert buildings were there, I wondered why this row of embassies had never been a target of violence. It appears to me that causing a disruption along this row of embassies would cause untold chaos.

As I exited the car, it was apparent Mira wanted to come with me. I was unsure how that would go with the Monsignor, but thought why not. When I rang the doorbell, Mira sat on the stoop and seemed satisfied to stay right there. A young priest welcomed me and asked me to follow him. He introduced himself as Brother Silva.

The embassy was not what I expected. An old structure, I believe it was built in 1938. It was filled with lovely furnishings, paintings and lots of gold crosses and other items on tabletops and bookshelves. Yet, it was dark and somewhat off putting. Just not what I had pictured in my mind.

We walked down a dark hallway and at the end Brother Silva knocked on an ornately carved wooden door. Monsignor Delacroix answered and ushered me into his private sanctum. Closing the door he asked if I wanted coffee, wine or something else.

I offered, "If there is a single malt in your closet that would be fine too."

The Monsignor opened what appeared to be a bookcase and before my eyes appeared bottles of every kind of liquor and liqueur. All were top shelf labels.

"I prefer cognac this time of day. What may I pour for you Mr. Vasile?"

"Monsignor, I prefer you call me Simon, and I will also enjoy your cognac."

"And likewise, you may call me Emile. I was named for my father and I rarely hear my name spoken."

He poured two snifters and handed me one. As he sat down across from me, "Simon, I'm sure you're curious as to the reason for my invitation."

"Emile, you read my mind."

"When we first saw each other I thought you looked eerily familiar to a gentlemen I knew back in Rome. When you said your name was Vasile I thought it was divine intervention that bought us together considering the difficulty of that evening."

"I assume you are speaking of my grandfather, Nicolae?"

"Yes. He and I met years ago during one of his business trips to Rome. He is an ultimate professional and one of the best banking minds I have ever met. He was gracious enough to take on a project for the Vatican and the results he obtained were outstanding. In fact, I have recently been tasked with a project that may again require his expertise. Tell me, is he still in the business?"

"Most certainly Emile. I just returned from a visit with him in Budapest and he is quite well and very active in his business. I'm sure you can call upon him at any time. I have his direct number if you need?"

"Thank you, but I have his private number. Now that I confirmed who you are, I would like to invite you to join a small group of business professionals with whom I work. There is a smattering of government officials in the group and we meet on a varied schedule depending upon what is happening in the world. If a crises has arisen, or possible trouble with a government, that sort of thing. We try to help."

I stood up and poured myself another cognac and offered Emile a refill. I walked to the window on the sidewall. It overlooked a magnificent garden filled with flowers that would soon bloom with the arrival of spring. Japanese Maples studded the slate pathway that led to a bench and small table. I stared at the beautiful scene, needing just a moment of mental quiet.

Walking back to my chair I asked, "Emile, do you have a name for this little group?"

"Odd you ask that question. It really isn't a formal group, but one of our members offhandedly coined us The Collective. Does that matter somehow?"

"Not at all Emile. Not at all. I was simply curious. Exactly what do you do in this group?"

"As I said, we offer competent assistance when countries or multi-national corporations are in desperate trouble. We pave the way for a variety of support for difficult times; we may supply manpower, money or advice. Whatever we feel will ensure a satisfactory result."

"And, who determines what result is satisfactory?"

"That would involve the unanimous consensus of The Collective, but the government or corporation involved would be asked for some input. We would not encumber any individual entity with our choice of a specific outcome. We seek only what is best for the collective participants."

"Emile, I am curious. Do you know a Mr. Melosh?"

"I don't believe so. The name is not familiar. Why do you ask?"

"No particular reason. What about Daphne Cosic Delaine?"

"That name rings a bell, but I don't believe I know her. Quite a while ago there was an Anthony Russo in Rome that did some work for the Vatican. I think his wife's name was Daphne or something quite similar. I don't believe I ever met her. Again, why do you ask?"

"Simply curious about people that travel in similar circles. Well Emile, do you need my answer this moment or may I take a day to consider my other commitments?"

"Simon please, take your time. The papal contingent is leaving tomorrow morning with the monsignor's casket. I am staying for a week to finish up some business items. Please give me a call in a day or two with your decision. It would be fortuitous for us to welcome into our fold the grandson of such an intelligent and business savvy man in our group."

"I must be going now. I will call you in a day or so with my answer. Thanks for the drink."

"Simon, it was my pleasure. I look forward to hearing from you and hope it is a positive conversation."

As I exited the front door, Mira immediately leaned and touched my leg with her side. We walked to the car and when I sat down, a deep tiredness covered my body. A nap seemed in order, but I asked the driver to leave us at Dupont Circle. A cool breeze and solitude was what I needed at this moment.

Quietly sitting on the north side of the Circle, Mira stood up and stared ahead. There was Leslie sprinting across the grass likely running some errand for Mel.

Mira strained slightly and I thought she might need some exercise. Unhooking the leash I let her go.

I wondered if Mel would miss Leslie?

GGG

Journal #7 - Grace
Entry 89

89 - THE ASSESSMENT

It had been non-stop since we arrived back in DC. Jet lag had not yet had a moment to ravage my body, but I was sure it would attack at the most inopportune time.

Mira and I returned to the condo. The girls were not there, but my voicemail light was blinking.

Accessing the tape I heard, "Simon, Simon, we have moved most of Maggie's clothes and little things into the house. We have a bunch more to do, but are going to spend the balance of the day here in Georgetown waiting for furniture delivery and trying to get things sorted. If you need to, call me on my cell. Otherwise Baron, my brother, go out and have a good time tonight. You need to relax. Find a lady with whom to share a drink or dinner. Love you, Allya."

Having a good time was the last thing on my mind. Remembering my life before Budapest was mind-altering. All my lugging cameras, lined notepad and time and expense sheets seemed boring. And they were.

I started to think about what Anastas said about my father's behavior. I wondered if he had known what was expected of him. What challenges and total commitment were required of his young, inexperienced soul. Had the Count and Anastas adequately prepared him for his future duties? Had they taken the time to soothe his adolescent fears? Did they learn their mistakes with him and now I was the focus of their intensity? Am I their do-over?"

I wanted to know how my father died, why and by what hand? The Count alluded to the fact that his death in the mines was just "geography." I needed to know the truth. During my research the information implied when a Lycan died they became a member of the underworld of vampires. Should I consider the possibility? The consequences were more than I could deal with at the moment.

I felt I had aged twenty-five years since Grace died. There had been no choice except to mature with the new revelations, being privy to lifestyles I did not know existed and the horrific burdens now resident in my soul.

My life had changed so dramatically and I was unsure Simon Gautreaux from Jackson Creek, Georgia, ever existed. I had to find something that would allow me to remember being normal.

But, Grace was gone and I was unsure if anything else would keep me sane.

I was tired and I knew the trip to Mel's lodge in West Virginia in the morning would be long. I hoped it would not turn violent, but knew Daphne and Mel would undermine me at every turn. Maggie and Allya were doing fine, Mira was already on the corner of my bed and I was ready to collapse.

I knew the passages ahead would take all my strength and knowledge. It would challenge my conscience and likely tarnish my soul.

G G G

"We revisit our past and harshly assess our actions and perceived lack of judgment. The incredible weight we carry upon our shoulders is one of not only inheritance, but one we have generated and choose to bear. We convince ourselves the burden is penance for our guilt – be it the guilt of our soul or that of humanity. It is the only defense that allows us to rise each day and permits us to have a fragment of sleep."

...Baron Simon Nicolae Vasile